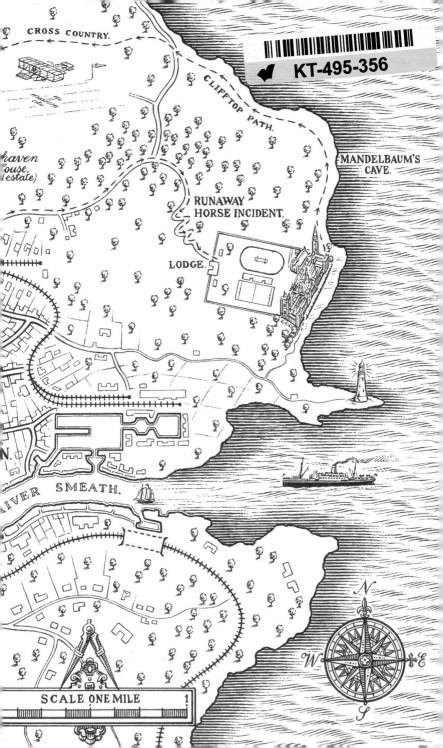

CROSS COUNTRY.

CLIFFTOP PATH.

MANDELBAUM'S CAVE.

...haven ...ouse. (estate)

RUNAWAY HORSE INCIDENT.

LODGE.

...N.

RIVER SMEATH.

SCALE. ONE MILE   1

N
W   E
S

John Morrison is a former foreign correspondent
and Westminster correspondent for Reuters

Also by John Morrison

**BORIS YELTSIN: FROM BOLSHEVIK TO
DEMOCRAT** (1991)

**REFORMING BRITAIN: NEW LABOUR,
NEW CONSTITUTION?** (2001)

ANTHONY BLAIR

CAPTAIN OF SCHOOL

'THEN SMITH RAN AND LAUNCHED HIMSELF AT THE HORSE.' *P71*

ANTHONY BLAIR

CAPTAIN OF SCHOOL

A STORY OF SCHOOL LIFE

BY

AN OLD BOY

WITH ILLUSTRATIONS BY DAVID ALAN HOPKINS

BLACK
PIG
BOOKS

LONDON SEVENOAKS BOMBAY

PREFACE AND ACKNOWLEDGEMENTS

Anthony Blair Captain of School would not have seen the light of day without my son Alexander's enthusiasm for collecting novels and magazines from the golden age of boys' popular fiction. This edition of what I hope posterity will see as a neglected Edwardian classic has been given splendid new illustrations by David Alan Hopkins. I am deeply indebted to both of them. I would like to thank my wife Penny for her meticulous proof reading, editorial advice and patience. I am also grateful to Vanora Bennett for her valuable comments, and to my son Nicholas for photographic help with the Black Pig Books website. This book could not have been published without the skill of Jane Tatam at Amolibros, who showed me the route to the finishing tape. Finally, I must pay tribute to the master of creative fiction at whose feet I learned so much.

I mean, of course, Tony Blair.

John Morrison
May 2005

DIFFICILE EST SATIRAM NON SCRIBERE –
Juvenal

CONTENTS

LIST OF ILLUSTRATIONS

CHAPTER I

A NEW BOY WITH PROMISE

The September sun glinted on the sea as Anthony Blair pulled the strap to open the carriage window. The train picked up speed as the line to St. Stephen's College followed the curve of the shore around the bay. Impatient for his first glimpse of his new school, he drummed his fingers on the windowframe as if to say, 'Faster, faster!' Carefully taking off his school cap, he gingerly stuck his head out of the window and craned his neck towards the engine. Just at that moment, a shower of soot and sparks covered his hands and face. A curse on these steam engines, he thought. Could nobody invent a gas-powered train, or even an electric one? As he closed the window and inspected the damage to his cuffs and neatly starched collar, he imagined himself lecturing to a rapt audience of experienced engineers about the new technical marvel he had single-handedly designed and built. Picking up his leather-bound diary, a farewell present from his mother, he turned to a page where he had already written 'Things to Invent' in a neat boyish hand. Underneath 'Automatic Translating Machine for Latin Homework' he wrote 'Electric Locomotive'.

Anthony Blair, or Anthony Charles Lynton Blair, to give the hero of our story his full name, was a boy of sunny disposition. A ready smile played around his mouth as he squinted into the mirror of the third class compartment he had occupied alone for the past hour. At fourteen he already cut a manly figure. On the platform where he changed trains, he had thanked the porter politely for carrying his trunk and tipped him half a crown. 'You are a proper young gentleman and no mistake,' the porter replied with a beam of satisfaction so transparent that Blair immediately wondered whether he had been over-generous. Perhaps a real gentleman would have given just a shilling, or even sixpence?

The Blair family was of modest origins, owing its position in society entirely to his father, who had by dint of study and application exchanged the narrow world of the counting-house for the broad vistas of the law. He was a Justice of the Peace and a man devoted to progress and good works. There were no shields, escutcheons or oil-painted portraits in the Blair household, but a tradition of useful endeavour inspired man and boy alike. It was only when the father, receiving a complaint from the curate about a boy trespassing on the church roof, detected signs of a mutinous spirit in his son that he decided to send him to complete his education in an English public school. St. Stephen's was chosen for its fidelity to the precepts of the great Dr. Arnold, and for its healthy location on the sea coast. Mr. Blair and his wife decided that their son's tendency to mischief-making would best be kept in check at an establishment remote from the temptations of our larger towns and cities.

The train stopped at a small station. The door of the compartment opened and a boy of around fifteen, wearing a Norfolk jacket of a greenish tweed, entered and sat down opposite him with a show of studied indifference. Some boys might have hesitated before addressing the newcomer, but not our hero.

'Hallo,' he began, stretching out a hand. 'My name's Blair. Anthony Blair.'

The response was crushing. Between a fifteen-year-old and a fourteen-year-old, there is a gulf that yawns as wide as anything demarcated by the Almanac de Gotha.

'Don't you grin at me, you young muff,' said the boy in the Norfolk jacket. 'Address fifth formers only when spoken to.' A sharp flush rose to Blair's cheeks as he withdrew the proffered hand in disarray. But he had no wish to provoke his travelling partner, and continued to smile genially in his direction.

'I'm sorry I don't know all the St. Stephen's rules yet. Anyway, you've spoken to me now, so I imagine I can say something in return.'

The boy took a large gold hunter from his pocket and consulted it. 'Only another ten minutes,' he declared. 'The first day of term is such a waste of good shooting. The grouse are just everywhere at the moment.'

Blair nodded. The assertion was not one he would have dreamed of challenging, though his own experience of field sports was limited to an occasion some three years past, when he fired his catapult unsuccessfully at a rabbit and broke a pane of glass covering the strawberry patch. He told his mother that he had seen the rabbits break the glass during their early morning jumping practice.

For the first time, the boy looked him straight in the eye. 'My name is Archer,' he vouchsafed. 'Since the last Sports Day everyone at St. Stephen's knows who I am. What house are you in?'

' "MY NAME'S BLAIR. ANTHONY BLAIR." '

'Hardie's,' Blair answered, relieved that the ice had been broken.

'Too bad for you. I'm in Salisbury's. We've been Cock House for ages. We thrashed your lot at cricket and rugger last season and we intend to carry on. If it wasn't for Salisbury's, St. Stephen's would be in a bad way. We bagged all three Cambridge scholarships last year.'

Blair felt unmoved by this sally. With no family tradition to draw on, he knew nothing of the different houses and did not care much where he ended up. If Hardie's was packed with duffers, then he would do his best to redress the balance. And he might make his mark more quickly than in a house full of swells and swots.

Archer looked at him critically. 'A word of advice, young fellow. Make sure you change the knot in your tie. Only sixth formers can use a Windsor knot. And don't forget the rule about jacket buttons, or you'll really be in hot water with the prefects.'

Blair's hand rose to his tie. That was something he could easily correct, but the rule about jacket buttons was a different matter. How was he supposed to know it?

Archer was reading a magazine full of advertisements for motor cars. Blair's gaze turned again to the window, and there beyond the lighthouse, perched upon a windswept cliff, was St. Stephen's, his home for the next four years! The stone walls shone the colour of gold in the autumn sunlight and the Gothic turrets and spires stood proud above the green sward of the playingfields. A flag fluttered, proclaiming loyalty to King and Country and defiance to any intruder who might brave the choppy waters of the sea. Blair was still admiring the scene when the train plunged suddenly into a tunnel and he was forced to close the window to keep out a cloud of smoke and cinders.

When the train emerged from the tunnel the sun was still shining but the view had changed. The line ran past suburban gardens, and then over a narrow bridge that crossed a dirty-looking river. There were small mean-looking red brick houses, a gasometer and what appeared to be a brickworks. The train slowed down and crossed a canal where urchins were throwing stones at a stray dog. There were barges full of coal and cement, and on one of them a coarse-looking woman was pinning out some washing.

When the carriage came to a stop at Coalhaven station, Blair clasped his portmanteau and his grub-box, and waited on the platform for his trunk to emerge. There was a gaggle of other boys, some smaller, some larger than himself. He was relieved to discover that no negotiation with cabdrivers and porters would be required, for the school had sent a motor lorry and a horse-drawn omnibus to meet them.

'Jolly good show,' he exclaimed to Archer as they walked down the platform, but his companion broke away as they passed the cab rank. 'I shall take a fly. It's a deal faster, and there's tea in ten minutes.'

When the omnibus finally reached the school, there was no sign of Archer. Most of the boys dispersed towards their familiar houses, leaving Blair face to face with an imposing red-faced figure in a black moleskin coat and silk stockings who was giving directions. 'Excuse me, sir, can you show me the way to Hardie's house?' he asked.

The man grunted and pointed to an archway across the courtyard. Blair heard laughter from behind him. A ginger-haired boy of about his age tapped him on the shoulder. 'That's Irvine. He's the Famulus. You don't call the old brute sir. You call him Irvine.'

'Well, I got that wrong, didn't I?' Blair replied with a broad grin. His mother had warned him not to take himself too seriously, not to show 'side' and to help other boys less fortunate than himself. He hoped that by taking her advice he would soon be surrounded by friends.

The boy guided him up a long flight of stairs, where he left his trunk to be unpacked by Matron Boothroyd. 'Old Betty' was a legend at St. Stephen's, and had outlasted most of the teaching staff. Her empire comprised a labyrinth of backstairs passages and echoing corridors, where laundry-girls and other domestic staff kept an ear cocked for the sound of her jangling keys. Next to the sanatorium was the sitting-room where she spent her off-duty hours. Boys who knocked and followed her command 'Enter, enter!' would see a bottle of port and a packet of cigarettes in easy reach of the armchair where she dozed, kicking off her boots and placing her feet on a piano stool. Sometimes she would reminisce about her career as a variety artiste, besieged at the stage door of provincial music halls by a succession of 'Champagne Charlies'. The boys knew her as something of a 'card' and late at night in the dormitories they would exchange whispered speculation about her past.

Blair knew none of this. The Matron glanced down a list and told him brusquely: 'You will be sharing a study with Brown. I always try to put the little Bs together.'

There were endless staircases to negotiate and miles of corridors. There were poky little rooms and grand vestibules decorated with Gothic statuary, which seemed to serve no useful purpose. There were oil paintings and enormous fireplaces, carved oak panels and brass fittings. There were frescoes of St. George and St. Andrew, and of mediaeval heroes such as Richard the Lionheart and Henry V. It was easy to get lost.

St. Stephen's, despite the antiquity of its foundation and the Gothic style of its architecture, was relatively recent in its construction. It would have been unrecognisable to any Old Boy who experienced the cramped and insalubrious accommodation of the early nineteenth century. After the great fire and the decision to move to a new site by the sea, many of the old traditions were swept away. Instead of small individual boarding houses named after masters, there were just three houses – Salisbury's, Hardie's and Gladstone's. The new building was a single edifice, with a series of small courtyards. At the corner of the school was the chapel, with a great clock tower affording views out to sea and over the windswept countryside.

Observe our young hero, cheerfully dragging his grub-box along a corridor and knocking on a heavy oak door. Without waiting for a summons, he opens the door and announces himself. A dark-haired figure with an intense gaze looks up from his books and motions him to take a seat. There is a moment of silence as Blair looks around the sparsely furnished room. There are two armchairs, a small gas fire, a bookshelf stacked with heavy tomes, and a food cupboard containing a jar of Dundee marmalade and a tin of oatcakes. The view from the casemented window is of an internal courtyard. The desk and the floor are covered with books and papers and mugs of tea. The only decoration on the wall is an engraving of the Forth Bridge.

'Hallo. I'm Blair. You must be Brown, if I'm in the right place.' He had already divined that St. Stephen's was a place where Christian names were to be used sparingly, if at all.

There was a grunt from his new study companion.
'Aye.'
'Can I put my things in the cupboard?'
'Aye.'
Without more ado, Blair opened his grub-box, lovingly
packed by his mother with such delicacies as potted meat,
biscuits and plum cake. His new study companion had
plunged his nose into a book, and was writing furiously.
He seemed much older than his years.

'The mater's done us proud,' Blair said as he pushed a
slice of cake across the desk. The dark-haired boy put
down his pen and took the cake with his inky fingers.

'It's not bad.'

Blair detected a Scottish accent. 'I'm sort of Scottish
too,' he said. 'How ripping that we should be sharing a
study. Do help yourself.'

'You don't sound Scottish,' Brown replied. 'You could
be a Sassenach impostor.' For the first time, Blair could
detect the hint of a wintry smile. Perhaps he and the dour
Scottish boy would be chums after all.

Blair quickly ascertained that Brown was indeed a Scot
of the purest water. He inquired if he was by any chance
related to our late Queen's famous Scottish manservant.
Alas, he was not. Brown had been at St. Stephen's for only
two terms, but the son of the manse was already making
his mark.

'You're swotting early. It's only the first day of term,'
Blair remarked.

'I'm up for a scholarship exam in a few weeks. You
won't see much of me till it's over,' Brown replied.

'Rather you than me,' Blair confessed. 'How much is
it worth?'

'Fifty pounds a year. That's a lot of money in Kirkcaldy.'

Before the two fourth formers could discuss the thorny topic of money any further, there was a loud shout from along the corridor.

'F-a-a-g!'

'Oh, let them shout,' said Brown.

'Shouldn't we go?' asked Blair nervously, his desire to do the right thing overcoming his rebellious nature.

'It's Healey and Benn. We have to fag for them because they're in the sixth. But they seem to spend most of their time fighting and throwing things at each other. Then we fags have to clean up after them.'

Blair came from a small cathedral school where fagging was unknown, but he had read enough about public school life in boys' magazines to know what was required. At home he had learned from Mrs. Beckett the cook to make toast over a gas fire, to warm the pot when making tea, and even to wash up cups and saucers when the maid had her day off. One of his favourite hymns included a line about 'the trivial round, the common task' and he was determined to 'muck in and show willing,' as his father often instructed him.

There was a crash from the corridor and another shout.

'F-a-a-g!' came the voice. 'I want you here in five seconds.'

Without hesitating, Blair made for the door. 'You're swotting. Why don't I go?' he said to Brown.

'Good chap,' came the reply. 'Down the corridor, and third on the right.'

He found the door and knocked boldly. From inside the study there was another crash and the door swung open. A tall boy with a fixed stare strode past him carrying a large model aeroplane.

There was glass all over the grate and the mantelpiece

where two framed photographs had been smashed to smithereens. The remaining occupant of the study heard Blair's polite knock and scratched his head.

'Hallo, new fellow. What's your name?'

'Blair.'

'Cut along and get a broom and brush. Wedgie has flown his wretched plane into my photographs and refuses to apologise,' Healey continued. 'It was deliberate, of course. He's a complete cad.'

Blair did as he was told. 'I'll have it straight in two jiffs,' he promised the sixth former with a cheery smile. Within five minutes, he had swept up the broken glass and washed the teacups. He returned to his study thinking that fagging was not as bad as he feared, but worried that all was far from well among the senior men in Hardie's house.

Brown confirmed his suspicions. The captain of Hardie's was a distant figure known as 'Old Footer' who sat in his rooms writing essays on history and literature, and rarely visited the dormitories or the studies. In his absence, the prefects had no authority and bullying and other vices were widespread.

'I met a swell called Archer in the train. He told me Salisbury's is Cock House and wins everything. Is that true?'

Brown nodded and frowned. 'Archer isn't much of a swell. He's just a fifth former who can run fast and loves making up tall stories. But he's right about Salisbury's. They've stolen our thunder.'

The life of an English public school ebbs and flows like the tide, as all Old Boys know. For a year or two an outstanding captain of house or school can quickly stamp his moral authority on other boys by forceful example, but when the shining figure of old Smithers leaves for Oxford or Cambridge, the rot quickly sets in. As the reader of these pages will discover, a boy whose character is shallow can do serious damage if he is promoted to a position of responsibility. There will be both triumph and disaster in our narrative, and it is well known that not all school stories have a happy ending.

'Can't we do anything?' Blair asked. 'I want Hardie's House to be the best house in the best school in all the world!'

'So do I,' replied Brown. 'But we're only in the fourth. Everything depends on those fellows in the sixth form. At the moment they're all fighting each other. There's drinking and smoking and all kinds of beastliness. One day it'll be up to us to put that right.'

The tall, saturnine Scottish boy exuded such confidence that Blair felt encouraged. At that moment if Brown had told him to pick up his rifle and march forward into a hail of machine-gun fire, he would have gladly followed orders.

At that moment the bell rang for callover. Blair followed Brown down the stairs with a crowd of other boys into the huge panelled hall known as Big School. The boys clambered over the green leather benches, hailing old friends, whooping and waving like tribesmen doing a war-dance. He was momentarily separated from Brown, and found himself squeezed among a rough crowd of boys. The only one he recognised was Archer, who had now swapped his Norfolk jacket for the same Eton collar and black jacket as his fellows. 'Well, if it isn't young Sooty!' Archer jeered. 'He's spent the hols down a coalmine!' Blair realised that the smuts from the train were still decorating his starched collar in conspicuous fashion. 'Sooty! Sooty! Bring us a sack of coal!' He realised he had unwittingly landed among the Salisburians, who were keen to make the most of his discomfiture. They were self-confident boys with fancy waistcoats and watch-chains. Suddenly he felt very alone. 'Sooty needs a wash! Sooty needs a wash!' came the chant. Blair was new to this kind of ragging, but he was determined not to show it. Most new boys joined the school in the third form, and he was a year older, so for him there was no safety in numbers. He stared straight ahead, fighting the prickling feeling in his eyes, and wondered how long his ordeal would continue.

The big oak door at the far end of the hall was opened by the richly garbed Famulus, and in strode a phalanx of masters wearing mortar-boards and gowns. The boys stood up, then resumed their seats. One of the younger masters began reading out lists of names, and soon his own was called out.

'Blair.'

'*Adsum*,' he answered confidently.

He felt a tap on the shoulder and turned round. Behind him a large fleshy boy flicked something towards him. Blair blinked as something wet landed on his face. He raised a hand to his cheek and found it covered in black. It was an ink pellet! A red mist rose before his eyes. He rose from his bench, swung round and caught his tormentor a heavy blow on the cheek.

'You, boy, stand up!' came the stern voice of the master. 'Yes, you with the dirty collar. You will do two hundred lines by tomorrow. What is your name?'

'Blair, sir. I'm sorry, I was provoked by this boy here and lost my temper.'

From behind him came a whispered chant: 'Peach, peach, peach. Sooty's going to peach!'

His despair was total. Luckily his tormentors, having

achieved their object, lost interest in him and within a few minutes the savage tribes of boys dispersed to their separate corridors.

Dejected, he spotted a crowd of other fourth formers, and tagged along. 'Come and I'll show you the faggery,' said the small ginger-haired boy who had spoken to him earlier.

The faggery was a small day-room for the fourth formers in Hardie's. There were leather armchairs, framed prints of famous cricketers around the walls, a fireplace and a shelf full of jigsaws and chess sets. Blair hoped that after his ambush by the hated Salisburians, he would find himself among friends.

'Well done, new bug! You landed one on Fatty Soames!' came a shout as he entered. 'Well done, Sooty! Never mind about the lines.'

The nickname was not one he would have chosen for himself, but Blair knew well enough that there was no point in arguing for a better one. Schoolboys are sticklers for precedent and tradition, and a nickname, once bestowed, tends to hang around a boy's neck for life.

Blair's spirits immediately lifted. 'Come on, Sooty, we're having a rugger practice!' shouted a small fellow who led the way into the corridor. 'Let's see if you'll make the fifteen.' Blair was reluctant to confess that his experience with the spheroid ball was non-existent; at his last school he had played Association Football, a game in which his skills were well developed. But rugger was a different kettle of fish.

The game of corridor rugger involved taking a pass, evading a tackle by a gang of other boys and then taking a drop-kick at a statue of William the Conqueror which stood at the end of the corridor. The boys took it in turns to run full tilt down the corridor, relying on momentum to get past the tacklers. Sheer weight of numbers brought most of them down in a flailing mass of limbs. When it was Blair's turn he caught the ball neatly, set off down the corridor at a steady trot and tapped the ball with his foot over the waiting tacklers. Swerving past them, he caught the bouncing ball and managed a creditable drop-kick towards the statue. As the ball spun forwards, he heard a shout from behind him: '*Cave! Cave!*'

Alas! The moment of triumph was not to be. After striking the inert stone helmet of William the Conqueror, the ball bounced sideways and into the hands of a muscular grey-bearded figure wearing a gown, mortar-board and clerical collar.

Blair stood with a look of horror on his face. After the incident in Big School, here he was again in serious trouble. What would he tell his parents if the school were to expel him after only one day?

'Thank God, it's only Flogger!' shouted one of the boys. 'Three cheers for old Flogger!'

Blair and the school chaplain 'Flogger' Williams stood facing each other. Williams had been an Oxford rugger blue and an army officer in his time, and did not believe that boys came to St. Stephen's to be mollycoddled. He believed in the virtues of robust physical activity, including boxing, running and cold baths. In his sermons he often told the boys they were footsoldiers for Christ, and should learn to use their fists if the situation de-manded it. As his nickname indicated, he used the cane liberally to punish serious misdemeanours, but in Flogger's book Blair's crime was of scant importance.

'Nice dropkick, young man,' the padre said with a smile. 'Now get back in your room and keep quiet, you

young baboons.' With a stern glare he was gone. The boys
retreated to the faggery in good spirits.

Blair's first day was nearly over. His confrontation with
the Salisburians had not gone unnoticed, and his corridor
dropkick had been a triumph. It was dangerous to be at
the centre of attention, but it was fun. He sat down and
wrote out his lines, feeling that St. Stephen's was not so
bad after all.

After the evening snack of milk and buns, followed by
prayers, the boys trooped off to their dormitories. Blair
put on his pyjamas, cleaned his teeth and tried to wipe
the ink off his face. The stain appeared to be indelible,
but his conscience was clear and he was far from down-
hearted. When the gaslight was turned out and he laid his
head on his pillow, he was buoyed by the thought that he
was now a St. Stephen's boy, ready to defend the honour
of his house and his school against all comers.

CHAPTER II

SOME EARLY SCRAPES

Blair's corridor exploits with the oval ball had indeed been noticed. Within two days, despite his ignorance of the rules, he was playing in a trial game ahead of the first house fixture of the term. The Hardie's boys were to face their old rivals the Salisburians, who were already boasting that they would administer an exceptional licking. In the trial game, our hero's footer skills and his quick eye for the ball compensated for his inexperience. Brown stood next to him in the line of backs and taught him the rudiments of the game. When Brown suddenly passed him the ball, Blair ran hell for leather towards the posts and, if he had not been tackled a yard before the line, would have succeeded in touching down a try.

'We can use a youngster with speed and pluck like you,' came the firm Welsh voice of Kinnock, captain of the Hardie's side. 'We wouldn't normally bring in a fourth former, but I'm thinking of giving you a chance next week.' Blair kept Brown's copy of *The Rules of Rugby Football* under his pillow, and spent many a spare minute glancing sidelong at the noticeboards to see if he had been chosen. At last, on the day before the big game, a sheet of paper was pinned to the board in Kinnock's handwriting. There was his name, just below Brown's!

In his first few days Blair had been too busy finding his way around the school, with its miles of staircases and corridors, to consider whether he was happy or unhappy. He smiled readily at his fellows, and even chatted amiably to boys from Salisbury's in the queue for the tuck shop. He had just bought two jam puffs and given one of them to a Salisburian who was short of funds, when a menacing blow on the shoulder made him turn round. It was a sharp-featured boy named Scargill, the leader of a group of fifth formers in Hardie's who took full advantage of the laxity of the prefects to pursue their own nefarious interests.

'All right, all right. Give me those. They're confiscated,' said Scargill with a leering grin. 'Nobody lets down the house by sharing tuck with the enemy.'

Blair looked around him for assistance. But his fellow fourth formers were nowhere to be seen. Scargill and his three companions tapped their boots menacingly on the stone flags. One of them lunged for the jam puffs, which fell to the floor.

'Pick them up, little Sooty,' jeered one of the gang. 'We'll teach you not to chum up with the enemy.'

Blair's cheeks went white with anger and he clenched his fists. But he saw he had no real chance of putting his tormentors to flight on his own. It was four to one, and he faced the real prospect of a thrashing if he resisted. Scargill and his friends were notorious bullies, and the smaller boys of Hardie's were used to seeing their prize tins of salmon and pots of jam being 'borrowed', never to be seen again.

As he bent down to retrieve the jam puffs, a picture postcard fell from his jacket pocket. In an instant, Scargill snatched it.

'Aha, what have we here? A card addressed to "Darling Anthony"!'

The other Scargillites crowded round. 'There are kisses!' exclaimed one of them.

'Kisses from Lizzie! Who's Lizzie, then? I bet she's a bit of all right! Is she your little fancy piece?'

Blair blushed, but with an iron effort of will retained his self-control. The card was from his eleven-year-old sister, and he was sorely tempted to hit Scargill on his prominent nose to defend her honour. But a glance at the four sets of boots aimed at his shins made him think again.

'She's just an actress I happen to know. She's promised me a set of signed photographs. When it comes you can have one, if you like.'

The hasty promise appeared to do the trick. Scargill's large fists returned to his pockets and his followers relaxed their threatening demeanour. 'I'll hold you to that,' he said as he returned the card.

Blair sauntered away with a spring in his step, glad to have talked his way out of trouble. His powers of persuasion and his ready tongue had been put to the test, and to his surprise, they had proved effective.

That night he tossed and turned in the dormitory, thinking ahead to the big match against Salisbury's. He wondered where he was going to obtain a signed photograph of an actress for Scargill, but decided to postpone that ticklish problem until a later date. Something, he was sure, would turn up. He knew that if he wished hard enough for something to come true, it generally did.

When the two teams took the field next day, there was no mistaking the air of confidence in the Salisburian camp. Almost the entire house was on the touchline, waving their mufflers. It was a beautiful autumn day, with the first leaves starting to fall from the high trees that flanked the drive.

On the other side of the pitch, a straggle of Hardie's boys lined up, but they were heavily outnumbered. The Scargillites were nowhere to be seen, and many of the senior men had sloped away into town or had stayed in their studies. Old Footer was there, hobbling on his gammy leg and waving his stick, but his shouting failed to rally the ranks.

Blair had read enough boys' magazine stories to know that rugger matches could be won against near-impossible odds. Alas! His naïve hopes were quickly dashed. Salisbury's were three tries up in the first ten minutes. Without teamwork, a rugger side might as well stay in the pavilion, as any experienced player will tell you. Teamwork was sorely lacking in Hardie's ranks, though Kinnock shouted himself hoarse encouraging his side.

'Come on, boys, get stuck in there! Come on! Forward, forward! Now after it! Tackle him, now! Keep your position and mark your man!' Unfortunately the double effort of chasing the ball and exhorting his team left Kinnock out of breath. The fiery Welsh boy found himself upended and flattened as the Salisburian forwards rushed the ball upfield.

When the halftime whistle blew, the boys of Cock House were already celebrating. With a lead of five tries to none, their superiority was clear. But adversity brings out the best in the British character, and the boys of Hardie's were no exception. They fought manfully to stem the tide, with Brown and Blair in the forefront of the battle. For most of the second half honours were even, until a flash of uncontrolled Welsh temper from Kinnock led to a penalty goal. Their captain's lack of self-discipline silenced the ragged cheers from the Hardie's touchline, while the other side whooped and cheered, led by Archer, who strode up and down the touchline blowing a copper hunting horn.

Suddenly the ball came hurtling backwards from a scrimmage where a stray boot had hacked it. It bounced towards Brown, who caught it neatly and set off to the left. Blair kept pace with him, sprinting a few paces behind. The Salisbury's backs were caught napping, with only the fullback barring Brown's path to the line. 'Pass!' shouted Blair. Brown lunged towards the fullback, drawing him forward, then flicked the ball neatly sideways. Blair plucked it out of the air and scrambled over the line. A try for Hardie's! The old house had gone down to defeat, but its honour had been salvaged.

As the boys tramped back to the pavilion, their limbs aching and bruised, Blair found himself clapped on the back by all and sundry. 'Good show, young 'un,' said Brown. 'I didn't do much,' said Blair modestly. 'It was all thanks to you. You taught me everything. You're a real chum.'

The house match did much for Blair's standing. There were still shouts of 'Sooty' when he appeared in the faggery, but the tone had changed. It was now 'Good old Sooty!' and the Scargillites left him well alone.

On the day after the match, Blair and Brown, by now inseparable, were walking together under the clock tower after morning school when Smith, one of the brainier boys in the sixth and a house prefect, hailed them.

'BLAIR PLUCKED IT OUT OF THE AIR AND SCRAMBLED OVER THE LINE.'

'Who are you two fagging for? I think you boys deserve a leg up in the world. Brown, you can fag for me, and Blair, you can fag for Kinnock. How do you like the idea?'

The two fourth formers agreed enthusiastically. At first there seemed something rather grand about washing up the tea things for two such swells as Kinnock and Smith. Blair could not, however, contain his satisfaction and when he enthused once too often about Kinnock as 'a topping fellow' he found the other inhabitants of the faggery less than impressed.

If truth be told, his admiration for the house rugby captain began to wane after a few weeks. Although sixth formers by custom did not hold conversations with the boys who fagged for them, Kinnock was one of those boys who found it difficult to remain silent in the presence of another person. Blair was at first flattered by the uninterrupted flow of Welsh eloquence in his direction, but soon realised that he was not expected to respond.

Brown had no such problems with Smith, a fellow Scotsman, and found his fagging duties were light. Smith would frequently tidy up his own biscuit crumbs and wash his own tea cup. With their shared roots north of the border, the two boys needed only a few choice words to understand each other perfectly. Blair could not for the life of him puzzle out these Caledonian exchanges, as impenetrable to him as smoke signals from a Red Indian reservation.

Brown was working furiously for his scholarship exam when Blair was approached by a large boy named Maxwell, a sixth former whose ample frame was sustained by weekly food parcels from home. Few of the other boys in Hardie's liked him, but few could resist an invitation to a 'feed' when Maxwell's hamper arrived. There was ginger beer and plum cake and chocolate creams, which could be smeared on toast like bloater paste.

'Hallo Blair,' Maxwell began, drawing his interlocutor aside into a panelled alcove where they would not be overheard. 'Have a brandy ball.'

From Maxwell's capacious pockets came a paper bag. Blair dipped in and took one.

'Your chum Brown – I wonder how his swotting is going?'

'Pretty well, I think. He's construing Latin like an ancient Roman. And he's well up on the Crusades and the Tudors. I couldn't help him with the maths because he's way beyond what we do in class.'

'Well let him know if he wants a good steer on what to expect in the exam, I might just be able to help him,' said Maxwell meaningfully.

Blair thought no more of the remark, and took his leave. Brown was the most brilliant boy in the house, and was unlikely to need assistance from Maxwell. But it was far from certain that the scholarship was in the bag. There were clever boys in other houses as well, and the Salisburian favoured for the scholarship was a tall young man named Redwood who was reputed to have learned Greek at three.

At callover that evening, as the boys assembled in Big School, an excited whisper went round. 'The Doctor himself is coming!' The headmaster, Dr. Bush, had devoted his life to composing a concordance to a series of ancient Hebrew texts whose intricacies had baffled the best minds of Oxford and Cambridge. But this devoted Biblical scholar was popular among the boys; the more infrequently they saw him, the more they respected him.

To be summoned to the Doctor's study for a disciplinary reason was a rare event, but his manner was always kindly and his use of the cane was sparing.

There was a sudden hush in Big School as the Doctor strode into the room, preceded by Irvine the Famulus in his black uniform. His air was perplexed and preoccupied. The smaller boys craned their necks to watch the Doctor place his gold 'nippers' on his nose. Would there be an extra half-holiday? Alas, the news was bad.

'A most serious event has occurred,' said Dr. Bush. 'Tomorrow is the day of the scholarship exam. The papers were left in a sealed brown envelope on the desk in my study. When I returned from my morning walk along the bay I discovered that the envelope had been tampered with.'

There was an excited buzz along the lines of oak benches. Dr. Bush looked over his pince-nez and his brow furrowed. 'Does any boy have any information about this matter?'

Silence reigned in the room. 'The examination will take place on time tomorrow, starting at nine. But there will have to be an investigation. This is a very serious matter.' Blair looked at Brown and squeezed his hand. 'How awful if some rotter has stolen the paper!'

'Very well,' said the Doctor. 'Any boy who owns up will be treated leniently. But if I find the culprit, there will be no place for him at St. Stephen's!'

The Famulus bowed to the Doctor and followed him out of the room. The hush was over and the boys, among whom were many avid readers of the adventures of Sherlock Holmes in the *Strand Magazine*, began to puzzle out the mystery. All eyes were on the exam candidates Brown and Redwood as they returned to their studies.

Sherlock Holmes was a particular hero to young Blair, who often imagined himself as the violin-playing detective, using his powers of observation and deduction to solve the most complicated and bloodthirsty crimes. But unless the Doctor were to invite him to make a forensic examination of the scene of the theft, it would be hard for him to investigate.

The examination went ahead as planned, and the boys waited on tenterhooks for the results. At chapel Blair listened to the ringing Old Testament voice of Dr. Williams exhorting him to 'fight the good fight' and said a silent prayer for his friend. Success for Brown in the scholarship would mean not only financial relief for his family but a defeat for the Salisburians and a signal that Hardie's house was on the path to greatness again.

At prayers next morning the Doctor appeared in person. There was a buzz of anticipation as he grasped the lectern. Blair closed his eyes and crossed his fingers. 'Here is the result of the scholarship examination. Redwood seventy-nine per cent. Brown ninety-six per cent. The scholarship worth fifty pounds per annum is awarded to Brown of Hardie's house.'

There was cheering from the Hardie's boys and glum looks among their rivals. Brown showed little emotion, but that was part of his Caledonian character. A dry smile played around his lips.

It was not until morning school was over that Blair and Brown realised something was wrong. They were leaving the tuck shop, where Brown, in a rare moment of extravagance, had purchased two bottles of ginger beer to celebrate, when two Salisbury's boys walked past.

'Now we know who pinched the exam paper,' one of them remarked. 'It's a beastly shame for Redwood.' At first they laughed it off, but then the talk started spreading in Hardie's house, and even in the faggery. How could Brown have scored ninety-six per cent? No boy since time immemorial had managed a result like that. The young Sherlock Holmeses were convinced that they had solved the crime.

'It's a case of *cui bono*,' said one learned denizen of the faggery. 'Who stands to benefit?' The next day, when Blair and Brown headed for the tuck shop, other boys began to look the other way. There was a faint hissing sound from the back of the queue as they went past.

'What I can't understand,' Blair confided in his friend, 'is why our own chaps have turned against you. I could understand it if the Salisburians were cutting you.'

'That's the way it is, Sooty,' Brown said with a sigh. 'When someone steals your jam puff, it's normally the person you least expect. It's not your enemies you have to watch out for in this place, it's your friends.'

The cloud of suspicion did not seem to affect Brown over much, for he knew he had won the scholarship fair and square. He was by nature suspicious of others, and was not bothered or surprised by their suspicions of him. Any anger he felt was bottled up inside. Blair, however, wore his heart on his sleeve. His easy intercourse with the other boys, his popularity as 'Good old Sooty', his hopes of making his mark as a Hardie's boy – all this was under threat from his position as Brown's best friend.

One morning his spirits were so low that he deliberately sat at the other end of the lunch table from his friend, choosing instead a place on an oak bench next to Cook, the ginger-haired Scottish boy who had given him directions on his first day. Cook was giving an expert summary of the racing season which was drawing to a close, and boasting about the odds he had obtained on the Derby winner.

Blair found the account so fascinating that he sat with Cook long after the plates were removed. He failed to see the glowering expression on Brown's face as he left the hall.

'So you're cutting me in favour of wee Cookie!' he said gruffly to Blair when the two were alone in their study. 'I suppose he was telling you he saw me through his field glasses, stealing the exam paper.'

Blair smarted. How unfair it was of his friend to accuse him when he had done nothing wrong! 'There's no need to get into a wax, old man. I don't see why I can't talk to Cook,' he replied. 'I shall stay on good terms with everyone I can around here.'

Brown snorted. 'That's my point. You can't do that. You have to choose.'

Blair frowned. It was not a piece of advice he wanted to hear, but he was afraid that Brown might well be right. He had assumed, wrongly, that all the Scottish boys were as thick as thieves. He would have to work out who his real friends and enemies were. Once again he began making notes in his diary.

The next day he was surprised to be accosted by Redwood, the unlucky scholarship candidate whom he had instinctively placed in the 'enemies' column. 'Don't worry, I'm not bearing any grudges,' Redwood said by way of introduction. 'I'm not half as clever as people think I am. I'm a frightful duffer, if the truth be known. So I'm not surprised that your chum Brown bagged the scholarship ahead of me.'

'What do you want?' Blair asked, an unaccustomed note of suspicion creeping into his voice.

'You know that boy Maxwell? The day before the exam, he offered me help in working out which questions to expect. I thought no more of it, but now it seems dashed peculiar. I wonder if he said anything similar to Brown.'

Suddenly Blair remembered his own conversation with Maxwell in the alcove. Of course! How could he, a student of Sherlock Holmes, have missed such an obvious clue? Without pausing to give Redwood a reply, he ran back upstairs to the study.

'Brown, old man, I've been a complete sausage!' Blair exclaimed. 'Of course it wasn't you who looked at the exam paper.'

'Did you think it was?' came the reply.

'Of course not. But I think I know who did it. It was that blackguard Maxwell all along!'

'Can you prove it?'

Blair recounted the exchange with Redwood, and his conversation with Maxwell before the exam. Not even the most bungling Scotland Yard inspector could have missed the implications of the fat boy's offers of information.

'We'll have to go and tell the Doctor,' Blair expostulated. 'It's wrong, absolutely wrong, and you and I have ended up sent to Coventry as a result. The right thing to do is to expose him and ensure he is suitably punished.'

'That would be sneaking. Boys don't sneak on each other, surely you know that?'

Blair hesitated. 'But it's such a caddish, mean thing to do. We can't cover it up.'

'Don't worry,' said Brown. 'The fact that we know Maxwell did it may turn out to be useful in the long run. We may need him on our side one day.'

At that moment there was a loud shout of 'F-a-a-g!'

from the corridor. As Blair applied boot polish to Kinnock's shoes, a close observer of his furrowed brow would have concluded that the young fourth former was unusually preoccupied. Life at St. Stephen's was proving more complicated than he could ever have imagined.

CHAPTER III

A TRIP INTO TOWN

As the term progressed, the fuss over the scholarship exam faded away and most boys began to talk of other things, notably the annual rugger matches against St. Wilfred's School, whose rivalry on the sporting field with St. Stephen's College was of long standing. But Blair's hopes of playing in the fixture were dashed when he accepted a sixpenny bet from 'wee Cookie' that he could not clear a whole flight of stairs in one leap. He landed awkwardly, twisted his ankle and hobbled forlornly up the stairs to Matron Boothroyd.

'Is it broken?'

'Of course not, silly boy! But I might break it myself if you don't sit still and let me bandage it. And don't play rugger for two weeks.'

Thus it transpired that on the afternoon when Brown and many other boys travelled by train to St. Wilfred's, Blair was left in his study, looking out at the rain and feeling sorry for himself. The school was largely deserted, and Blair was wondering how to occupy his afternoon when there was a commotion in the corridor.

'We want a rag, we want a rag!' went the chanting.

Curiosity getting the better of him, Blair opened the door of the study. It was Scargill and his gang of malcontents, evidently up to mischief.

'Why, if it isn't young Sooty!' exclaimed one of the chief lieutenants. 'Let's have some fun with Sooty.' Within seconds, the gang of fifth formers was inside the study and ransacking its contents. One of them picked up Blair's diary and waved it in triumph.

'I say, give me that, you swine!' he shouted. But by this time three of them had pinned him down, bending him backwards over the table and twisting his arms. Blair prayed they would not find his list of enemies, on which Scargill figured in a prominent position.

'You'll catch it from Kinnock when he comes back. He's very down on bullying in the house.'

Blair's invocation of Kinnock's name produced a chorus of jeers from his tormentors, who were rifling through his grub-box. He lashed out with his foot, only to receive a violent kick on his bandaged ankle. Within a second he was blindfolded, with a cushion cover over his head. He was in darkness and suffocating. The tears welled up. Never had he been so alone, so humiliated. Then he had a brainwave.

'I say Scargill, are you still interested in a photograph of my actress friend Lizzie?'

The leader of the gang motioned to his colleagues to release the prisoner. 'Perhaps I am. All right, you hand over a signed picture and we'll leave you alone.'

'She doesn't exist. And if she did, she wouldn't be interested in a milksop like him!' piped up the nasal whine of a junior Scargillite named Livingstone.

'She jolly well does exist. And I'll get you her picture by next Friday!' Blair heard himself exclaim in desperation. How he hated these boys! His mother and father had filled him full of the milk of human kindness, telling him to rub along with all his fellows. But how could he ever be friends with Scargill and his gang?

'Next Friday? I shall hold you to it,' said the gang leader. The cushion cover was removed from his head and the group ran off, heading down the corridor to find another target.

Blair reflected ruefully on his predicament; he had escaped from the bullies once, but next time he would not be so lucky. Where was he to find a signed picture of an actress at such short notice? The Blairs did not move in thespian circles, and in any case he could hardly send a telegram to his parents with such an unusual request. His only picture of his sister Lizzie showed her clearly to be a girl of tender years rather than a star of Drury Lane.

Somehow he would have to use his wits to find a photograph. He did not dare explain his problem to his friend Brown or any other inmate of the faggery. He knew, however, that among the town shops there was a photographic studio, highly recommended by Healey and other boys in the school photographic society. But there remained two substantial hurdles.

Firstly, he was low in funds. How he regretted that half-crown given to the railway porter on the first day of term! His liberality was catching up with him, and he could hardly write home for more money. The unpleasantness over the scholarship exam had led him to be even more generous than usual in treating his friends to jam puffs from the tuck shop. His entire wealth now came to only ten shillings, while he knew a set of photographs would cost upwards of three pounds.

The bigger headache was how to find a suitable model. He needed a girl who could simper for the camera and who could be relied on to keep her expedition to the photographer's studio a secret. Blair knew little about girls, though from observing his sister he was persuaded that keeping secrets was not their forte. But there were no girls at all on the horizon at St. Stephen's, apart from the laundrymaids.

His train of thought appeared to have hit a blank wall, but then he realised that his last reflection was not strictly true. There was one girl at St. Stephen's. Irvine, the school Famulus (a title which he preferred to the more mundane one of porter), lived in a small lodge by the school gates. In the kitchen garden behind the house, Blair had glimpsed a dark-haired girl of about his own age weeding the vegetable plot. On one sunny afternoon, walking with Brown towards the rugger field, he saw the girl sitting on a garden bench receiving a Greek lesson from one of the masters.

'Who's she?' he asked.

'Irvine's daughter. She's swotting for some scholarship exam or other, and her name's Sherry, like the drink.'

Nothing ventured, nothing gained, thought Blair as he seized pen and ink and constructed a letter. He was not used to writing to girls, and wondered how to broach the ticklish subject. Should he address the object of his missive as Miss Irvine? After a moment's reflection he decided that the rules of Victorian etiquette could go hang. His letter would be simple and direct, as if he had construed it directly from the ancient Greek.

> *Dear Sherry,*
> *I am a fourth former in Hardie's house and my name is Anthony Blair. We are preparing an end-of-*

term concert party and need a photograph of an actress. As we don't have an actress to hand, would you oblige us by pretending to be one? Do be a sport and say yes. I shall meet you outside the photographic studio in town at three o'clock on Tuesday. If you can come, leave a hat on the garden bench this afternoon.

Yours,

Anthony Blair

P.S. You can keep the photograph.

He sealed the envelope and set off down the school drive towards the lodge. It was lunchtime, and he knew that Irvine would be busy in the dining hall, where he performed the duties of butler to Dr. Bush and the senior masters. At the wicket gate he looked round nervously, strode down the path and dropped his note through the letterbox.

A few hours later, he retraced his steps. There on the garden bench was a large straw hat! Blair's spirits rose, and he reflected on the fact that not all girls were as useless as the general opinion in the faggery held them to be. They might perhaps not be the equals of boys in all respects, but they were fellow members of the human species, he decided.

There remained just one problem. How would he pay for the photographs? He could hardly ask Brown for money, for his studymate often lectured him on the evils of debt. 'Neither a borrower nor a lender be!' Brown would proclaim as he collected ginger beer bottles from neglected corners of the faggery for return to the tuck shop at a halfpenny a time.

Should he perhaps ask Maxwell, one of the few boys in Hardie's who seemed to be always flush with cash?

After the examination incident, he was very loath to put himself under any obligation to the fat boy with the bulging wallet. In Salisbury's most of the boys seemed to have sovereigns and half-sovereigns to spare. But Hardie's was largely made up of scholarship boys and a sizeable number of 'day bugs' from the nearby town, who were known contemptuously as the natives. Occasionally Blair wondered whether, if fate had made him a Salisburian, he might have been happier than as a recruit to Hardie's house. But it was too late to ponder such might-have-beens.

'I say, Sooty, old fellow!' came the sound of a familiar voice. It was Cook. Blair smiled back.

'Sooty, do you have a half-sovereign on you? I have a rock-solid tip for the three o'clock at Newmarket on Saturday, and I'm short of funds. It's Cannonball at twenty to one, so we could share a tenner if she wins.'

Blair looked dubious. Betting on horses was frowned upon in the Blair household.

'I mean, when she wins. It's a dead cert.'

'Are you sure?'

'Scotsman's honour.'

Still he hesitated. He had never thought of himself as a gambler. But the thought of arriving at the photographic studio without the wherewithal to pay filled him with dread. Sherry would laugh at him and the story would probably find its way around the school in no time.

'All right, Cookie. When will you have the money?'

'Monday afternoon. Don't worry. The slip won't have your name on it.'

Blair handed over his last ten shillings. The deed was done.

That evening he was unusually industrious when the time came for prep. He did his Latin twice over and

practised a few Greek words under his breath in case
Sherry should seek to test his progress in that ancient
tongue. Half asleep in the dormitory, he prayed to God
to ensure that Cannonball won the three o'clock at
Newmarket. Then he awoke with a start. Did God have
any power to affect the outcome of a horse race? And even
if He did, was it His custom to intervene in such matters?
Dr. Williams would no doubt have an answer to this
theological dilemma, but he could not possibly risk asking
him.

On Monday morning Blair was eating his breakfast
when Cook swaggered up to him with a grin. 'Cannonball
won it by two lengths,' he whispered. The first part of his
gamble had paid off!

The next afternoon young Blair, still excused rugger
because of his injured ankle, could be observed sauntering
along the road into the town of Coalhaven, with five
sovereigns in his pocket and a look of confidence on his
well-washed face.

The road into Coalhaven led downhill through the
suburbs. Boys were allowed into town on free afternoons,
but were only permitted as far as the High Street. Beyond
this point lay the industrial area between the river and the
canal, known as Mesopotamia. It was strictly out of
bounds.

Blair realised he was five minutes early, so he turned
away from the High Street and rejoined it closer to the
river. Then he walked back up past the Italian café owned
by Signor Berlusconi, whose ice-creams were deservedly
popular among the boys of St. Stephen's. The swarthy
Italian was allowed to park his ice-cream cart by the
school pavilion on summer cricket afternoons and did a
roaring trade.

Opposite the café was the grandest establishment in the street, Mr. Thatcher's grocery and provision store, a world of marble counters, polished glass and exotic delicacies such as crystallized fruit. Boys whose grub-boxes were depleted could replenish them with Mr. Thatcher's famous veal and ham pies and his special selection of pickles. A small cohort of assistants in striped aprons and straw hats scurried behind the counters, and the grocer's daughter sat in a mahogany booth, operating a giant American cash register of polished brass.

Blair pushed stray thoughts of veal and ham pies out of his mind and arrived at the photographic studio just as the church clock was striking. There waiting by the door was Irvine's daughter. He took a deep breath.

'Awfully good of you to come, Sherry. I'm Blair, but you can call me Anthony if you like.'

'Hallo. It isn't Sherry, actually. It's Cherie. You spell it C-H-E-R-I-E. Still, *nil desperandum*. I'll forgive you. You're only a boy, after all. One can't expect too much.'

Blair was momentarily discomfited. Somewhere in a magazine he had read about these educated New Women who were agitating for votes and chaining themselves to railings. Perhaps this girl was one of them.

'Sorry. I'll write it out two hundred times if you like.'

He smiled and she smiled back.

He opened the door for her and they entered the shop. The photographer understood immediately what was required, and produced a backdrop with the words 'Drury Lane' in large letters. 'Now smile like a Gaiety Girl,' he said. He took three plates of Cherie in different poses, and offered one extra for no charge.

'I should like a picture of you in your uniform,' said the girl. Blair posed grasping the steering wheel of a large

'BLAIR POSED GRASPING THE STEERING WHEEL.'

wooden replica of a motor-car. He took three sovereigns out of his pocket, and agreed to collect the photographs the very next day. Feeling very pleased with himself, Blair offered to buy ice-creams in Berlusconi's café.

'I've never been in here,' Cherie confessed as she licked the last traces of coffee ice off her spoon. 'My stepfather is awfully strict.'

'Your stepfather?'

'Yes. Mr. Irvine is my stepfather. He married my mother when she was a widow, but now she's dead as well. I'm an orphan, you see.'

Blair had never met a real orphan before, though he knew all about them from novels.

'How unfortunate. Are you unhappy?'

'Oh no. I will be going away to school next term. Miss Beale has offered me a scholarship, you see. The Latin in the exam was mostly Caesar and the Greek was only Thucydides, and I'd done all that, so it was as easy as pie.'

Blair was impressed, but tried not to show it. Cherie then questioned him about the concert party which he had cited as the reason for wanting her photograph.

'It's going to be at the end of term. I shall be in it, and I'll make sure you're invited. How rotten that you are going away and we shan't see each other again!'

The following day Blair collected the photographs, signed the one of himself and slipped it in an envelope with one of the pictures of Cherie. He slid the envelope through the letter-box at the lodge, and then wrote 'With love from Lizzie' on another picture, and delivered it to Scargill, who caused him no further trouble. The third picture of Cherie he kept for himself and placed it, wrapped in tissue paper, at the back of a drawer in his study. He was about to make a new entry in his diary, but thought better of it. Diaries could so easily be read by other boys.

Blair resolved to husband his resources for the remainder of the term. To remove temptation he accepted Brown's offer to keep his cash under lock and key. *'Radix omnium malorum est cupiditas,'* his study companion muttered. 'Money is the root of all evil.' Brown entered the sum of two pounds in a ledger, and gave him an IOU, a grand piece of paper which bore in copperplate the word 'Investment'.

At the back of Blair's mind, however, there was a problem. On the spur of the moment he had thought up the idea of a concert party, and now he would look a fool if no such event were to take place. There was no alternative but to set about organising one.

Consultations began in the faggery that evening. Blair proposed that the concert would be open to all third, fourth and fifth form boys. An organising committee would be established to compose a programme, obtain the use of Big School on the last evening of term, and handle other arrangements.

With a slight show of reluctance, Blair agreed to preside over the committee himself. At the next meeting, to which all interested boys were invited, Archer was chosen as treasurer and immediately proposed that any surplus funds from what he called 'our smoker' should be given to a charitable cause.

The school was responsible for a Christian mission in one of the back streets of Mesopotamia, where Dr. Bush often preached on Sundays. It was agreed *nem con* that buying footballs for the mission would be the most suitable cause.

In the next few days Blair used all his persuasive skills

to winkle out a list of those ready to perform their party pieces. Piano players tinkled the ivories, conjurors and magicians inspired by *Chums* and the *Boy's Own Paper* competed for the right to do their tricks before an audience, and several boys revealed an unexpected vocal talent.

Brown held himself aloof; there was something in his Calvinist character which made him reluctant to put on the motley and entertain others. Besides, he was doubtful about the choice of Archer as treasurer for the venture.

'I wouldn't leave that character in charge of collecting the money,' Brown warned. But Blair ignored him. Archer was a gentleman, no doubt about that, and though he was not universally popular, Blair felt his presence added to the lustre of the event.

The programme drew on the talents of as many boys as possible, and several sixth formers agreed to help. Kinnock was to rehearse the choir in singing 'Men of Harlech' while Smith was to organise a dramatic tableau on a Scottish theme. The Salisburians would sing 'Hearts of Oak' and a selection of sea shanties, while Blair himself volunteered to recite some extracts from Shakespeare.

With a week to go, Blair learned that with 'please' and 'thank you' and judicious compliments he could charm the birds off their perches. A boy with a new printing set agreed to produce programmes if someone else would bear the cost of paper and ink. Blair immediately thought of Maxwell. Perhaps it was time for the fat boy to do him a good turn.

'Maxwell, what are you doing for the concert party?' Blair asked.

'Nothing much. I can't sing, I can't act, I'm no good with conjuring tricks. You don't need me for your bally concert.'

'Why not cough up for the programmes? You can afford it.'

'Not at this stage of the term, old man,' responded Maxwell. 'You think the walls of my study are lined with five pound notes?'

'No, I always thought they were lined with scholarship exam papers. At least, that's what Brown and Redwood believe to be true.'

Maxwell turned pale. Beads of sweat dotted his brow. 'All right, how much do you need?'

'You cut along and speak to Campbell. He's the one with the printing set.'

Maxwell meekly did as he was instructed, despite being told by a younger boy to 'cut along' as if he were a fag. Blair was beginning to be a little scared by his own powers of persuasion. How much he had learned in just one term!

Invitations to the concert were sent to masters and to the parents of boys who lived close to the school. Blair made sure that Matron Boothroyd and the Famulus were included and delivered one in a separate envelope for Cherie, with a handwritten dedication signed with a large A.

Rehearsals coincided with the last examinations of term. Blair was suddenly aware that he had neglected his studies, relying instead on Brown to help him with his daily prep. For three mornings running he got up before dawn, lit a candle and swotted away before breakfast. On the last afternoon of the exams, his head began to swim and his forehead felt clammy. He put down his pen and rose to his feet, but his knees gave way underneath him and he sank to the floor.

He awoke to find Matron Boothroyd peering over him in the sanatorium. 'Complete rest,' he heard her say. 'No more excitements until the end of term. You've been over-working your brain, what little there is of it.'

'But Matron, I have the concert to prepare! They can't do the dress rehearsal without me.'

'Out of the question, my boy. You will remain in the sanatorium until the end of term, or I won't answer for the consequences. You have heard of brain fever?'

Blair gulped. Of course he had heard of brain fever. It was an ailment that came on suddenly and there was no cure. Was he going to be its next victim?

Matron patted him on the head. 'Don't look so alarm-ed. I've never lost a boy yet, though I can think of a few I wouldn't have minded losing.'

And with that she closed the door of the sanatorium and turned the key firmly in the lock. Blair flung his head on the pillow. All his hopes for a triumphant end-of-term concert were shattered. No Romeo could ever have felt such dark despair.

CHAPTER IV

BRINGING THE HOUSE DOWN

Blair sat up in bed in his pyjamas and sighed with frustration. After two whole days in the sanatorium, he was fairly sure that he was not going to die of brain fever after all. Matron Boothroyd had agreed to allow him a single visitor, and Brown climbed the stairs twice a day from the faggery to bring him news of the outside world. On his first visit he brought him Gibbon's *Decline and Fall of the Roman Empire* as light reading. Blair was too polite to reject the well-intentioned gesture, but asked his friend if he might not rustle up some Jules Verne as well.

'How's the rehearsal going?' he asked impatiently.

'Don't worry, it'll be just fine without you.'

This was not the reply for which Blair had been hoping. He had counted on his absence provoking a certain degree of disorganisation, if not outright chaos in the preparations.

Brown silenced his protestations. 'Everything's going like clockwork. Prescott's stepped in and taken charge.'

Prescott was a 'day bug' in Hardie's who came to school on a bicycle, his cap awry and his scarf trailing in the

wind. He was a budding poet and something of an aes-
thete, with hair flopping over his collar and a volume of
verse stuffed into his pocket. He was notorious for losing
his prep, forgetting his books and being generally absent-
minded.

'You're chaffing me, aren't you?' Blair addressed his
visitor.

'I'm afraid so,' Brown replied. 'Here's a jam puff. It'll
take your mind off the concert. If it's a disaster, you won't
be responsible.'

After Brown left, the winter light began to fade and a
few snowflakes swirled outside the window. In an hour or
so, the concert would begin without him. Blair wondered
if Prescott had remembered to reserve some seats at the
front for Cherie and other important guests.

His meal arrived on a tray carried by one of Matron's
assistants. When she reappeared to collect it, he flashed
her a smile and asked her to leave the door of the room
unlocked.

'I'm sorry, sir. Matron gave strict instructions about
locking up.' With that she turned the key, and he was left
alone 'in durance vile'.

To a fourteen-year-old boy with pluck and determination, a locked door is a challenge. Blair wondered
what Francis Drake, Lord Nelson or the Duke of Wellington would have done in his place. Would they have
meekly stayed in bed, listening to the faint sounds of
laughter and applause drifting up from Big School? Of
course not.

He pushed the bedclothes aside, donned his dressing
gown and slippers, and made for the window. The arched
casement opened on to a leaded roof just below one of
the spires. Blair swung his legs out into the cold evening

air, and looked over the parapet. The ground was four stories beneath him. Any thought of knotting two sheets together as boys so often did in novels began to seem hopeless. Suddenly, a gust of wind blew the window closed behind him. He was trapped! The wind was icy cold and the snowflakes began to tingle. He had read all about polar exploration and the Esquimaux, and knew that to avoid frostbite he would have to find a means of escape.

Blair climbed carefully along the roof to where a chink of light emerged from a window and pressed his face against the glass. Between heavy curtains he glimpsed two familiar figures in relaxed mood, enjoying mince pies and rummers of port. Seated together on the sofa were Matron Boothroyd and Irvine the Famulus, deep in conversation.

Blair moved quickly away from the window, but not quickly enough. The Matron had spent half a lifetime observing boys and their antics, and she had spotted him. The casement opened and she peered out.

'All right, young Blair. What are you up to?' she enquired.

'Matron, I opened the window because it was stuffy. I thought I'd take a look at the snow.'

'Don't tell crams, young man. You were looking to get out. Well, you're out now. Are you satisfied?'

'I can't open the window. Could you let me back in?'

'There's no pleasing some young gentlemen. Isn't that right, Mr. Irvine?'

'Indeed, Matron, indeed,' replied the Famulus.

Back inside the sanatorium, his teeth chattering, Blair stood face to face with Matron Boothroyd. 'I really feel completely better. Won't you let me go? The concert's about to start. After all, you seem to be enjoying a pretty cosy evening yourself.'

Matron Boothroyd glared at him, but there was a faint ghost of a smile on her face.

'I remember when I was fifteen, I climbed down a drainpipe to go and see the famous Leotard on his flying trapeze at the old Alhambra. Young people always have this idea that rules are there to be broken. Now get back into bed, you young scamp.'

She moved towards the door. 'And whatever you do, don't look in that cupboard,' she said sternly, gesturing towards a wooden door with 'Fire Equipment' painted in red on the outside. With that she was gone, turning the key behind her.

Blair needed no second invitation to open the cupboard. Inside was a bucket, an axe and a large coil of rope. It was the work of a moment to tie the end of the rope to the iron bedstead, push the rest out of the window and climb after it. Blair looked to see if the coast was clear, then tossed the rope over the parapet. Like an alpinist he tugged the rope a couple of times to make sure it was firmly tied, then swung himself over the edge.

O! The happy foolhardiness of youth! How easy it is to believe we are immortal when our experience of real danger is so slight! A real mountaineer would have thought twice before attempting the descent, but pluck and determination carried him through. At first he swung wildly on the rope, then managed to balance his feet against the stone wall and lower himself downwards. At the bottom of the rope there was a drop of about ten feet. Looking down for the first time, he let go and fell into two inches of snow. He was free!

Behind the curtain at the end of Big School he found

'HE LET GO AND FELL INTO TWO INCHES OF SNOW.'

his chums in the final stages of preparation. A cry went up: 'Sooty's here!' and they crowded round him, slapping him on the back. A programme was thrust into his hands. Campbell and his printing set had done them proud! He sneaked a glimpse through the curtain. Among the parents and the masters' wives sat Cherie, wearing a blue dress trimmed with lace and carrying a Christmas rose.

Even the Salisburians had a cheerful greeting for him. Soames put down the top hat he was to use for his conjuring act, and shook him warmly by the hand. Archer acknowledged him with a wave, and other boys from the rival house smiled as if he was one of them. Only Brown looked down in the dumps. 'Hallo, Sooty, I've been learning a speech from *Macbeth* because I thought you wouldn't make it. I was going to take your place in the second half.'

'Jolly decent of you, old man. But it won't be necessary. Here I am, as large as life!'

Brown turned his back and walked away.

'Well, I suppose you can always hand out the programmes,' Blair said. 'Better still, be a brick and fetch me my togs from the dorm.'

The big clock struck seven times, and the audience hushed in anticipation as the gas jets were turned down. The curtain was pulled back with a flourish, and the pianist launched himself into the overture.

There is nothing like an end-of-term school concert to persuade parents that their hard-earned income is being well spent on the fees at an English public school. There is nothing to touch the sight of a choir of freshly scrubbed boys, with the mud of the rugby field removed, singing their hearts out and making the rafters ring.

The Salisburians were singing sea shanties and a

selection from *HMS Pinafore*, finishing with a rousing chorus of 'Hearts of Oak' that would have carried all the way to Portsmouth. From behind the curtain Blair glimpsed Cherie applauding enthusiastically. Behind her a small boy in a sailor suit, probably someone's younger brother, jumped up and down and shouted 'Hurrah!'

Would Hardie's be able to compete? Blair suppressed a feeling of panic as Prescott took the stage to read a selection of poetry. There was a titter of laughter from the back of the hall as he placed himself behind the lectern, dressed in a velvet smoking jacket with a large floppy tie. Prescott was a devotee of the Aesthetic Movement, and would have been more at home in the last decade of the nineteenth century than in the new world of aeroplanes and motor cars summoned up by the twentieth.

The laughers were stilled momentarily as Prescott recited verses by Browning and Swinburne. He raised his arms with a flourish and mopped his brow with a silk handkerchief, acknowledging the polite applause from the ladies at the front. 'Well done,' Blair hissed at him in a loud whisper. 'Don't give them any more.' But Prescott feigned not to hear him. 'I shall now read a selection from the prose of John Ruskin and Walter Pater,' he announced. After a few minutes, there were sounds of restlessness from the audience. 'The Stones of Venice seem particularly heavy this evening,' one master murmured to his neighbour. Prescott responded by quickening his pace and increasing the volume. Pater's theories of beauty had never been broadcast in such stentorian fashion, and the murmur of laughter turned into a full-scale roar.

Prescott began to stumble over his words. From the back of the hall, a shout of 'Down with the natives!' was followed by a slow handclap. From the side of the stage,

Blair gesticulated furiously at Prescott, who by now was faltering.

Many a boy would have lacked the presence of mind to handle such a tricky situation, but not Blair. With a broad grin he marched out from behind the curtain, applauding as he walked up to Prescott and clapped him warmly on the shoulders, then gestured to the audience to rise to their feet. The effect was akin to that of a conjuring trick. The audience rose from their seats and clapped furiously. Prescott and Blair bowed low towards them, leaving the stage to the sound of cheers.

'Thanks, Sooty,' said Prescott.

'Never let them see you're nervous,' Blair responded. 'It's not what you're saying that counts, but how you say it.'

After this shaky start the concert went well. A small Spanish boy named Portillo performed a song with castanets and an exotic dance in which he stamped his feet to a guitar accompaniment. At the end the fiery-tempered youth bowed low to the audience and swirled his black cloak proudly in the direction of the applause. Then came a sketch set *'Among The Natives'* in which the inhabitants of a coral island prepared to cook a visiting missionary in a large iron pot. The natives, clad in grass skirts and with their faces blacked with cork, danced around a wooden replica of the school clock and a street sign marked 'Coalhaven 2 miles'. After boiling the hapless missionary with parsley sauce, the chorus of natives from all three houses burst into a medley of music hall songs including 'A Bicycle Made for Two' and 'Who's Your Lady Friend?'

At the interval there was a rush for the tombola stand and for Signor Berlusconi's lemonade and buns at the back of the hall, with many of the smaller cork-blackened boys ignoring the prefects' injunction to be polite and let the audience be served first. From behind the curtain Blair could see Matron Boothroyd and the Famulus joining the throng of masters and parents. Then the crowd parted, and the illustrious figure of Dr. Bush himself entered the hall.

Nobody, least of all Blair, had dreamed for an instant that the headmaster of St. Stephen's College would abandon his Biblical studies for an hour to watch an informal entertainment staged by junior boys. A space was quickly made in the front row as the audience returned to their seats.

As the lights were dimmed, Archer jumped on stage. 'Dr. Bush, ladies and gentlemen, parents, masters, friends and boys of the school! I have an extra special announcement to make,' he said with the air of a man about to announce the coronation of a monarch or the discovery of a new planet. There was an expectant silence.

'I am delighted to announce that the income from tombola and ticket sales has broken all records,' he declared. 'As treasurer I originally hoped we might be able to buy a few footballs for our mission in the impoverished quarter of Coalhaven. Now, however, I am proud to tell all of you tonight that according to my calculations we will now be able to purchase no fewer than one hundred footballs!'

As a unit of currency, the football may have some drawbacks compared to the gold sovereign, or even the cowrie shell. It does, however, have the advantage of being instantly comprehensible to even the dullest boy. There were cries of 'Bravo!' and shouts of 'For He's A Jolly Good Fellow!' which Archer acknowledged with a bow that Blair found slightly too prolonged. As the applause continued, Blair consoled himself with the knowledge that Archer was only basking in his reflected glory. The audience might not know it, but the whole concert was Blair's idea in the first place. It hardly seemed above board for Archer to take the credit.

In the second half of the concert the boys of each house staged their historical pageants. The boys of Gladstone's house appeared in suits of armour to celebrate the signing of the Magna Carta at Runnymede. The Gladstonians had uncovered some mediaeval costumes buried in a basket in one of the school attics and laid claim to them. The boys of Salisbury's had wanted to stage a tableau involving Richard the Lionheart, but with the armour and costumes all spoken for, they had to settle for King Alfred burning the cakes instead. When he saw the blackened cakes appear on a tray, Blair understood the origin of the acrid burning smell which had wafted up to the sanatorium the previous evening.

The boys of Hardie's had been practising hard for their tableau, which portrayed Robert the Bruce and the battle of Bannockburn. This provided roles for all the Scottish boys in the house, who marched on stage swathed in brown blankets and armed with claymores. Blair's knowledge of history was far from all-encompassing, but he knew enough to understand that from the English point of view Bannockburn was a defeat. Should Hardie's really be celebrating it? It was too late to ask the question. Smith of the sixth form had taken charge of this particular tableau, rallying the Scottish boys with the promise of a real bagpiper. And now, lo and behold, there burst forth from the gallery of the great hall the skirling sound of the pipes. There was much craning of heads to see where the noise was coming from, but the piper remained invisible.

On stage Brown and Cook took advantage of the commotion to poke each other viciously with their claymores. There was a bloodthirstiness about the Scottish boys which Blair, nurtured in the gentler climes of England, could never quite bring himself to admire.

Next came a violin and piano duet by two small fourth formers, who were greeted with polite applause. Some of the audience, including the Famulus, looked at their pocket-watches. Soames performed his conjuring tricks, all three of them. Then Archer took the stage to read a story of his own composition, which he introduced with a reference to the great works of Dickens. The story was an adventure set in the French Revolution and betrayed a recent perusal of *A Tale of Two Cities*. The plot was convoluted and the attention of the audience began to wander. The small boy in the sailor suit was seen dozing on his mother's arm, and Matron Boothroyd shook her head. She cast a sideways glance at the Famulus, whose attention was also fading, and elbowed him gently in the ribs. Archer's story reached its climax with a scene in which the innocent hero escaped from the clutches of his wicked half-brother and returned to clear his name and complete his education at St. Stephen's College, meeting a warm welcome from the wise headmaster.

Blair found this part of Archer's story a little contrived, and he was not sorry when he saw Dr. Bush frowning and shaking his head for a second before he raised his hands to applaud. His own performance of extracts from Shakespeare was to conclude the evening, and he left the crowded backstage area to steady his nerves. He caught only a fleeting glimpse of the Salisburians' final offering, a comic song and dance routine about fox hunting, performed by Soames and five other boys. It seemed only a minute or two before a long burst of applause and a whisper of 'Sooty, you're on!' told him his big moment had come.

Most of the boys in the audience knew that he was locked in the sanatorium suffering from suspected brain fever; there is nowhere news travels faster than along the corridors and through the dormitories of an English public school. So there was an audible gasp when Blair appeared on stage. 'Friends, Romans, countrymen, lend me your ears!' he proclaimed. There was no hesitation in his voice, and no question of him stumbling over the lines, which he had learned by heart during those long hours of incarceration. There was a hint of shy modesty in the way he delivered the famous speech that captivated the audience, and out of the corner of his eye he saw Matron Boothroyd looking at him with warm approval. He dared not look in Cherie's direction for fear of losing his composure, but his eyes took in Dr. Bush, who peered at the programme through his pince-nez to check the name of this talented young Shakespearean. He bowed slowly to the audience and walked off the stage to a tumult of clapping. There really was nothing to match this – not scoring tries at rugby, not winning scholarships, not even writing novels like young Archer. He had not felt such intense happiness since the day his father lifted him onto the footplate of a locomotive at the age of eight to be instructed by the driver, who presented him with a badge in the colours of the Great Western Railway and a lump of coal. For a few moments, he had held the audience in the palm of his hand, and he knew that having captured their attention, he did not want to lose it.

The clapping was still going on when he reappeared on stage. With a swift gesture of his hand, he bade them be still. His eyes surveyed the audience; Cherie was on the edge of her seat, looking intently at him. 'But soft! What light through yonder window breaks? It is the East, and Juliet is the sun!' There was a catch in his voice, and a boyish hesitation which melted the hearts of several mothers in the audience, who turned to each other and wondered aloud why their own offspring were so uncouth and untalented compared with young Blair.

Unfortunately for Blair, the mothers were outnumbered. While a dramatic critic could not have faulted his performance as Romeo, the presence of several score of his fellow schoolboys meant that his choice of material was perhaps not of the wisest. Boys of fourteen and fifteen are not the most romantic of creatures, and speeches about girls and vestal livery tend to bring them out in goose bumps. Worse still, Blair had made a fatal error in signing up one of the smaller fourth formers to read the part of Juliet. The boy in question had refused to go on stage, insisting on uttering his lines in a piping treble from behind the safety of the curtain. At the line 'O Romeo, Romeo! Wherefore art thou, Romeo?' there was a burst of giggling from the back of the hall.

'Who's your lady friend?' shouted one wag. There was a gentle murmur of suppressed laughter, which like a stream bursting its banks gave way to a small torrent of noisy mirth. 'Shall I hear more, or shall I speak at this?' Blair realised he would do better to cut short his recitation, and was wondering how to get himself off stage when he saw a rose flying upwards in his direction from the front row of the audience. In a single movement he plucked it from the air, placed it between his teeth and bowed low to a storm of applause.

When he resumed with 'Once more into the breach,

dear friends, once more!' Blair knew that he had won the audience back again. In his mind's eye he was no longer a boy in front of a curtain reciting Shakespeare. He knew that from far away the spirit of Henry V was lending him strength. He was at Harfleur, calling on his men to stiffen the sinews and conjure up the blood, to set the teeth and stretch the nostril wide. 'On, on, you noble English, whose blood is fet from fathers of war-proof!' He no longer felt he was acting; he had left the stage, left the hall, left St. Stephen's and was suddenly somewhere else. 'The game's afoot! Follow your spirit; and upon this charge, cry "God for Harry, England and Saint George!"'

At that moment Blair stood very still for at least five seconds, then bowed his head. The audience clapped wildly. Some of them jumped to their feet and shouted. Out of the corner of his vision Blair caught a glimpse of a girl in a blue dress raising a handkerchief to her eyes.

CHAPTER V

THE TOAST FAG

'F-a-a-g!'

The voice is a familiar one, though deeper and more manly than when last we heard it.

'F-a-a-g! I want you here in ten seconds!'

More than two years have passed since we last heard the voice of Anthony Blair echoing in the corridors of St. Stephen's College. But now the voice has a new authority, for it belongs not to a lowly fourth former, but to a young man enjoying his newly acquired fagging privileges.

Much water has flowed under the bridge since that famous school concert. The stone walls of St. Stephen's still tower proudly over the clifftop, and boys have exchanged their school caps for straw boaters, for it is summer and the cricket pitches ring to the noise of willow striking leather. Much has changed in the school, and Blair and Brown are now members of the lower sixth, allowed to button and unbutton their jackets at will. Both of them are regarded as 'coming men' and have recently been made house prefects. The two chums, once so inseparable, no longer share the same cramped study. Each has his own quarters, at opposite ends of the corridor known as the

'Pilgrim's Way' to generations of St. Stephen's boys – or so the current denizens fondly imagine. For it is the young, not the old, who cherish obscure names, customs and traditions. The end-of-term concert before Christmas is now a fixed item in the annual calendar, and fourth formers have been heard to tell third formers that its origins are lost in the mists of time. No house at St. Stephen's is more wedded to hallowed custom and precedent than Hardie's, and the prefects know that they interfere with such matters at their peril.

Old Footer, Healey, and Benn have all left the school. So has Kinnock, who is now a subaltern on the Northwest Frontier, from where he sends the school regular letters about his progress in introducing rugby football among the Pathans. Maxwell has been withdrawn from the school after a family financial disaster. The captaincy of Hardie's has passed to Smith, but the boys of Salisbury's still rule the roost. Their ascendancy over the school is waning, but their swagger of natural authority is still ever-present. The boys of Hardie's have struggled to overcome the expulsion of Scargill and his cronies for fighting in the streets of Coalhaven. The incident which led to the imposition of this severe penalty has been so enhanced in the telling that, as in the great Norse sagas, no two accounts coincide exactly. According to one well-embroidered version, it was Thatcher the grocer who applied his leather belt to the Scargillites after one of them broke a shop window. According to another, even more fanciful, the boys were rounded up by the grocer's daughter, who escorted them to the police station herself, armed only with a knife and fork normally used to cut slices of ham off the bone.

'F-a-a-g!' Blair's voice betrayed a hint of steel. It was no use becoming a house prefect if the junior boys could not learn to respect authority. There was still too much slackness in Hardie's, he decided. He was reading a novel about a boy kidnapped by pirates in the Caribbean, which reinforced his view that the present generation of third formers enjoyed rather too many of the amenities of modern life. Instead of ship's biscuits full of weevils and barrels of salt pork, there were three square meals a day. Instead of the cat-o'nine-tails, they risked only an occasional encounter with 'Flogger' Williams' cane. Instead of climbing the main-mast in all weathers, the young mollycoddles at St. Stephen's were subjected to nothing worse than the occasional Hare and Hounds race across the fields. And even this was cancelled when it snowed. When younger, Blair had always done his best to avoid taking part in such events himself, but age had brought him wisdom and at seventeen he was now their fervent advocate.

Vexed to find his shout unanswered, Blair sprang out of his armchair and marched down the corridor. A few dozen steps further on, he caught the sound of a low moaning coming from the floor above. Strictly speaking, the dormitory floor was out of bounds until after evening prayers, but he knew this rule, like so many others at St. Stephen's, was often ignored. He turned, climbed the stairs and flung open the door to the dormitory.

The sight that met his eyes was a distressing one; to be more exact, it would have been distressing to most eyes, but not to a hardened veteran of Hardie's house such as Blair, who had seen many similar scenes before. A small boy was being held upside down by his feet. His head was invisible inside a metal firebucket full of water, which clattered against the iron bedframe as he tried to wriggle free from the vice-like grip of his four tormentors.

'He's in a funk,' said one of the four, an Australian boy named Murdoch, who spoke with a broad colonial twang. 'This should teach the little fella to put his fists up and fight when he has to, instead of threatening to peach.'

Murdoch, whose family was reputed to own a sheep farm as big as the whole of the United Kingdom, found the confines of St. Stephen's too narrow and its customs too quaint. He was no respecter of traditions, or of prefects. He would sit of an evening whittling sticks with a large bushknife and telling tales of his encounters with the duck-billed platypus and other exotic creatures.

The victim's head emerged from the water spluttering and moaning. Blair looked more closely and recognised a fourth former from Hardie's who had recently arrived at the school. He had few friends in his own house and was often seen consorting with older boys from Salisbury's.

'Put him down,' Blair heard himself saying. 'None of you should be in the dormitory before prayers. Besides, he looks as though he's had enough. Cut along.'

Murdoch smirked at him. 'You're only a house prefect and I'm not in your house, so I suggest you cut along yourself, young Sooty.'

Sooty was a nickname that Blair now found unfitting to his new station in life, but he was determined to hide his irritation at hearing it used in this mocking tone.

Blair heard footsteps behind him and looked round. In the doorway stood Smith, the captain of Hardie's, who was a school prefect. Never had he been so pleased to see reinforcements arrive. 'Let the wee chap go this instant,' said Smith. 'Is this what ye do with yirselves on yir sheep farm? Well, there's nae place for yir sort in this school.'

Murdoch nodded to the other members of his gang, who let go of the small boy's feet and allowed him to crumple in a sodden heap on the floor. They sauntered out of the dormitory and down the stairs.

'Oh thank you,' said the boy. 'They took my pressed flower collection and wouldn't give it back.'

'What's yir name?' asked Smith. 'Dinna blub like that.'

'I'm Mandelson, but they all call me Mandy. You can call me Peter if you like.'

'I don't like,' said Smith. 'Just run along, Mandelson, or you'll be late for prayers. And put the bucket back afore ye go.'

'Thank you, Smith,' the boy replied, and disappeared red-eyed down the stairs.

'Nasty business,' said Smith. 'What do you think we should do?'

Blair hesitated; he knew that Smith was testing him, and he was keen to give the right answer. 'Someone should sit down and have a man-to-man talk with Murdoch. I suppose he can't help being a bit rough. After all, he grew up in the outback.'

Smith peered back through his spectacles and shook his head. 'Fiddlesticks. He'll take nae notice. If ye need to sup with the de'il, make sure ye take a lang spoon. We canna let that wee boy go around crying his eyes out. Invite him for tea in your study and see what his problem is.'

Blair nodded. He was secretly glad that he would not be asked to confront Murdoch and his gang. He did not like encounters where his newly-minted authority as a prefect might be flouted.

Two afternoons later, young Mandelson was seated in the leather armchair in Blair's study, admiring his collection of books of adventure on the high seas, and devouring a pile of buttered crumpets from the tuck shop.

'And what does your pater do?' Blair enquired solicitously.

'He was in the Indian Civil Service, but he's dead. They buried him in the churchyard at St. Stephen's church in Ooty. Mother decided to send me here to St. Stephen's because of the name.'

'That's a terrible shame about your pater. But now you're here you must stick up for yourself. Take my advice and forget about the pressed flower collection for a while.'

Mandelson nodded. 'I suppose you're right. But I don't seem to have any friends. They all make fun of me and hate me. Especially Murdoch and his beastly crowd. Did you know they have a secret den in the basement for drinking and smoking?'

Blair did not wish to show his ignorance. 'Yes, we know all about that,' he interjected.

'Would it be a good idea if I kept an eye on them for you? They've promised to give me my pressed flowers back if I'll be their lookout. But I don't mind telling you what they're up to. You've been jolly decent.'

Blair hesitated. He had just been reading a story about a boy in Canada who spied for the Mounties on a gang of crooked gold prospectors. Mandelson was clearly more than just a mamma's boy if he was prepared to risk spying on the Murdoch gang.

'You're a plucky lad. But be careful.'

'Thank you, Blair. You're a real brick. Do you know what I would like to be more than anything else in the world? I want to be your toast fag.'

Under the reformed fagging system at St. Stephen's only the captain of school and the captains of the three houses were allowed to appoint their own toast fags. In the days before modern gas fires, each boy in the upper sixth would pick a toast fag from the third or fourth form. It was the younger boy's duty to cut bread from a large loaf, toast it with a fork before a roaring log fire and butter it, then run upstairs to the study floor with the product of his labours. If the toast was burnt or cold on arrival, he was sent back to do it again.

'You see, Blair,' Mandelson continued, 'You're bound to be captain of Hardie's before too long. I'd wager a half-sovereign you'll be captain of school as well. The boys in Salisbury's are all talking about it. So if I come up here in the afternoons and make your toast and tea, I can tell you what they're saying about you behind your back.'

Blair nodded gravely. Loyalty was a virtue which his father had always taught him to prize highly. A toast fag might indeed be a useful acquisition, especially one who had Mandelson's gifts. No doubt the boy had inherited the talents of his late father, who had probably run agents in the native bazaars of the Indian frontier towns.

'Yes. Consider yourself appointed forthwith. I don't have a badge of office, but I think you're better off without one. Put out your right hand and we'll shake on it. And if you like, Peter, you can call me Anthony.'

'Thank you, Anthony. That's topping. Now I won't have to worry about the Murdoch gang any more. I shall know there is someone to protect me.' With that, the young secret agent departed as discreetly and silently as he had come.

Blair shut the door of his study and began pacing up and down. Young Mandelson's confident predictions about his future had not come as a complete surprise; he had been wondering idly, at moments when Horace and Virgil were more than usually tedious, what the next year might hold in store for him. He had shared the general assumption that his old friend Brown would follow Smith in due course as captain of Hardie's. But now he wondered whether things would really turn out the way everyone expected. Or whether they really should.

Brown, of course, was an excellent fellow, now the proud holder of the school's most important scholarship and a star of the rugby fifteen and the cricket eleven. A year ago, Blair would have supported him through thick and thin. But now some doubts were creeping in. Brown, with his studious and meticulous character, was famous for undertaking the administrative drudgery which other boys shunned; he was now treasurer of nearly every sports club, entering the boys' contributions in a series of ledgers and keeping a close eye on expenditure. When a new box of cricket balls was required, Brown would carefully collect the old ones and take them personally to be sold at a shop in Coalhaven. *'Facta non verba,'* he would say. *'Praetio prudentia praestat.'* When subscriptions fell due, boys who were in arrears would receive a note in his neat copperplate handwriting, reminding them that their continued participation in rugby practice and cricket nets would be in jeopardy. He was also secretary of several school societies, taking great pleasure in the organisation of meetings, dramatic evenings and other events. Any boy trying to assemble a group of like-minded fellows at short notice for a draughts competition or a talk on birds and their nests would be abruptly reminded by Brown of the need to consult him in advance; not, of course, to obtain his permission, but merely to ensure the smooth operation of the school calendar.

Outside Hardie's, Brown was less popular. The boys of Salisbury's and Gladstone's held him in respect, but in little affection. Blair could not help reflect on the contrast with his own easy acceptance by the boys of the other houses. As he walked across the school courtyards, his cheery demeanour and friendly greetings were almost universally reciprocated. Whenever a group of younger boys was gathered together for a serious purpose, such as exchanging postcards of locomotives or practising conjuring tricks, Blair would stop to indicate his interest and drop a few words of encouragement. Thanks to an ability to remember the names even of obscure third formers, his reputation as a good-humoured fellow and a credit to the school continued to grow. *Sum amicus humani generis,* he thought. He was indeed a friend of the human race. Alas, our hero was not equipped with the equivalent of a miner's canary to help him detect the perils ahead.

Brown, he recognised, would do well as captain of Hardie's, but was he really the right choice to lead his housemates to the ultimate prize? Could he turn Hardie's into Cock House instead of Salisbury's? Was he really the right boy to become captain of school? Until now, Blair had shunned such thoughts, but his talk with Mandelson had opened wide a door that he had privately kept closed. He could not help wondering if the smaller boy's prediction might be right. By some strange coincidence, the boys of the lower sixth were studying *Macbeth* in the summer term, and Blair wondered whether his new toast fag Mandelson was, like the three witches, a servant of a higher purpose.

Since Blair and Brown had moved into separate studies, the two boys had lost their former intimacy; within a short while they abandoned the habit of sauntering down the Pilgrim's Way to drop in on each other for a chat. The estrangement left Blair feeling uneasy and he considered it high time he made amends. The next afternoon, he picked a book off his shelf and walked down the corridor. Pausing only to knock briefly on the study door, he entered to find Brown enjoying a mug of tea and a slice of buttered gingerbread.

'Come in, Sooty old man,' said Brown with a wave of the arm. *'Quid novi?'*

'Nothing in particular,' said Blair. 'I've got a topping new story I thought you might like. It's about a Scottish boy in Africa; he joins a pioneer column and they get ambushed by the Matabele. Cracking stuff.'

'There's no time these days for reading stories,' Brown replied. 'But thanks all the same. I'll keep it by my bed in case the Matabele attack St. Stephen's.' He offered Blair some tea and gingerbread.

'You're well supplied these days,' his visitor commented. 'A parcel from home?'

'No. There's a new boy in the fourth who's insisted on becoming my toast fag. I told him I didn't need a toast fag, but he took no notice. His name's Mandelson. Do you know him?'

Blair felt like a ship's captain on the bridge spotting a small dark cloud on the horizon. But his face did not move a muscle.

'No, I don't think I do,' he replied.

After leaving Brown to his textbooks and his accounts ledgers, Blair reflected on whether he should confront Mandelson and insist that he resign as Brown's toast fag. But a moment's thought sufficed to persuade him that this would be both foolish and superfluous. He did, however, drop the most casual of hints to the younger boy that he was fully aware of the state of affairs; some prefects might be inclined to raise objections to sharing a toast fag, but not he. Of course, he added, it would be better if Brown remained unaware of his toast fag's other duties. And if any useful scraps of information on house matters were to come to Mandelson's attention during his visits to Brown's study, then he, Blair, would certainly be interested to learn them.

Mandelson proved to be a fountainhead of interesting observations on his fellow-pupils and their weaknesses. He had little to impart about Brown that Blair did not know already, but he knew everything that Murdoch and his gang were getting up to in their den. The Australian boy and his growing band of fellows had forced the lock of a room in the basement which was used for storing old furniture. They would sit around on the broken armchairs, smoking and drinking beer, and even gambling at cards. By the light of a guttering candle, the boys would swap stories of life in faraway corners of the Empire. One would tell the tale of how he had driven away a pack of dingoes with his own gun; another would describe his father's tiger-hunt in India; a third would recount how he had personally tracked an elephant in Natal. But, as Mandelson reported to Blair, the den was also a centre for school gossip, particularly about the misdemeanours of boys in Salisbury's and their debts to local tradesmen.

'You won't believe the latest things, Blair,' announced the toast fag one afternoon. 'Murdoch is organising a syndicate to place money on horses, and he's going to start printing a newspaper.'

Blair was not shocked by the revelation of secret gambling; after all, he had more than once used 'wee Cookie' as an intermediary to place his own bets when his funds were low. He could not for the life of him see anything wrong with the practice, providing the intentions of all concerned were pure. *Exitus acta probat,* as the ancient Romans expressed it. And in his case, there could be no question that the end justified the means. He had used the money on one occasion to buy a birthday present of some handkerchiefs for his mother.

He was far more interested in the mention of a newspaper.

'Does this have anything to do with Campbell?' he enquired of Mandelson.

'Yes, they're going to use his new printing set with proper movable type and everything. But it's going to stay secret because they don't think the prefects will allow it.'

Armed with his knowledge, Blair decided he should tell Smith. The captain of Hardie's was walking out of the school gates in the direction of Coalhaven when Blair caught up with him. Smith squinted owlishly at his companion, and Blair noticed his spectacles were missing. 'I'm off tae order a new pair in town,' said Smith.

'What happened to the old ones?'

'Some bright fellow trod on them at the cricket nets,' came the reply.

'What a terrible bore. Can you see?'

'I can read a book, but I canna make out that sign across the street.'

Blair began telling Smith all that he had learned about Murdoch and his acolytes, including the mooted plan for a school newspaper. 'I shall have to discuss it with Major. Though he wilna do anything. He's afeart of Murdoch and his set.'

Major was the captain of school and of Salisbury's house. Despite his exalted standing, he was looked down on by many of the 'swells' in his own house and wielded little authority. His academic attainments were modest, and it was only his prodigious achievements on the cricket field that had won him the captaincy.

'If I was ever captain of school, I wouldn't take old Major-minor for a model,' Blair exclaimed. 'He lets all the other prefects in Salisbury's sit around in endless discussions. No wonder the old school's in such a mess.'

'Don't I know it,' said Smith.

'The newspaper sounds interesting, though,' Blair interjected. 'I don't think we should stop it entirely. Why don't we offer to let them pin it up officially on a noticeboard? In exchange for us checking what it says, of course.'

'What did I say about supping with the de'il?' Smith replied.

Before Blair could respond, there was a sound of hooves and wheels, and from round the corner came a small dog-cart, travelling at a perilous pace. Blair and Smith caught a glimpse of two young ladies screaming and hanging on for dear life as one of the wheels mounted a culvert. The runaway horse's harness was hanging askew and the reins were twisted around the shafts. The boys turned and watched in horror as it gathered speed at the beginning of the long descent into Coalhaven. Blair scanned the pavement, but there was nobody else within sight, and no obvious way of halting the cart's descent.

Then Smith ran and launched himself at the horse, flinging both arms out in an attempt to grab the reins. Without his spectacles, he was fatally unsighted and lost his footing, catching a glancing blow from the shaft and falling beneath the wheel. Blair's hand went to his mouth as the two women cried out for help. Within a few seconds, the cart had swerved sideways and clipped a gatepost, grinding to a halt in a confusion of dust and stones. The horse stood sweating and distressed, tossing its head and pawing the ground as the two terrified passengers alighted.

There in the middle of the road lay the prostrate form of Smith, with Blair cradling his bloodied head in his arms. He was still alive, but his laboured breathing and the gash on his brow betokened the worst. 'Fetch some water!' shouted Blair. The young ladies knocked on the door of a nearby cottage, and returned with a cloth and a jug. The wait was agonising. Blair mopped Smith's brow, and the injured boy seemed to come to.

'Dammit, I couldna' see the reins,' he groaned. 'You may have to play the cricket match without me.' With that his head fell back and he was silent.

CHAPTER VI

THE REWARDS OF VIRTUE

The June sunshine dappled the lawns and cricket pitches. Horatio, Dr. Bush's elderly labrador, lay stretched out as usual on the stone flags that led to his master's lodgings. But the normal morning bustle of St. Stephen's was nowhere to be detected. Instead, the sound of a hymn drifted across the courtyard from the chapel, where the entire school had assembled to pray for Smith's recovery. As the organ fell silent and the boys knelt in prayer, Blair looked sideways at Brown, who was next to him in a pew near the front. Brown's eyes were red from weeping at the fate of his friend and fellow Scot. Blair had also wept copiously – not immediately after the accident, but alone, after he and the injured Smith had been transported back to school by a passing motor car. Smith was taken on a stretcher up to Matron Boothroyd's sanatorium, where Coalhaven's leading physician, Dr. Munro, was quickly summoned to make a visit. That evening he left the school looking grim. Small knots of boys stood around, robbed of their customary high spirits by the news.

Inside the chapel, Blair closed his eyes and listened as

'Flogger' Williams led the prayers for Smith. His faith in the power of divine providence was hedged around with question marks. If God really wanted to save Smith, then surely He would have prevented the horse from bolting in the first place? Then there would have been no accident. Or was everything that happened predestined? If so, there was not much point in praying to change it. God, after all, was not the kind of person who was given to second thoughts.

After the service, as the boys dispersed to their classes, Blair's thoughts were interrupted by two young ladies, who dabbed their eyes with handkerchiefs as they approached him. 'Good morning,' one of them said. 'Aren't you the boy who helped save our lives?'

'It was Smith who saved your lives, not I,' came his modest rejoinder.

'Oh no. You are just as much a hero as your friend. We saw you hanging on to the reins at the risk of your own life. We have told our father about you, and we came this morning to thank you in person.'

'To whom do I have the honour...?'

'I am Hetty, and this is my sister Clementine. Our father is the Marquess of Coalhaven.'

Clementine, the younger of the two, stretched out her hand. 'Call me Clemmie,' she said with a smile. 'I am sorry we are meeting on such a sad occasion. When your friend is fully recovered, you must both come to tea.'

'Oh yes,' added the older sister. 'Father wants to meet you. Will you please give our very warmest wishes to young Smith when you see him? We understand visitors are not allowed for the moment.'

Blair promised to do as he was asked. Was this meeting also part of God's great pattern for him, he wondered as he watched the chauffeur help the two young ladies into their motor car. 'I say, Blair, could I have a word?' came a voice at his elbow.

It was Campbell, the proprietor of the famous printing set, whose ink-stained fingers were clasping a pencil and notebook. 'Could I have a word about the accident? I couldn't help overhearing your conversation.'

'Is this by any chance for Murdoch's newspaper?' Blair enquired.

'You're in luck. It's our first issue this week and the accident is going to be the story on the front page. Murdoch's already written the headline.'

'What's it going to say?'

'Heroes of St. Stephen's.'

'I'm not a hero. I just did what anybody would have done. Smith was the real hero.'

Campbell sucked his pencil. 'Yes, but I can't talk to him. I already tried to get in, but Matron threw me out. So you'll have to do.'

Blair reflected for a moment, and then clapped Campbell on the shoulder. 'Very well. Come to my study at four.'

Two days later, the first issue of the *St. Stephen's Rocket* was pinned to the noticeboard outside Big School, with a crowd of boys craning their necks to get a glimpse of it. Blair waited for them to disappear at the bell, then approached.

'OUR HEROES' said the headline. The account of the accident, accompanied by a pen and ink sketch, was highly dramatic, and bore little resemblance to what Blair remembered. It described how he and Smith had simultaneously flung themselves at the runaway horse, hanging on for dear life as it careered for a hundred yards down the road. There were numerous quotations from eyewitnesses, who claimed to have seen the whole tragedy from beginning to end. Lady Hester and Lady Clementine, it said, were praying daily for the life of their injured rescuer. Blair himself was said to have behaved with cool composure in summoning medical attention. 'I am no hero,' were the words which the *Rocket* reporter chose to head the second part of his account.

There was a discreet cough from behind. Blair looked round to find Campbell watching him nervously. 'Is it all right?' he enquired.

'It'll do,' Blair replied. 'Come with me to the san. I'm hoping we may be allowed to visit Smith.'

When they arrived outside the sickroom Brown was already waiting in a state of distress. 'It looks very bad,' he said. 'Munro says he's weakening.' The three boys looked at each other in dismay. The door opened, and Matron Boothroyd emerged. 'He's asking for you. Dr. Munro says you can go in for two minutes.'

Blair, Brown and Campbell, who was still clutching his notebook, filed in to the room. Smith was propped up in bed, his head bandaged and his face a deadly shade of pale. 'Come in, you fellows. Where have you been?' he asked.

'We wanted to come earlier. But it was better to wait until you were on the mend,' said Blair. 'The two girls are very concerned about you. They want us to come to tea.'

Smith shook his head, as if to rule out the possibility. 'You can go on your own, Sooty. Don't worry about me. I shall be fine, whatever happens. I want you two to promise me something.'

Blair and Brown nodded silently. The meaning of Smith's words could no longer be disguised.

'Promise me you'll both stay chums. I don't want you

to be fighting each other. And promise me you'll make Hardie's into Cock House. And make sure you never let the old school down.'

'We will,' said Blair. 'We promise,' said Brown. At the far side of the room, Campbell sat scribbling in his notebook.

'It's a fine place, St. Stephen's,' Smith continued. His voice was getting weaker, and the boys leaned forward to catch his words. 'Yes, it's a fine place. But I'm going somewhere that's better by far. Next term, you'll forget that I was ever around here at all.'

'No I won't,' said Blair. 'You can trust Sooty. Cross my heart and hope to die.'

At that moment, Smith's eyes closed and his head sank back on the pillow. He was breathing, but had slipped out of consciousness. Dr. Munro motioned to the boys to leave the room. They did not speak as they descended the stairs and walked into the sunlight. But Blair slipped quietly into the chapel to pray.

Smith passed away the next morning, in the presence of his parents, who had been summoned by telegram from Scotland. The school flag with the portcullis emblem was at halfmast and a guard of honour composed of Boy Scouts and the school Rifle Corps stood to attention as the carriage bearing his coffin and his relatives left for Coalhaven station. The short ceremony was supervised by the Famulus, who in his early years had been apprenticed to an undertaker. It was agreed that Brown would travel with the family and attend the funeral on behalf of the other boys.

The next edition of the *Rocket* carried a series of tributes to Smith, and a tastefully written account of the scene in the sickroom, in which Blair's fervent pledge 'You can trust

Sooty' figured prominently. There was also an appeal for contributions to place a stained glass window in the chapel in Smith's memory. Because of Brown's absence, Blair was named as the person to whom contributions should be addressed. In bold type, the editor of the newspaper called on the boys of St. Stephen's to put aside their grief and faithfully carry out Smith's dying wish to make their school the best in all of Great Britain. This applied particularly to the boys of Hardie's, who had been robbed of their captain of house. Luckily for them, the editor wrote, there was no shortage of suitable successors, including Blair, the surviving hero of the fatal incident with the runaway dog-cart.

'You're going to have to put your name forward now,' Mandelson told Blair the next day as he cleared away the teacups. 'I've been asking around, and most of the chaps want you as captain of house. You can't just hide your light under a bush, or whatever the bally Old Testament proverb says.'

'But Brown is the obvious choice, everybody knows that. He's been preparing for it for years.'

'I know. I happened to come across his diary,' Mandelson confided.

'Well, Dr. Bush has the final say. And Brown and I promised Smith we would work together, not fight each other.'

Mandelson put down the teatowel and looked Blair straight in the eye. 'You know very well that if a name emerges among the senior boys, the prefects and the chaps with cricket and rugby colours, the old Doctor won't go against it.'

The younger boy was speaking the truth, and Blair knew it. At St. Stephen's, unlike some public schools, the senior boys were encouraged to take as much responsibility as possible. The leadership qualities which this generous regime encouraged would be doubly valuable when the boys entered the real world. In whatever far corners of the Empire St. Stephen's old boys were to be found, they were second to none in their pluck and initiative, in their gentlemanly conduct and their honesty.

'You don't have to fight each other,' Mandelson continued. 'I agree, that would be rotten. One of you has to withdraw. And I don't think it should be you.'

Blair began to protest, but fell silent as Mandelson continued. 'You think Brown is cut out to be house captain? Well, he might do quite well. But if we want Hardie's to be Cock House and to have our captain head the school, then we jolly well have to pick a man who will have support all over the place. Gladstone's and Salisbury's don't have much time for Brown. That means you, I'm afraid.'

'He won't agree to withdraw. I know him,' Blair said.

'Leave it to me. I think I can persuade him. Look at what Campbell's been writing about you in the *Rocket*. He's on your side, you know. And old Murdoch seems to have taken quite a shine to you as well.'

Blair knew better than to interrogate his young toast fag about the sources of his information, which almost always turned out to be accurate.

By the time Brown returned from Scotland two days later, the idea that Blair was going to be the new captain of Hardie's had spread around the school like an indelible inkstain on a clean white shirt. From a possibility, it became a probability, and then a certainty. The first meeting between Brown and Blair was an awkward one.

Neither boy wanted to visit the other's study, so they arranged to meet in the cricket pavilion, where they were sure to be undisturbed. There was a summer rainstorm, and the building was deserted as Brown arrived to find Blair scanning the photographs of past school teams which hung on the walls.

'The poor man's not yet cold in his grave,' said Brown with an icy stare. 'You ought to be ashamed, flaunting yourself around as his successor. I know what's been going on behind my back!'

'Nothing's been going on behind your back! Nothing has been decided, and I've nothing to be ashamed of,' Blair retorted. He had always deferred to Brown before, but this time he was determined not to give in to his Presbyterian hectoring.

'What about all that stuff in the *Rocket*? Don't tell me you had nothing to do with that. You know Smith wanted me to take over from him next term. We discussed it.'

'I don't control what Campbell writes. Some of it's sheer fiction. All I will say is that there are lots of boys in Hardie's who want me as captain and I've told them I'll go for it. I can't pull out now.'

'You remember what Smith said. He asked us not to fight each other.'

'Correct,' said Blair.

'So you want me to withdraw instead of you?'

'I want you as my friend. Together we can do great things for Hardie's and for the school. I shall need you, Brown. And who knows, if something awful happens, or I get expelled in disgrace or something, you'd be the ideal man to take over.'

'You're not planning to get yourself expelled, are you, Sooty?'

'I certainly hope not. I mean it, old chap. You can trust me. You can take charge of everything else, all the societies, all the sports clubs. And if we make a big effort this term Hardie's will win all the cups and come top in all the exam results, and we'll be Cock House after all.'

'Very well, I'll think about it.'

The next day Mandelson came into Blair's study with a note in Brown's copperplate handwriting. 'What does it say?' he asked.

'He's agreeing to withdraw,' Blair replied. 'Will you take back a note in reply?'

'I can't,' confessed Mandelson. 'He's in a foul mood. He told me never to come near his study again. I think he suspects I was your toast fag all along and blames me for everything.'

'That's jolly unfair,' said Blair.

'He still keeps an enemies list in his diary,' Mandelson continued. 'You're at the top of it, and I'm in second place. I just thought you should know.'

The choice of Blair as the new captain of Hardie's was confirmed by a meeting of house prefects and senior boys. The next day his appointment was announced at morning prayers by Dr. Bush, who referred to the tragic circumstances in which Smith's successor was taking over, and asked all the boys of Hardie's to give Blair their support. If the boys of St. Stephen's were to serve their country and the Empire, then they had to assume leadership and the authority that came with it; honour was the reward given to virtue, but honour also required modesty and humility.

Blair went to the chapel to pray. He looked up at the stained glass window proclaiming *Veritas Prevalebit*. The truth would prevail. It was pointless criticising the

Almighty for the way He arranged things, he decided. It was more modest to accept that certain events which might seem to be mere accidents were in fact manifestations of some far greater divine plan. So it was with his elevation to the house captaincy.

As he left the chapel, he bumped into 'Flogger' Williams, who gave him a stern look. 'I hope you prove to be the right choice, young Blair,' he said meaningfully.

The next issue of the *Rocket* gave pride of place to Blair's promotion and speculated on the chances of Hardie's snatching the laurels from Salisbury's in the remaining weeks of the summer term. Young Mandelson confided to Blair that he was now penning articles for Murdoch under a *nom de plume*. The first such column, signed 'Horatio', suggested that things were going from bad to worse in Salisbury's.

Brown made a public show of loyalty to his new house captain. He continued as a house prefect and the majority of Hardie's boys were pleased to see Blair in charge. There were, however, mutterings of discontent among the 'natives', or day-boys, who felt their interests had been overlooked because none of them had been present at the meeting where Blair's name had been agreed. In order to silence the grumblers, Blair decided that Prescott, the long-haired poet and leader of the native contingent, should deputize for him in his absence. 'Of course,' he explained to Brown, 'being my deputy doesn't mean anything. It's just to keep the Coalhaven boys happy.' Prescott was invited by Murdoch to compose a poem for the *Rocket* entitled 'The Runaway Horse'. After some judicious editing, it duly appeared.

THE RUNAWAY HORSE

It takes a knight in armour bright
To save one maiden fair
It takes a rather special boy
To bravely save a pair.

Now gather round and pay good heed
Pray tender me your ear
A song I sing of pluck and speed
And how to conquer fear.

That day upon the clifftop road
A boy became a man.
He's now the subject of my ode
I'll try to make it scan.

Two boys are strolling into town
They hear the sound of hooves
A huge black horse is hurtling down
How speedily it moves!

Between the shafts the horse runs free
The girls are in despair
A cry for help, a tearful plea
Cuts sharply through the air.

But one brave boy has heard them shriek
Alone he makes his stand.
The horse's breath is on his cheek
He leaps with outstretched hand!

With all his strength he hangs on tight
The foaming beast slows down
The awful hooves are rendered quiet
Their cargo safe and sound.

The girls cry out 'Sir Galahad!
Who are you, youth so fair?'
The boy replies: 'A college lad.
Trust me – my name is Blair.'

J. Prescott

Blair called a house meeting in the senior dayroom. Third and fourth formers from Hardie's filed in and huddled together on the floor, looking up in awe as their new house captain explained that there was a tide in the affairs of men. So it was in the affairs of the school, which was nothing but a microcosm of the world outside. *Fortes fortuna adiuvat!* If Hardie's was to become Cock House again, then every boy would have to pull his weight both on the sports field and in the examinations. Blair pointed to the extraordinary record Brown had set in winning scholarships, and urged the younger members of the house to emulate him. Then Prescott recited 'The Runaway Horse'. The meeting ended with shouts of 'Hip Hip Hooray!' and the singing of 'For He's A Jolly Good Fellow'. Blair cut short the singing, telling his audience: 'I think that can wait. We're not Cock House yet.'

The Hardie's boys went away with a fresh determination to do well. They rose early to translate Virgil, carried their mathematics books with them to breakfast, and queued at the cricket nets to practise their batting. Major and the other boys in Salisbury's were preoccupied with their own rivalries, and failed to notice what was going on. Small boys from Hardie's learned the verses of Prescott's heroic poem by heart, especially the line describing how Blair clutched the reins and brought the foaming beast to a halt. They recited it boldly at the tops of their voices when the swells from Salisbury's were in earshot.

At last 'Vic Week', the week of the inter-house cricket matches for the Victoria Cup, arrived. Gladstone's put up a brave fight, but succumbed by three wickets to Hardie's and lost the next day by a remarkable seven wickets to Salisbury's. The winners of the match between Hardie's and Salisbury's would carry away the Cup and become favourites in the race to be Cock House.

The deciding match was expected to be close. Salisbury's had ruled the cricket square for so long that the Victoria Cup had not been won by any other house for some ten years. But this year's match had the makings of a real contest; two of Salisbury's best bowlers had gone on to Cambridge and were now winning Blues. Dr. Bush, wearing a striped blazer of a violent hue, welcomed his guests. Pride of place went to the Marquess of Coalhaven and his daughters, who were seated in wicker armchairs. Behind them on wooden benches sat parents and local tradespeople connected with the school, such as Thatcher the grocer, who left his daughter in charge of the shop, and Signor Berlusconi, the owner of the town café and licensee of the school tuck shop. As an Italian, he claimed no special understanding of cricket, but explained to enquirers, touching his straw boater as he spoke, that he was intending to learn.

The Salisbury's team won the toss and batted first. Major scored 40, but after Brown sent his stumps flying, the innings began to falter. The Hardie's team fielded like demons, and cheers went up around the ground when Clarke, one of the most feared batsmen, proved too slow between the wickets and was run out. The innings closed on 129, a target which looked well within reach. Archer was keeping the score for Salisbury's and initially credited his team with 139, but the error was spotted and the total corrected by the umpires.

Blair, however, was not taking any chances. 'Don't tempt fate and don't take anything for granted,' he told his team as they prepared to bat. 'Just play safe.' Even Prescott, who was known for his emotional style of batting, paid heed. The mood was one of grim determination as Blair and Brown walked out to the crease to open the Hardie's innings. The runs came steadily, though an attentive observer might have detected a certain lack of warmth between the two opening batsmen. Once Blair and Brown had survived the first four overs without mishap, a certain tetchiness began to infect the fielding side. Heseltine, the team's star bowler, looked rusty from lack of net practice. Clarke tried running after the ball but was forced to give up with a fit of coughing. 'Too many cigars, old man!' shouted a voice from the pavilion. The score crept along to 38 without loss when Brown edged a ball behind third man. 'Yes!' shouted Brown, charging down the wicket. 'No!' cried Blair in horror as the fielder scooped up the ball. He set off down the pitch in a doomed attempt to reach the crease, but was still two yards out when the wicketkeeper whipped off the bails. Run out for 24! After that Brown dug in like a limpet, making a half-century, while the less experienced batsmen pinched singles and twos like veterans. Suddenly the scoreboard read 126 for four. Small boys on the touchline

'HE SET OFF DOWN THE PITCH IN A DOOMED ATTEMPT TO REACH THE CREASE.'

were cheering themselves hoarse, only falling silent when told by sixth formers that shouting during a cricket match was bad form. The Salisbury's fielders were by now standing around with folded arms, sighing as the ball ran past them and trotting casually in its pursuit. A murmur of excitement was heard from the spectators. 'Come on, Hardie's!' shouted the younger boys. 'Hit it for six!' It was Brown's turn to take strike against the bowling of Major, but he was not to be tempted into anything rash. *Praetio prudentia praestat* was his motto. He prodded his bat forward to the first four balls of the over, left the fifth one alone, then turned the sixth delicately behind square leg. Four runs!

The cheers from the Hardie's boys sent the rooks flying out of the trees. Brown was the hero of the day with 75 not out, and a rare smile of satisfaction played around his lips as he received the congratulations of the Marquess of Coalhaven. Salisbury's had surrendered the Victoria Cup and Hardie's had won it in fine style. 'Splendid, young man,' said the Marquess as he put the trophy into Blair's hand. 'You must come to stay before next term. My daughters are insisting on it. We will send Ecclestone with the motor to meet you.'

The boys of Hardie's celebrated their famous victory with foaming bottles of ginger beer and lemonade. Wee Cookie, who had been taking bets from the swells of Salisbury's backing their own side to win, collected a tidy profit. From Archer he accepted a promise to settle up on the first day after the long vacation.

The rest of the summer term passed in a blur of examinations. For day after day the boys sat in Big School, where the only sound was of three hundred pens scraping across three hundred sheets of paper. The Hardie's boys swotted as if their lives depended on it. Monsieur de Chirac, the French master, who had almost given up in despair at the inability of his charges to learn the language of Voltaire, found to his astonishment that boys from Hardie's were asking him to stay behind and go through the present tense of *avoir*.

Even the despised natives were doing their best, walking or cycling back to Coalhaven with satchels packed with books. For they knew that to become Cock House, the valiant footsoldiers of Hardie's would have to score higher on average than their counterparts in Salisbury's. 'Good old Sooty, we'll do it for him,' they whispered to each other as they filed in to the hall.

A week later, when the papers were marked and the results calculated, Mandelson rushed excitedly up the stairs to Blair's study. 'We've done it!' he confided in a conspiratorial whisper.

'How do you know? The Doctor is only announcing it tomorrow.'

'Never you mind how I know. We've beaten their average mark by eight per cent. It's unheard of! I'm off to tell Murdoch, in strictest confidence, of course.'

Thus it came to pass that a special edition of the *Rocket* was posted on the noticeboard early the next morning, announcing that Hardie's had won the contest to be Cock House fair and square. So when Dr. Bush rose to read out the result at the annual prizegiving, there was no great sense of surprise. 'I am happy to announce that when the school returns in September, the position of captain of school will be filled by Blair of Hardie's house,' he proclaimed. The good doctor was about to continue, but his voice was drowned in a chorus of cheers from the Hardie's boys. They jumped on to the green benches of Big School, threw their hats in the air and made the oak beams ring with shouts of 'Hip hip hooray!' and 'Three cheers for Sooty!'. The Salisbury's boys were dumbfounded at being supplanted as Cock House, a role which they had held since time immemorial. Now they were to surrender their status as the Brahmins of St. Stephen's College to a lesser caste. Dr Bush, unable to silence the tumult, put down his Bible and joined in the applause.

Blair bowed his head and closed his eyes. There *was* a divine plan after all, and he was privileged to be part of it. *Veritas prevalebit*. He felt very humble.

CHAPTER VII

STAYING THE COURSE

The summer holidays seemed to flash past like an express train. Blair's parents were delighted by the news that their son was to be captain of school, though his sister Lizzie spoiled the celebration by pulling his ears and exclaiming: 'I expect, dear brother, that you will now become unbearably pompous!' The Blair family spent their usual two weeks in Weymouth, accompanied for the first time by young Mandelson, who became a firm favourite with Lizzie after buying her a large shrimping net and challenging her to repeated games of 'shrimp cricket' on the sands.

After Mandelson returned to his mother and the family was once more at home, Blair asked his father where he might find a copy of Burke's Peerage. 'Come with me to the Constitutional Club. I expect it is in the library,' his father replied. 'But why do you need it?' Blair explained that before term started, he would be staying the weekend with the Marquess of Coalhaven at his country seat not far from St. Stephen's. 'I have to reply to a letter, and I need to know the correct way to address the daughter of a marquess,' he confessed.

'YOUNG MANDELSON, WHO BECAME A FIRM FAVOURITE WITH LIZZIE.'

Though the letter he had received on crested notepaper was signed just 'Hetty', Blair followed Burke's advice to the letter and replied 'Dear Lady Hester'. He confirmed his time of arrival at Coalhaven station, and said he was looking forward to the weekend with great anticipation. What he did not say was that the anticipation was mixed with increasing nervousness. It was a sharp climb up the social ladder from the Blairs' modest villa to the rolling acres of the Fairhaven estate, ancestral home of the Coalhaven dynasty. His father's view, shaped by his years as a Justice of the Peace, was that true gentlemen were to be found in every station of life. This approach seemed to Blair admirable in theory, but of little practical help in preparing him to be the Marquess's weekend guest. He was partially reassured by Hetty's kindly instruction to bring just his school luggage. 'Don't bother with lots of country togs. We can lend you anything you need,' she wrote.

Blair began his research in Burke's Peerage, imagining the first Coalhaven splashing ashore with William the Conqueror just in time to be depicted in the Bayeux Tapestry shooting the fatal arrow at King Harold. His descendants had probably gone on a crusade or two, defended their battlements during the War of the Roses and been chased by Roundheads during the Civil War. Younger sons of the family had no doubt distinguished themselves at Blenheim, Waterloo and Balaclava. But a quick perusal of the red-bound volume revealed no evidence of blue blood trickling down the generations. The father of Lady Hester and Lady Clementine, a widower, was the first and only holder of the title. His family name was Jenkins.

When the day of his departure from home dawned, Blair paid extra attention to the packing of his clothes. He knew that the greatest social solecism that a country house guest could commit was to unpack his own luggage instead of leaving the staff to do it. 'Speak up and be polite, and remember to comb your hair,' his mother admonished him. Blair's mother, like all representatives of the maternal species, could never get used to the fact that her son was now seventeen years old, rather than twelve.

When the train pulled in to Coalhaven station, Blair was met by a uniformed chauffeur who sprang to take his bags. 'Just climb in while I get her started, sir,' the man said, as he loaded the luggage and swung the handle. A Rolls-Royce! Blair did his best to look as though he travelled in this fashion regularly as the magnificent vehicle swung into the street, attracting admiring glances. At St. Stephen's the subject of motoring, like aviation, was endlessly debated by the boys, who pored over magazines to glean the latest details of the new machines which were favoured for the Tourist Trophy. The Simms-Welbeck, the Arrol-Johnston and the Thornycroft all had their passionate supporters. But majority opinion held to the view that the Rolls-Royce held the crown. As the magnificent silver vehicle cleared the outskirts of Coalhaven and approached the open road, the chauffeur handed him a pair of motoring goggles. 'You'll need these, sir. Let me take you for a little spin. Hang on tight!' Blair felt the wind whistling past his face as the motor climbed the hill towards St. Stephen's and the bend where the horse had bolted. Now they were on the level, travelling along the clifftop. 'She's doing at least thirty!' the chauffeur shouted over his shoulder. This was the right way to travel! A cloud of dust billowed behind them as the horn sounded, scattering the seagulls. Blair looked ahead to see a female pedestrian taking swift avoiding action. There was something familiar about the half-remembered face covered with a scarf. It was Cherie! He turned round and waved vigorously, but she looked away without a spark of recognition. He realised that his face was hidden by the goggles.

The car crunched to a halt on the gravel drive and Blair looked out on Fairhaven. It was a surprisingly modern and spacious country house in red brick, rather than the Palladian mansion he had expected. Hetty and her sister skipped down the steps to greet him, followed by two dogs, and a few steps behind came the Marquess himself. 'You're on time, lad. Hope you enjoyed the ride.'

'Very much, sir. This is the new six-cylinder model, isn't it?'

The kindly host clapped Blair on the shoulder, delighted to find an attentive audience for his story about how the Silver Ghost had been delivered to Fairhaven by the great Mr. Royce himself, an engineering genius whom he was proud to call a personal friend. 'My last motor was a Panhard, but there's no comparison. Don't you agree?'

Blair nodded enthusiastically. His own experience of motoring was restricted to occasional journeys in taxicabs, but he did not want to show ignorance. The Marquess was not at all the languid aristocratic figure he was expecting, but a forceful personage who was used to being obeyed instantly. 'My girls will show you round the place. There's tea on the terrace in a few minutes.' Blair was ushered upstairs into a well-equipped bedroom which opened into an equally spacious bathroom, fitted with the very latest American designs of bath and shower. All the lighting was electric and there was an elaborate system of bells and buzzers for summoning staff.

At tea Hetty and Clemmie explained that the Marquess

was a busy man; he was the owner of the Coalhaven Collieries, founded by his late father-in-law, and of the Black Pig Brewery, whose products quenched the miners' thirst after every shift. In the space of twenty years he had sunk new mineshafts, built whole colliery villages, dredged the estuary and expanded the port. He was the patron or president of a dozen local organisations and a generous benefactor to all of them. 'Papa's very keen on people who make their own way in the world as he did,' Hetty explained. 'He's rather down on the idle rich.'

'Don't worry, I'm not one of those,' Blair replied with a grin. 'I have been accused of being idle, but never of being rich.' His worries about the weekend were beginning to recede as the two young women put him at his ease. After a walk around the grounds and a brief game of croquet he went upstairs to change for dinner, to find his best suit laid out neatly on the bed. He reflected with satisfaction that the role of charming weekend guest was one that he could play without too much difficulty. It was certainly a lot easier than performing Shakespeare.

At dinner they were seated at a long oak table. After a glass of champagne and two glasses of claret Blair's conversation began to sparkle; Hetty and Clemmie laughed uproariously at his impersonation of the Ancient Mariner who had taken them boating at Weymouth. Even the Marquess was amused. After dessert the conversation took a more serious turn, and Blair was questioned about school matters and the tragic accident in which he had played so heroic a part. 'I shall raise a toast to the young man who stopped the runaway horse and saved my daughters,' the Marquess said. Blair looked modestly down at his plate and said nothing as Hetty and Clemmie raised their glasses in unison. 'To Anthony!' they exclaimed.

Over the port and nuts Blair began to feel a little drowsy as the young ladies engaged in a spirited argument with their father over the merits and demerits of riding side-saddle. The Marquess rose from his chair to signal that the discussion was at an end. 'Hunt rules are hunt rules for everybody. I don't care if you wear breeches to ride around Fairhaven, but tomorrow you'll be riding side-saddle like all the rest.'

'But father!' protested Clemmie.

'If you fall off, young Anthony here will rescue you, I'm sure. Goodnight.'

Suddenly Blair realised the full implications of what had been said. His equestrian experience was very slight, and nowhere in his wildest imagination had he considered the possibility that his weekend programme might include galloping across the countryside on a horse.

'I'm not sure...' he began. 'I don't have riding boots or anything.'

'But of course you will come!' said Hetty. 'What else will you do tomorrow? You can borrow Ernie's togs.' Ernest was the sisters' elder brother and heir to the Coalhaven fortune. He was presently somewhere on a remote Canadian farm, learning to make his way in the world.

Within five minutes, Blair was led by the hand into Ernest's bedroom and equipped with everything he needed, from riding hat and black jacket to tailored breeches and well-polished boots. As he tried them on in the privacy of his bedroom after the sisters had waved him goodnight, he reflected that he cut rather a dash. But then his heart sank as he looked in the mirror and realised that this was not just a stage costume. He went to sleep dreaming that he was a fox, pursued across open fields by a pack of hounds and a hollering band of riders. There would be no escape.

It was a beautiful late summer morning for the Coalhaven Hunt's first outing of the season. Blair came down to breakfast to see the Marquess reading *The Times*. 'There's bacon, liver and kidneys. Tuck in now, it's going to be a long day. God knows why the Coalhaven Hunt always has to start the season a month before everyone else.' Unlike the usual run of condemned men, Blair had little appetite for a hearty breakfast, but he piled his plate from the silver chafing-dishes as instructed, so as not to seem impolite. He was rescued by Hetty and Clemmie, who summoned him to the stables to choose a mount. Blair followed them, with the two chocolate-coloured labradors Huntley and Palmer bringing up the rear and licking his hands.

'Anthony's the same height as Ernie. I'd love to see him up on Emperor,' said Hetty, as they approached what seemed to Blair a very large brown-coloured animal which was glaring at him and making contemptuous snorting noises. 'I have to confess, I'm rather out of practice. Have you something a little smaller?' Blair was reluctant to reveal that his last excursion on horseback had been on a bad-tempered pony when he was about ten years old. Why the pony was so bad-tempered when it lived in one of the most beautiful corners of the Dorset countryside with no visible dependants to support was unclear. But the memory was not a happy one.

'There's always Pumpkin, I suppose,' said Clemmie. 'Not really the right mount for hunting and he's only fourteen-two. But at least he's no trouble.' Pumpkin lived in a far corner of the stable and even Blair could see that he was the sort of animal who lived to eat, rather than ate to live. Breakfast, lunch and tea were the high points of his day, and locomotion in between these feasts was kept to a minimum.

Blair looked Pumpkin straight in the eye, smiled and patted him on the nose. There was no reaction. 'Come on, Pumpkin,' he heard himself say. 'There's a good chap.'

The groom had Pumpkin saddled in no time, and held him still while Blair placed his foot in the stirrup and mounted him. So far, so good. Pumpkin stood still, all four hooves apparently glued to the cobblestones. Hetty and Clemmie were waiting for him on their mounts by the gate. 'You'll have to give him a good poke now and again,' said Hetty. 'Once he gets moving, he'll start to enjoy it.'

With a couple of sharp taps on his broad rump, Pumpkin was persuaded to follow the others. Perhaps this expedition down the lane might lead to some kind of al fresco equine picnic, he wondered as he fell in step behind the larger horses. After a few minutes Blair began to feel that things were not turning out quite as badly as he feared. His mount was lagging a little behind and stopping occasionally to nibble the vegetation, but he felt broadly in control of the situation. However he was well aware from the jolly scenes depicted in sporting prints that hunting was not generally conducted at walking pace.

When they reached the village square, Blair had a chance to look around him. The scene was as pretty as a picture, with the hounds spilling across the green, the riders touching their hats to each other and the horses clattering on the metalled road. Pumpkin seemed less than enthralled by the turn of events, though he perked up a little when Clemmie gave him half a carrot. 'Look, Anthony,' she said. 'Just follow me and you'll be all right.

You won't have to jump anything if you don't want to. When in doubt, open a gate.'

The huntsman sounded his horn and they all moved off. Soon the long straggle of riders became even longer. By the time they entered the third field, they had lost sight of the hounds, who had disappeared into a covert. The field was a triangular one and Blair was uncertain what would happen if he encouraged Pumpkin to trot down the steep slope towards the noise of baying hounds. 'There's no way out down the bottom there,' said Clemmie. 'They're all going to have to come back. Let's head for the top corner.' They reached it just as the leading riders came into sight, heading up the hill towards them. 'Better hang on and let them pass,' she told Blair. He was starting to feel more at ease with Pumpkin, though he was not sure that his confidence was fully reciprocated. The animal was starting to slow down and consult its internal clock, which told it that the next meal was probably some hours away and it might be advisable to look for a midmorning snack. Pumpkin moved to the corner of the field, where an old dry stone wall had collapsed, just leaving room for a horse and rider to pass. He put his head down and began to eat.

All manuals for young riders will tell you that the best ponies are always grass-fed. Pumpkin agreed whole-heartedly with the manuals and was determined to prove them right. He was still eating contentedly, moving on from the hors d'oeuvres to the main course, when Blair became conscious of a commotion behind him.

'I say, move over!' came a shout. 'Out of the way!' came a stentorian female voice. He looked round to see a lengthening queue of sweating animals and riders, all heading for the gap in the wall. There was a note of urgency in the requests, explained by the fact that the hounds had taken a short cut through the covert and were several hundred yards away. A horn sounded. Blair tapped Pumpkin on the rump with his riding crop and jerked the reins, but there was no reaction. He tried using his knees, but it was hard to get much leverage on the broad expanse of Pumpkin's middle regions. Was this the fetlock or the withers, he wondered? Either way, Pumpkin would have to show some manners and shift himself. 'Come on, Pumpkin!' he shouted. 'Come on, old chap!' But the animal was not to be moved. His legs were rooted in the grass like young oak trees and he took no notice.

'Young idiot!' said the female voice, followed by a chorus of imprecations. 'Can't you see I'm doing my best?' he shouted in return. 'It's not my fault!' Blair looked around for Clemmie, but she was nowhere to be seen, having passed through the gap ahead of him. At that moment a middle-aged man with a red face and white whiskers levelled his riding crop at Blair and spat out a stream of oaths. 'The worst display of horsemanship I have seen in fifty years!' he shouted. 'You are holding up the hunt!' Blair jerked the reins again, but without result. The red-faced man raised his riding crop, and Blair thought for a split second the man was going to lose control and strike him across the face. He let go of one rein and put his hand up to protect himself. At that instant, the riding crop landed, not on him but on Pumpkin, with a resounding noise.

Nothing in Blair's extensive library of adventure stories had prepared him for what happened next. Wherever these stories were set, from the Argentine pampas to the Australian outback to the sunburnt veld of South Africa, their heroes had one thing in common. They were expert horsemen who never lost control of their mounts. Snakes, crocodiles, buffalos, lions, kangaroos and woolly llamas popped up regularly on the printed pages and sometimes in coloured illustrations, and might occasionally provoke a horse to rear up in surprise. But that was as far as it went. What was about to happen to him and Pumpkin was quite different.

Pumpkin was not used to having his mealtimes interrupted. His head jerked up and he twisted round to see where the blow had come from. He then swiftly engaged reverse gear, leaving Blair to fall forwards and grab hold of his neck for dear life. Then he looked around, spotted the gap in the wall and charged towards it, gathering speed. Blair's right boot caught the wall a painful glancing blow and his grip on the reins vanished altogether. Pumpkin was showing unusual acceleration for a pony of his size and shape. Within twenty yards he had moved from a standing start to a gallop, bypassing the walk, the trot and the canter. Blair decided it would be better to part company with his mount voluntarily and live to fight another day. With his right foot out of the stirrup, he executed what he hoped would be an elegant leap to his left. But Pumpkin's progress was by now too swift for such manoeuvres and Blair fell to the ground, landing heavily but breaking his fall with his hands and rolling over into a cowpat. As he sat on the grass in humiliation, head in hands, the rest of the hunt trotted past him, for all the world as if he was a clump of bramble.

As the riders vanished into the distance, Blair picked himself up. His bones were unbroken, but his right wrist was very painful and his eyes were smarting. Pumpkin was standing some thirty yards away, munching the grass as if nothing had happened. Blair picked up his riding crop, brushed the cowpat off his coat and breeches as best he could, grabbed the animal by the reins and headed back in the direction of Fairhaven.

An hour later Pumpkin was back in his stall concentrating on the next meal of the day. Blair was sitting in the bath inspecting his bruises and reflecting on the morning's unpleasant events. Never, never would he allow this to happen to him again! Never mind what foxhunting did to the fox! Its effect on people was quite beyond the pale.

Before dinner Hetty and Clemmie bandaged his swollen wrist. During the meal they were determined to avoid all mention of his misfortune and competed with each other to be as tactful as possible. Whenever the Marquess allowed the conversation to stray back to matters equestrian, one or the other of the sisters would glare at him silently while the other changed the subject. By the end of the meal Blair's spirits had recovered somewhat and he allowed the Marquess to pour him a tumbler of whisky and show him how to smoke a cigar. While the young ladies retreated to the drawing room, Blair expounded his plans for the coming term at St. Stephen's. After many years of drift and slackness, there would be a tough new spirit sweeping through the old college. It was important to send the proper signals from the start, and he had already identified a number of boys who would help him put things on the right track. Within a term or two, the school would be running like a Rolls-Royce.

'Do let me know if there's anything I can do for the school,' the Marquess said as he bade his visitor farewell on the afternoon of the next day. 'I always like a good cause to support. Though in my personal opinion, engineering is what you young lads should be studying, not Latin and Greek.' Blair thanked his host, promised to send him news of college life and allowed Huntley and Palmer to lick his luggage all over before it was loaded into the Rolls-Royce. Hetty and Clemmie each planted a kiss on his cheek in farewell.

As the magnificent vehicle gathered speed down the drive, Blair thought it was not a bad thing that the age of the horse was coming to an end. Good riddance to the beasts, he muttered to himself. One day, every Briton would have his own Rolls-Royce to drive and then things would be quite, quite different. The modern world, with its cylinders and its brakeblocks and its carburettors, its magnetos and its thirty horsepower engines was now unstoppable, and he was determined to be part of it.

CHAPTER VIII

A NEW BROOM

There was a spring in Blair's step as he alighted from the Rolls-Royce and tipped Ecclestone a shilling for his labours. A shout of 'Fag!' produced a gaggle of boys jostling for the right to carry his luggage upstairs. Matron Boothroyd passed him in the corridor and winked at him conspiratorially, as if to recall memories of past complicities. Blair spent his first afternoon back at St. Stephen's moving his belongings from his old study to the one reserved for the captain of school. The room occupied a corner turret and commanded a view in two directions, along the clifftop and over the playing fields. It had solid oak furniture, a leather sofa and two armchairs, and a wardrobe which smelt strongly of linseed oil, for it was the place where Major had kept his cricket bats. *Sic transit gloria mundi,* Blair thought as he contemplated the oblivion into which his predecessor had quickly fallen. He was determined that he, unlike Major, would leave his mark upon St. Stephen's College in a way that would be remembered by generations of boys. Within an hour or so, his new study was looking shipshape. 'I found this in your old desk,' said one of the helpful fags, handing him

'A SHOUT OF "FAG!" PRODUCED A GAGGLE OF BOYS.'

a dusty package wrapped in tissue paper. It was his photograph of Cherie, taken by the town photographer. Since her departure for Miss Beale's boarding school for young ladies he had not seen her, apart from a brief glimpse on the clifftop road. Would they ever meet again? His reverie was interrupted by the Famulus, who bore a message from Dr. Bush inviting him to dine that evening.

'Thank you, Irvine, that will be all.' The Famulus left the coffee on the sideboard next to the stilton and glided out of the room. Horatio slumbered peacefully on the Persian rug. Blair waited expectantly for Dr. Bush to begin the real business of the evening, a discussion of his tasks as captain of school. But the good doctor was still in the middle of a rambling story about how he had outwitted the Oxford University Press in an argument over Old Testament scholarship. 'Excuse me, sir,' Blair interrupted. 'I was hoping I could outline some of my ideas about the new term.' Dr. Bush stopped his discussion of Deuteronomy and encouraged him to say his piece.

'There's been an awful lot of slackness in the last few years,' Blair declared. 'Among the senior boys especially, and once the rot sets in, it goes all the way down the school. There's drinking and smoking and breaking bounds and not turning out for house matches, and so on.'

Dr. Bush nodded. 'If you say so, then it must be happening. I expect college rules to be obeyed without question and wickedness to be punished. *Thou shalt therefore keep the commandments, and the statutes, and the judgments, which I command thee this day, to do them.* It's all in Deuteronomy. What do you propose we should do?'

'Well, sir, I want Prescott as my deputy, because he's a day-boy and the other day-boys are rather expecting it. And here's a proposed list of new prefects. That will clear up a lot of the problems, particularly in Hardie's. Between ourselves I think Smith may have taken his eye off the ball now and then. And there's a particular problem with the fifth form, sir. They're too young to be prefects and too old to be fags, so they tend to be a law unto themselves. I think we need some way to keep an eye on them. Have you ever thought of a system of fifth form monitors?'

'That sounds a splendid idea. Do you have any particular names in mind?'

'Well, sir, I've been very impressed by young Mandelson. He's very loyal and upright, and he seems to have the knack of knowing what's going on.'

'Very well, Blair, I will announce it tomorrow morning. And Murdoch? Should I make him a prefect?'

Blair had been expecting that question. The Australian boy's role as editor of the school newspaper made him an influential figure at St. Stephen's, and giving him a prefect's cap would only increase that influence. 'I don't think he really wants to be a prefect, sir. He's not really a great respecter of college rules.'

'You do read his newspaper, of course, before it goes on the noticeboard?'

'Indeed, sir, without fail. The captain of school has authority over what goes on the noticeboard at all times.'

'I think a school newspaper is an excellent thing, providing it is well supervised. Naturally I would have preferred it to be partly in Latin, but I suppose the vernacular will have to suffice. Make sure you keep a close eye on it.'

Horatio woke up, rolled from side to side on his back with all four paws in the air, yawned, staggered to his feet and shook himself. Dr. Bush gave the dog a Bath Oliver and Blair took this as a signal that the meal was at an end.

The next morning at breakfast he found himself sitting next to Fatty Soames. 'Morning, Blair. Done something to your wrist?'

'Oh, it's nothing. I was out all day with the Coalhaven on Saturday. My mount was tired and I took a tumble towards the end.'

'Good sport, was it?'

'Splendid. Do you know the Marquess? He's a decent enough old soul when you get acquainted.'

Soames did not appear overly impressed by Blair's new social connections. 'Salt of the earth, Billy Jenkins. Another coalowner who bought his title off the peg. My pater says you can't move a yard in the Lords these days without bumping into a brewer. He says he's expecting Thatcher the grocer to get a peerage one of these days for his veal and ham pies.'

'There's nothing wrong with being a self-made man, Soames. Look at your own captain of house.' Blair was referring to Hague, a lower sixth boy chosen to general surprise as the head of Salisbury's. His father owned a ginger beer and aerated water business, and young Hague was sometimes spotted in the school holidays delivering crates of bottles from a dray. 'And you know that the Marquess has two rather charming daughters?'

'Be careful! Jenkins will invite you into his front parlour and ask if your intentions are wholly honourable. At which point you know the game's up and you have to marry one of them or run away to sea! Excuse me, I'm going up for some more toast. Tally ho, Sooty!'

Blair had mixed feelings about being chaffed in this fashion. He had not expected Soames to show so little respect for his new status as captain of school. But Soames and the other prefects from Salisbury's meant no harm and provided good company in a light-hearted way. Especially compared to Brown, who always appeared to take life a little too seriously. Blair's heart sank as he thought how difficult his relations had become with his old chum. He had wanted to have a heart-to-heart chat and clear the air at the start of term, but the moment never seemed right.

The new list of prefects contained a few surprises; some of the grander figures who sported their first fifteen rugby colours were eclipsed, and gasped in astonishment when the names were read out. In their place were boys who were generally undistinguished, but reliable and loyal. There was Byers, a bespectacled boy of no great attainments, and 'Tiger' Hoon, a dullish fellow who said nothing in class and only came to life when the college Rifle Corps, which he commanded, held its weekly parade. Hoon's voice lacked the authentic gravitas of the trained soldier, but he made up for it by gesturing with a large silver-topped ebony cane. At inspection time he would prod the ill-fitting uniforms of young recruits and criticise their turnout. If a boot was insufficiently polished, he would accept no easy excuses. 'You didn't have time? Time, boy, is something you must find for yourself, not something I give you credit for not having!'

The list also included some Scottish boys whom Blair hardly knew, but whose names had been given to him on a slip of paper by Brown, who made clear their qualifications for being prefects were beyond discussion. When all the twelve prefects assembled for their first weekly meeting in Blair's study, he quickly put them at their ease by making a joke about the Apostles. He adopted a brisk tone, imagining how a self-made man like the Marquess of Coalhaven might conduct his business affairs. The

Marquess would hardly tolerate endless discussions with minor shareholders about how to run his collieries or his port. 'I know you're all busy men, so I've decided to change a few things. In future I shall only hold prefects' meetings like this at the beginning and end of term. In between, you can come and see me individually when we agree it's necessary.'

Next on his agenda was a tightening of discipline. The weekly prefects' meeting had always been preceded by a session known since prehistoric times as 'E4', a term borrowed from some long forgotten basement room where rough justice was dispensed. Miscreant boys were summoned to face their accusers and had the chance to defend themselves before the prefects. In nine cases out of ten the verdict was guilty as charged and the errant pupils were soundly thrashed with a cane. Occasionally a boy was found innocent. Blair told the prefects that it was time to abolish E4 because it was timewasting and archaic, and announced that henceforth they would be expected to impose instant penalties for misbehaviour. It was bad for the school's morale when everyone expected a boy to be punished, only for him to be found innocent for some trivial reason and let off.

Punishment of young wrongdoers began to be a competitive sport among the newly appointed Apostles, who would exchange notes on how many victims they had personally thrashed. Some of the prefects went further, and devised their own punishments. Reid, a Scottish boy who had seen his share of scrapes in his young days, was found pushing the head of a third former named Filkin through the banisters for 'being cheeky'. Blunkett, another keen disciplinarian, decided to revive a device dating back to the days before Dr. Arnold, and imposed silence on a rowdy day-room or dormitory by arriving equipped with a red-hot poker. The fagging system, previously a matter of give-and-take among older and younger boys, was rigidly enforced. When one recalcitrant fourth former was tied up in a bath of ice-cold water for refusing to fag for a new prefect, it was the straw that broke the camel's back.

The next afternoon the cry of 'Fag!' echoed along the corridors of St. Stephen's but went unanswered. Word quickly spread that the fags had gone on strike, an event unprecedented in the history of the school. Mandelson came to Blair's study and sat down on the sofa with a furrowed brow. 'It looks serious. They had a meeting last night and held a unanimous vote. There's been a lot of talk about free-born Englishmen, and the Magna Carta, and *habeas corpus.* Some of them are saying it would never have happened under Smith. And there are one or two who think Brown is secretly on their side.'

Blair frowned. Historically, it was the senior boys of Salisbury's who had always upheld the fagging system, while many in Hardie's had wanted to change it. But he had no intention of giving in to the mollycoddlers. Because he came from Hardie's house, it was especially important that he should be seen to uphold the thin red line of authority. Blair had just finished reading an account of the siege of Mafeking and he knew that Baden-Powell had always imposed iron discipline, without which the defenders would have been overwhelmed.

'We're not going to give in,' he said. 'But I think I'd better talk to them.'

Blair arranged a meeting of all members of the third and fourth forms, to be held at a time when not only boarders but day-boys, who were not generally involved in the fagging system, would be present. He sent Mandelson off to discover who the ringleaders were and then went to see Brown. 'What do you think we should do?' he asked. Brown delivered a long reply which indicated he knew a great deal more about the origins of the strike than Blair did. 'Of course, I know who's put them up to this. It's Livingstone.'

Blair remembered that Livingstone had been a member of the Scargillite gang which had made his life such a misery two years earlier. Livingstone was now a member of the upper sixth, but was notoriously hostile to prefects and adept at undermining their authority. If there was one subject on which Blair and Brown could agree, it was that Livingstone was a rotter and a bad influence in the school.

'How do you know all this?' he asked. Brown pointed to a note on his desk in faint brown handwriting.'I have my sources of information,' he said mysteriously. 'It's invisible ink, if you haven't noticed.' Blair persuaded Brown to come along to the meeting. 'If I invite you to speak, what will you say?' he asked.

'You'll find out soon enough,' was the cryptic reply.

Blair had one more important interview to conduct. He despatched Mandelson to find Murdoch and ask him to visit his study. Murdoch was not often to be found in the usual haunts of St. Stephen's sixth formers; he shunned the day-room and the sports pavilion and avoided the tuck shop. After half an hour Mandelson came panting up the stairs.

'He wants you to go and visit him instead.'

'But that's ridiculous. I'm captain of school.'

'I told him that, but he took no notice. I think you'd better go.'

Blair realised that there was no point in standing on ceremony. 'Very well. Send out a scouting party if I don't come back.'

Following Mandelson's directions, he made his way down to the basement and entered a cavernous corridor. On either side there were vaulted brick arches, some containing coal for the boilers. Shafts of light from ground level illuminated old desks and broken chairs, iron bedsteads and a series of padlocked doors. A small black mouse scurried past him. The passageway turned to the left and revealed a door marked with a neatly printed card, just readable in the darkness. 'St. Stephen's Rocket Editorial Office', it said.

From behind the door Blair could hear the sound of a pianola playing 'Two Lovely Black Eyes'. He knocked and walked straight in. Murdoch was sitting in an armchair beside a potted plant. At the back of the room Campbell was sitting at a table in front of a typewriter. 'G'day, Sooty,' said the rough-hewn colonial boy, motioning him to a stool. 'I'll stop the pianola if it bothers you,' he said. 'What's the trouble, mate?'

Blair outlined his concerns about the strike and said he was curious to know how the *Rocket* planned to report the affair. He hoped very much that the school newspaper would take the side of the school as a whole, rather than that of a small faction of boys who were bent on trouble.

'We're pretty even-handed, I think,' came the reply. 'You know Campbell – he writes the story without fear or favour. Just the facts.'

Blair said he understood the *Rocket* had to report events in a balanced fashion; nobody was more aware of the need for balance than he was; but he hoped that the authority of the school and its prefects would receive firm support in the newspaper's editorial column. He reminded Murdoch that as captain of school, he had the authority to bar anything that was placed on a school noticeboard, and this included the school newspaper. Naturally, censorship of the *Rocket* was the last thing on his mind, but he considered it useful for the avoidance of possible misunderstandings to remind Murdoch of where ultimate authority lay.

Murdoch rose from his chair and walked over to the table. 'I want to show you something,' he said, drawing back a cloth. There on the table was a piece of modern machinery and on the floor beside it, an empty wooden packing case. 'Do you know what this is?' Blair shook his head.

'It's called a Gestetner machine. My folks ordered it for me from the United States. We're going to use it for the *Rocket*.'

Blair let out a whistle of admiration. 'By Jiminy. How does it work? Gas or electricity?'

Murdoch pointed to Campbell, who was vigorously pounding the keys of a typewriter. 'He's cutting a stencil. We put it in the machine, with ink and paper, and Bob's your uncle. Out comes the newspaper, like a rat going down a dunny.'

'And then it will go on the noticeboard in the same way?' Blair asked.

'Oh no, we won't use the noticeboard any more. You see, this is a duplicating machine. We can print as many copies of the *Rocket* as we like. We could print one for every boy in the school, if we had enough paper. There's no limit to what we can do.'

The implications of what Murdoch was saying took a moment or two to sink in. If the *Rocket* was not going to be pinned on the school noticeboard, he would be unable to check and approve its contents in advance. Suddenly, Blair realised that his chief bargaining card had been blown away. A change of tactics was required.

"What are you going to say about the fags' strike?' he asked.

'I'm not sure I really approve of fagging. We certainly don't have it Down Under. Now what do you think we should write?' Murdoch's question was posed with a menacing smile, but Blair detected the faint glimmer of a useful compromise.

The intelligent reader will not be surprised to learn that the conversation ended in agreement. Nothing was written down, but some important understandings were reached, namely: that the *Rocket* would criticise the striking fags as un-British and their ringleaders as dangerous troublemakers; that the new duplicated version would be sold freely around the school at the price of one halfpenny per copy; and that the freedom of the editor would be fully respected. There were some additional minor points which Blair agreed to in a spirit of goodwill once he was confident that Murdoch had succumbed to his persuasive arguments. These points were to remain confidential: that the editor would be free to visit the town of Coalhaven to conduct interviews, meet potential advertisers and fetch printing supplies without interference from prefects, and would have access to the editorial offices in the school basement at all times; it was also understood that rival publications to the *Rocket* would be strongly discouraged. At the end of fifteen minutes, as in all diplomatic negotiations of high import, there was a handshake.

The meeting of the third and fourth forms took place two days later. The *Rocket* carried a strongly worded editorial warning that the fags' strike was undermining the foundations of the school. Severe penalties, including expulsion, were being considered for the ringleaders, it reported. Brown and the other prefects were already seated in the crowded day-room when Blair entered, wearing a splendid new waistcoat of the sort traditionally favoured by senior boys in Salisbury's. He began by announcing that there was a new and urgent matter on which it was vital to hear the views of all boys.

In his inspection of a school outbuilding he had found two ferrets incarcerated in a cage. The animals' suffering was indescribable! What boy, he wondered, could be so cruel and inhuman as to punish small animals by locking them up in the dark? He was pleased to tell the boys that he had immediately released the ferrets back into the wild, where they would roam freely as nature intended. There were sighs of relief at this announcement, and some clapping, led by Brown. 'Thank you. Now I want you to vote on whether prefects should in future enforce a ban on keeping ferrets in school. Would all in favour raise their hands?'

There was a murmur of excited approval. Some third formers, unaccustomed to the procedures of Athenian democracy, raised both hands. 'Against? None. Abstentions? None? Carried *nem con.* Now we move on to other matters.'

Blair spoke briefly and persuasively on the subject of how his one desire was for the school to be a better place. He made up an amusing anecdote about how he had once been thrashed as a fag for breaking a teapot, and told the day-boys he had decided, in the interests of fairness and justice, that in future they would be freed of all fagging duties. He omitted to mention that this was already the case, but most of the young Coalhaven 'natives' in the audience were too grateful to notice. They were quickly convinced by Blair's open manner and ready smile that he had their interests very much at heart. When he sat down, there was prolonged applause. Brown spoke next, making clear to any doubters that while he could understand the feelings behind the strike, it had to be brought to an end. Nobody loved and understood the traditions of St. Stephen's better than he did. Then Prescott read out an 'Ode to a Toast Fag' in his inimitable style.

ODE TO A TOAST FAG
(after Newbolt)

Come gather round me by the grate
Raise high your mugs of tea
Pile high the muffins on the plate
And lend your ears to me.

But where's the butter, where's the jam?
The fags are all on strike
There's no-one left to slice the ham
Or fetch the things we like.

The fags who used to lay the fire
And bring us a jam puff
Have gone and left us in the mire.
They say they've had enough!

But hark! A footstep on the stair,
A knock, a treble tone –
'Please let me be your toast fag, sir!
I'll do it on my own.'

The boy lifts high his toasting fork
Puts crumpets on the table
He knows that action outweighs talk
He's loyal, fearless, able.

For soon the boy becomes a man
School days are left behind
We fight the good fight while we can
And cherish ties that bind.

Our bullets spent, our captain slain,
Then round the shattered wheel,
Like Drake upon the Spanish Main
We draw our blades of steel.

There's fire upon the afterdeck
The rigging's all ablaze
The ensign's bleeding from the neck
But steadfast is his gaze.

'I'll be your toast fag, do not fret
As long as battle rages!'
His fork is now a bayonet
His name in history's pages.

That man was once the stripling youth
Who dared to toast a crumpet
He loved his school and told the truth.
For him we'll sound the trumpet!

J. Prescott

When the matter was thrown open to the floor, only two fourth formers called for the strike to continue. Their words were met with a low murmur of disapproval, a stamping of feet and a drumming of fists on table-tops. It was agreed without a vote that the fags would resume their duties the following day.

The next issue of the *Rocket* (price one halfpenny) began with the headline 'STRIKE OVER!' An article signed 'Horatio' described the outcome as a triumph for British common sense and said the new captain of school, who had already proved his courage by stopping the runaway horse, had now proved himself to be an exceptional leader of men and a wise conciliator. Blair put down his copy with a feeling of a job well done and went to wash the purple ink off his hands.

CHAPTER IX

BOYS WILL BE BOYS

Left-right-left-right-left-right...PICK those FEET up!'
The sound of boots crunching on gravel briefly
drowned out the cries of the seagulls, then slowly
faded as the St. Stephen's College Rifle Corps marched
away down the drive in the misty October sunshine. Blair
watched from his study window as the long column of
boys in khaki headed for the road, their bulky knapsacks
on their backs and their rifles shouldered. At the head of
the column marched 'Tiger' Hoon with his silver-topped
cane, looking straight ahead. The corps was heading for
its half-term camp, a ritual which normally involved a
long train journey to Aldershot for an event shared with
other schools. But this year the Marquess of Coalhaven
was allowing the camp to take place on his estate, a
generous gesture which Blair felt owed much to the
favourable impression he had made on the Marquess
and his daughters.

The captain of school was not, however, taking part in
the expedition himself. All St. Stephen's boys were
expected to join the corps, and few exemptions were
granted. One group of boys from Gladstone's house had

recently won permission from Dr. Bush to set up a patrol of Boy Scouts as an alternative to corps membership. Blair's experiences of corps discipline were less than happy and, once he was in the sixth form, he was happy to jettison his puttees and his boots in favour of missionary work. This involved assisting Dr. Bush in holding Sunday Bible classes for the urchins of Mesopotamia, the most wretched corner of Coalhaven between the river and the canal. It was an activity less taxing than nights under damp canvas, reveille at six and lumpy porridge. A leisurely Sunday breakfast was followed by the chance to ride with Dr. Bush in his trap to the college mission. After the good doctor's sermon, Blair and a couple of other boys would divide the urchins into small groups for half an hour of Bible study. At the end of the morning came a feast of milk and buns, an essential part of the proceedings if the urchins were to be persuaded to attend on a regular basis. Blair found that Bible study allowed him to employ all his thespian talents to the full, and he enjoyed the way the boys and girls in shabby clothes hung on his words. While Dr. Bush concentrated on the Old Testament, Blair preferred the New and did his best to bring it into the twentieth century by making Jesus turn water into ginger beer rather than wine, and introducing motor cars, telephones and aeroplanes into the gospels whenever he could.

On this particular weekend, however, he felt a twinge of nostalgia for the corps; he was particularly sorry to miss the opportunity to see Hetty and Clemmie and their father, who he knew was meeting most of the costs of the weekend camp from his own pocket. Boys who had attended previous camps at Aldershot had returned full of exciting stories about firing live ammunition on the ranges, cooking sausages in the open air and late-night ragging of contingents from other schools. Despite his elevation to school captain, Blair still nursed an adventurous streak, and he sighed as he thought of the weekend excitements he would be missing. Little did he imagine the awful spiral of events of which the half-term camp on the Fairhaven estate was to be the first episode.

Spirits were high as Hoon led his troops on to the camp site, a large field close to the Fairhaven home farm about a mile from the big house. Soldiers from the county regiment had erected a long line of big white tents, with a giant marquee for a canteen and a small one for the officers' mess. 'Flogger' Williams the school chaplain, wearing his major's uniform, was supervising proceedings. 'Fall the men out, sergeant-major. Parade in fifteen minutes,' he instructed Hoon. The boys were soon lined up in threes, hanging on the padre's every word as he outlined the programme for the weekend. For every boy knew that 'Flogger' was no ordinary weekend soldier. As a young subaltern he had fought the fuzzy-wuzzies at Tel-el-Kebir and helped pacify the warlike Zulus in Natal; the exploits of Captain Williams against the Boers at Ladysmith had been the subject of an article in the *Illustrated London News*. His bearing was still military, and only his big grey beard betrayed the fact that he was a part-time soldier in holy orders. 'You are now subject to military discipline,' he warned the boys.

The first two days of the camp passed in a blur of activity; there were field exercises, signalling lessons from a grey-haired sergeant, a cross-country march and a night map-reading exercise during which some boys were found in the snug of a local hostelry. 'We were lost and asking for directions, sir,' they answered. There were football matches and hearty meals of beef and potatoes, washed down with mugs of tea. After dark, sentries were posted around the canteen and the farm building which did service as an armoury. Inside the tents the Scottish boys sang 'The Campbells are Coming' and 'A Hundred Pipers', which the English boys countered with 'The British Grenadiers' and 'What Shall We Do With The Drunken Sailor?' The weekend camp was an event of which Lord Roberts would have been proud.

The final day dawned with bugler Bradshaw, a small third former, sounding reveille. The boys wolfed down their porridge, knowing that today's field exercise would simulate a real battle, with blank ammunition, smoke bombs and thunderflashes. The Marquess arrived as guest of honour and was welcomed with a skirl of the pipes. Hoon saluted him smartly, offered him a pair of military field glasses and escorted him to the top of a small hill to watch the contest between 'blue' defenders and 'red' attackers. Huge clouds of smoke drifted across the fields as the attackers advanced. 'Of course, in a real battle, we'd be using Maxim guns,' Hoon confided to the Marquess. 'That would polish them off in no time.' Then came the shouted command 'Fix bayonets!' and the 'red' forces ran forward, yelling in bloodthirsty fashion and jabbing the muzzles of their rifles at the defenders as they overran their positions. 'We don't actually use bayonets, it's just a figure of speech,' Hoon explained. 'But we've jolly well got them if we need them.'

There followed a parade at which the Marquess inspected a guard of honour, and a free afternoon for the boys to bathe in the nearby stream, climb trees and roam around the Fairhaven estate. After a copious final dinner, the boys sat around in groups in the dusk. The officers' tent was deserted, for 'Flogger' Williams and the other masters were dining at Fairhaven as guests of the Marquess. The drill sergeants from the county regiment, exhausted by three days of answering questions from excited boys, had repaired to a local public house, and the canteen staff had doused their field cookers and departed, leaving Hoon in charge of the camp. As the subsequent police investigation into the events of that night showed, this was a mistake.

'Let's have a camp fire!' shouted one boy. At this point in the narrative, it must regrettably be made clear to the reader, who is anxious to discover exactly which boy was responsible for what actions on that night, that he will be disappointed. There was no moon and the darkness cloaked the perpetrators in anonymity. Suffice it to say that boys from all three houses were equally responsible and sixth formers led the way. But the task of pinpointing the ringleaders, as Blair subsequently explained to the Marquess, was an impossible one. We are, however, in danger of getting ahead of our story.

It was a dry night and the fire was soon alight, fuelled by timber taken from the barn and a pile of old packing crates which, the boys agreed, could no longer be of any use to man or beast. There were songs galore: 'Green Grow the Rushes Oh!' and 'Rule Britannia', for which the boys stood. It was after about half an hour of singing that Hoon, who had been awake since long before dawn, felt his eyes closing. 'I'm going to cut along. You're in charge,' he announced to nobody in particular as he left the party to return to his tent. As he sank his head upon the straw bolster, the singing was as loud as ever, so he stuffed a piece of cotton wool in each ear, closed his eyes and was soon sound asleep.

There was a sudden shout of 'Sausages!' which the younger boys understood to mean 'Sausages will now be served'. They rose from their places and sniffed the air. But it quickly emerged that the cry was to be construed rather differently; the sausages were hiding and were to be hunted down in their lair. A boy with a bicycle lamp quickly untied the flap to the kitchen tent, which revealed an array of metal-lined boxes containing provisions for the next morning's breakfast. It was the work of a moment to find the sausages and the wherewithal for cooking them. Twenty minutes later, it was universally agreed amid cheers that, although a trifle blackened, they were delicious.

It was not long before a similar cry of 'Beer!' was heard, and further explorations of the tented area behind the kitchen were undertaken. Covered by a tarpaulin in a corner behind the drill sergeants' quarters lay several crates of ale and two whole barrels marked with the distinctive porcine insignia of the Black Pig Brewery. The beer was quickly consumed from tin mugs and billycans. By now the bicycle lamp had given out and the boys began to equip themselves with flaming torches, thanks to a tub of pitch which they found in one of the farm outbuildings. Old hands were already agreed that the evening was shaping up to be just as good a rag as the one at Aldershot two years earlier, which ended with the abduction of a regimental goat and its introduction into the sleeping quarters of a particularly authoritarian sergeant-major.

A mile away, in the dining room of Fairhaven, a most pleasant evening was moving towards its close. The Marquess's guests included not only the school padre and other masters in uniform, but a former Lord Lieutenant of the county and two officers from the local regiment, accompanied by their wives. Dr. Bush, who shunned alcohol, always retired to bed early and preferred the company of books to people, had declined the invitation. Hetty and Clemmie retired to the drawing room 'Away from your beastly cigars, Papa!' to fluttering expressions of regret from the former Lord Lieutenant, a widower. The first toast was to the health of His Most Gracious Majesty the King, a worthy representative of the royal line, a leader admired by all right-thinking Englishmen and a sovereign whose voice was always on the side of peace. Then followed toasts to the Army, the British Empire, the Volunteers, the gallant former Lord Lieutenant, to St. Stephen's College and its valiant Rifle Corps, and to the Marquess himself, not forgetting his delightful daughters. It was not surprising that with the windows fastened tight, the diners detected neither the sound of detonations, nor the smell of burning from the direction of the farm. It was Hetty who raised the alarm after Huntley and Palmer began to bark. 'Father, I can see a fire at the farm!' she exclaimed, bursting into the dining room.

Made dizzy by alcohol, the mob of boys with their torches let down the guy-ropes on the sergeants' tent, then paused for a minute while considering their next step. 'Let's hunt a sheep!' shouted one. 'I've got some blanks!' shouted another, displaying the cartridges he had secreted in his tunic pocket at the end of the morning's exercise. From there it was a brief step to forcing the lock of the armoury and distributing the rifles. The boys opened the nearest gate and rushed into the field firing blanks, panicking the sheep, who stampeded in formation down the hill to escape. One straggler headed the wrong way and was tackled by three members of the first fifteen, who drove the animal in triumph back to the farm. 'Put it in the officers' tent!' came the cry. There was a moment of hesitation, but the boys realised there was to be no turning back at this stage. The sheep was dragged inside the tent and the boys pressed forward to follow it. 'Mind that torch, you idiot!' shouted a voice, but it was too late. Within seconds the straw, the canvas and the wooden furnishings were alight. The boys scrambled out of the tent to safety, but the sheep was trapped. A piteous bleating sound rent the air as the flames billowed upwards, to be followed by the acrid smell of burning wool and frying mutton.

It was at this point that the mob was disturbed. The gamekeeper whose cottage adjoined the farm buildings heard the fracas and came sprinting across the field with his shotgun. Confronted by a scene comparable to the sack of Rome by the Vandals, he fired both barrels in the air, and the boys replied with a full half-dozen blank rounds. Hattersley the gamekeeper was a big, sturdy man but he was alone, faced with several score boys, some of them hardened by years of rugger and playground fighting. The gamekeeper was swept off his feet, his shotgun was waved aloft in triumph and his face ground into the earth. When he tried to kick his captors away, a schoolboy fist smashed into his face. One bespectacled boy, who in more sober times had won the Stubbs-Walker Prize for mathematics, began shouting 'Finish him off!' and waving a rifle around his head, but was restrained by his fellows before any fatal injuries were inflicted. Hattersley was quickly tied up, with a sack placed over his head as a precaution.

We shall spare the reader a detailed account of what followed: the arrival of the Marquess and the rest of his party at the scene of pillage; the unsuccessful attempt to douse the fire; the rousing of the sleeping Hoon; the ignominious departure of the St. Stephen's contingent at first light without breakfast; the tears of Hetty and Clemmie at the fate of the sheep; the injuries sustained by the gamekeeper; and the newspaper headline in the *Coalhaven Gazette* about a 'Hooligan Fracas Blamed on College Boys'.

On the final morning of half-term Blair was sitting in his armchair engrossed in a new adventure story about two English schoolboys who were spending their Christmas holidays in Russia; they had already saved the Tsar from a revolver-wielding assassin and were now being held prisoner by a gang of revolutionary nihilists somewhere in the depths of Siberia. Would Frank and Bob escape from their snowy dungeon in time to reveal the dastardly plot to blow up the Imperial railway train? As he turned the pages, there was a knock at the door. 'The doctor wants you in his study. It's urgent.'

Blair arrived to find Dr. Bush's brow more furrowed than usual. Sitting opposite him was the Marquess, with a face like thunder, and 'Flogger' Williams, still in his khaki uniform. Horatio the labrador, as if conscious of the gravity of the moment, was fully awake and standing at the headmaster's side. The padre summarised the results of the night's manoeuvres: 'A gamekeeper taken to hospital with cracked ribs, an army tent destroyed with the personal belongings of several masters, a sheep burned alive and some serious damage to farm buildings and equipment. Most serious of all, a dozen rifles appear to have vanished into thin air.'

Dr. Bush interrupted. 'Canon Williams has already offered his resignation to me as commanding officer of the Rifle Corps. I have accepted. But the wicked perpetrators of this outrage must be cast out. I have told the Marquess that the ringleaders will be expelled from College. Finding them, Blair, is your task.' Blair's jaw dropped. For once, he was speechless.

When the Marquess spoke, his tone was frosty and his gaze was penetrating. He growled at Blair. 'Young man, my generosity to the school has been ill repaid. My daughters are distressed and my staff are outraged. I shall not be allowing the school to use Fairhaven again and the footpaths crossing the estate will be closed forthwith. I shall be sending a bill for repairs. The constabulary are investigating, but if appropriate measures are taken within the school, I shall ask them not to press charges.'

Dr. Bush nodded gravely. He had never taken much interest in the Rifle Corps, regarding it like all other outdoor activities as a distraction from the study of the Bible. 'I have every confidence in you, Blair. These events were not of your making. But the responsibility is now yours.'

'You can trust me, sir,' he replied. 'It was an appalling outrage. I shall treat this as a personal crusade.' The Marquess's grim visage relaxed slightly and he nodded. But it was with a heavy heart that Blair returned to his study. He knew that it was a golden rule at St. Stephen's that boys did not peach on their fellows, and any captain of school who encouraged such conduct would quickly lose all respect. Then he thought of the glorious day on which he had sped along the clifftop road in a Rolls-Royce belonging to a peer of the realm. He knew that if the incident was not resolved to the Marquess's satisfaction, the gates of Fairhaven would be closed to him for ever.

His first consultation was with Campbell, to discuss how the *Rocket* would report on the weekend events. It was quickly agreed that in view of the sensitive nature of the affair, it would be better if the newspaper avoided all mention of the disturbance. Blair strongly suspected that Campbell himself had taken part in, or at least witnessed, the incident, because he was the Rifle Corps piper. But he did not think it right to question him further. He then summoned Mandelson, who as usual was able to furnish him with a full picture of what had happened. Apparently several prefects, including some from Hardie's, had been in the forefront of the riot. 'What are the boys saying about it?' Blair enquired.

'Most of them think it was a capital rag, the best ever. They're sorry about the dead sheep and they're ready to get up a collection for the gamekeeper. I think there's going to be an awful stink if anyone gets expelled. After all, pretty well the whole corps was there.'

'Were you there?'

Mandelson cast him a withering glance, as if to suggest Blair was being a trifle naïve.

'Do you really expect me to answer that question?'

Blair had never before faced such a dilemma. In the chapel he knelt to pray for divine guidance. What was the right thing to do? If he ignored his promise to the Marquess and Dr. Bush, there would be no more invitations to Fairhaven and rides in the Rolls-Royce. But if he found the guilty boys and reported them, his reputation in school would plummet to the ground like an aeroplane which had run out of fuel. He closed his eyes, but there was no word of guidance from above. In this sticky corner his faith was proving of little practical help. What was the point of being humble enough to be God's instrument, if God would not tell him what to do next?

When he consulted Brown, who had been absent over half-term visiting a sick relative, his advice was equally unhelpful. 'Those who make their bed have to lie on it,' Brown said pointedly. 'But you know I'll back you up, whatever you decide.' Campbell's counsel was more to the point: 'What's important is to maintain your authority as captain of school. Announce a subscription fund for the gamekeeper and offer to pay for the damage. Find out which boys are leaving the school at the end of this term and write to the Marquess telling him they were the ringleaders. Archer's leaving, though we don't know why. You can blame it on him.'

'What about poor old Hoon?'

'Don't let old Tiger resign, whatever you do. That would set the wrong sort of precedent entirely. Send him to visit the gamekeeper. That's something we can report in the newspaper.'

Blair decided to follow Campbell's advice and convened a special meeting of prefects. There were anxious looks on all sides of the room as he announced he was determined to do the right thing. No stone would be left unturned in the search for the truth. But, he added, he did not expect boys to start sneaking on each other. He threw open the discussion and Hoon rose to his feet. 'I suppose I'm for the high jump because I was asleep,' he said in a mournful tone. Blair quickly interrupted him. 'Not at all, old chap. What happened was outside your control. What is important is that your intentions were entirely pure. *Errare humanum est.* And I'm sure nobody wanted matters to end as they did. I shall tell that pompous old fool of a Marquess that it was just letting off steam. Boys will be boys, and so on. Trust me.'

And so Hoon was despatched to the cottage hospital with a large basket of fruit for Hattersley; Brown was persuaded to release emergency funds to pay for the damage; and Blair took it upon himself to write a lengthy letter to the Marquess explaining in confidence that several boys had been asked quietly to leave the school at the end of the Michaelmas term.

A few days later, Dr. Bush summoned Blair to his study. 'The Marquess says he won't press charges. But if the perpetrators are not to be publicly shamed, I feel that some kind of punishment is still in order. I have decided that the town of Coalhaven will be declared out of bounds to all boys until further notice.'

'That won't go down well, sir,' Blair replied.

'If you can find the missing rifles, we can look at the matter again. Perhaps we should offer a reward of ten pounds.'

'Very good, sir.' Blair patted Horatio on the head and returned to his study with a spring in his step. He had no doubt that, thanks to his deft diplomacy, the worst of the crisis was over.

CHAPTER X

THE FISH RISES TO THE FLY

As Blair predicted, the decision to declare Coalhaven out of bounds proved highly unpopular with the boys of St. Stephen's, who regarded the right to stroll into town on half-holidays as part of the birthright of every true-born Briton. But it also proved highly unwelcome in another quarter. The Coalhaven tradesmen and shopkeepers relied heavily on the 'young college gentlemen' to swell their takings. In the tailor's, the photographer's, the watchmaker's and the bootmaker's, there was anxious scrutiny of the amount owed on account by the boys, for very few purchases were made for cash. Instead, the magic incantation 'Put it on my account' was uttered each time a package was wrapped in brown paper. It was not long before the postman began to deliver plain brown envelopes to the school, all bearing similar tidings: Bloggs the hatter or Potts the shirtmaker presents his compliments and requests immediate settlement of the enclosed account, to the value of four pounds, eight shillings and ninepence. Loud groaning sounds were heard in the studies and day-rooms as the addressees screwed up the missives and lobbed them theatrically into the receptacles provided by a thoughtful school management. But to no avail. A second round of letters arrived, warning that if payment was not received, Bloggs and Potts would be communicating with Dr. Bush directly. Some tradesmen took their walking sticks and trudged up the hill to the school in person to chase the money owed them for bicycles and cricket bats. They were directed by the Famulus to the study of Brown, who received them courteously, and took careful notes of who was being dunned for money by whom, and for how much. The only tradesman with no debts to collect was Berlusconi the café proprietor, who did not give credit. Although his sale of ice-creams dwindled, his school tuck shop still did a roaring trade. The High Street establishment with the largest amount in monies outstanding was Thatcher's grocery, noted for its veal and ham pies. One day Blair was sitting in his study reading a magazine when the door burst open to reveal a woman in a bright blue dress and a large bonnet. With a start, he recognised the figure who had carved him sixpennyworth of ham during Vic Week – the grocer's daughter!

'Good afternoon, young man. I am here because I want my money back!' she exclaimed in an imperious tone, advancing without further invitation into the study and waving a piece of paper in his face. Resistance was impossible. Blair scrabbled in his pockets and, to his relief, found that he had just enough to meet his obligations. But not all boys were so fortunate. Young Mandelson, for one, was acutely embarrassed to discover that he was unable to locate sufficient funds to settle his debts. 'I'm in an awful hole,' he confided to Blair. 'I had a midnight feed in the dorm when I became a fifth form monitor, and it all came from Thatcher's. Silly old me, I suppose.'

'How much do you owe?' asked Blair.

'Four pounds and something or other,' Mandelson replied.

'That's a lot of money in Kirkcaldy. I'd help you out if I could, but I'm on the breadline myself,' said Blair. 'I'm sure you'll think of something.'

Blair's words proved truer than he could have imagined. A few days later, Mandelson poked his head around the door with his usual air of mystery. 'Let's go for a walk. I've found something very interesting.'

The two boys put on their overcoats, for winter was in the air, and headed down the school drive. Mandelson knew that at some point Blair would point out that the town of Coalhaven was out of bounds, and had his reply ready.

'It may be out of bounds, but you're captain of school. You have to make sure nobody is breaking the rules. *Dura lex, sed lex*, as I believe the Romans say.'

'But what about you?'

'I'm a fifth form monitor, that's almost as good as being a prefect. Besides, you're with me, so it must be all right.'

Blair felt there was probably a logical flaw somewhere in Mandelson's arguments, but could not immediately spot it. 'I'm surprised you're off to the shops. You said you had no money.'

'I'm not going shopping,' Mandelson retorted. 'I'm on the trail of the missing rifles. If I can find them, I'll get the reward. Promise me you won't breathe a word to any one.'

'You can trust old Sooty,' Blair replied. 'Cross my heart, my word is my bond, and all that.'

They were approaching Coalhaven High Street. 'Take your cap off and turn up your collar,' Mandelson whispered.

'Better if we're not recognised. There may be natives about.'

Natives, the day-boys who lived in Coalhaven and tramped up the hill to school each day, were of course exempt from the out-of-bounds regulation, a fact which served to enhance their lowly status in the school. Since half-term some of them had organised themselves to run errands into town for a small consideration, in competition with the bootboys and laundrymaids who also surreptitiously undertook such commissions.

They walked past Thatcher's grocery store and the photographer's studio and turned downhill towards the river down a narrow street. They passed secondhand clothes dealers, a tripe shop and a steam laundry. Hard-featured women stood on the doorsteps of their small terraced houses, casting curious glances at the two boys in smart overcoats as they hurried by. Ahead of them loomed the outline of the gasometer, and as they followed a rag-and-bone cart across the cobbled bridge by the Black Pig Brewery, Blair realised that they were entering Mesopotamia by a different route from the one he normally travelled with Dr. Bush to reach the mission.

Mandelson led him down a small alleyway to the towpath that ran along the River Smeath. They walked for another five minutes past barges and canalboats until they reached a boatyard. 'Leave the talking to me,' he whispered. Without knocking, he opened the door of a dilapidated brick building and entered, with Blair following nervously a step behind. In the gloom he caught sight of a large billiard table, some wooden tables and chairs occupied by workmen, and a counter presided over by a broad, slatternly woman in a dirty pinafore. There was a single gas lamp and a pervasive odour of beer and cheap shag.

'Hallo, Ma,' said Mandelson. 'I've brought a present for Oscar.' He withdrew a brown paper bag from his overcoat pocket.

'I'll fetch him and you can give it to him yourself,' the woman replied, disappearing out of sight.

'Who's Oscar?' Blair asked.

At that moment there was the sound of loud yapping and a small white terrier with a brown and grey patch on his left ear rushed at Mandelson, the picture of eager excitement. Mandelson opened the bag and gave the dog a bone, sending it into a frenzy of delight. 'He's all mine. But I can't keep him in college, so Ma is looking after him for me. Dogs are loyal, you see, unlike people. When the summer comes Oscar and I shall go ratting together.'

The slovenly woman came up and winked at Mandelson. 'I have two fellows coming in shortly who may be able to tell you something.'

'How will I recognise them?' Mandelson asked.

'They're Irish,' the woman replied.

Blair felt it was time to press his friend for an explanation; as captain of school he was prepared to go anywhere and meet anyone in the interests of St. Stephen's College, but this was the kind of low dive where he felt distinctly uncomfortable. He knew very well about the distinction between the deserving and the undeserving poor, and he felt he was now surrounded by the latter.

'What's going on?' he asked Mandelson. 'Who's that woman?'

'That's Ma Mowlam. Don't worry. She's the real salt

of the earth, and she's promised to help me find the missing rifles.'

The door opened and in came two working men with check caps, red mufflers, blue jackets and brown corduroy trousers. They walked to the bar, and Blair saw the woman gesture with her thumb towards their table. The two men approached, bearing glasses of porter in both hands. 'And which of you bully young lads is Peter?' enquired the taller of the two men, who had a black beard.

Mandelson put out his hand and greeted them. 'Just water for me, but I'm sure my friend Anthony is not averse to a glass.' The smaller of the two Irishmen, who had a mop of curly fair hair, thrust the porter into Blair's hand and sat down. He raised his glass in friendly fashion and launched into a long story about his recent troubles with 'the Peelers', and about the Irish people's desire for freedom.

Blair's nerves were suddenly on edge; was this some kind of trap? He had read accounts of Fenian outrages, and had always wondered whether Irishmen really resembled the sinister figures portrayed in newspaper cartoons. As if reading his thoughts, the curly-haired man stretched out his hand with a smile. 'Don't be alarmed, now. We're not planning to blow you up. Not for a little while, anyway. I'm McGuinness and this is my friend Adams. We're from the Shamrock Scrapyard round the corner. We may be able to help you find the rifles.'

Adams seemed cold and distant, but McGuinness talked for both of them. 'Ma, bring us some bread and cheese,' he shouted. Then he ordered more porter and, when Blair confessed he knew little of Irish history, McGuinness promised to remedy that omission forthwith. After half an hour Blair had learned about the grave of Wolfe Tone, the strengths and weaknesses of Parnell, and the interesting fact that the Marquess of Coalhaven had recently purchased an estate in Ireland and was planning to evict his tenants. Blair, keen not to give offence, raised his glass to toast something known as the Republican Brotherhood, and under the tuition of McGuinness gave a fair rendition of a jolly ballad about Irish people 'wearing the green'. McGuinness clapped him on the shoulder and congratulated him on his fine tenor voice, and Blair decided that the Irish were perhaps not quite as bad as they were painted.

At the other end of the table, Mandelson and Adams were discreetly discussing the missing rifles. Mandelson recounted the circumstances of the half-term camp, and Adams made him explain in detail what kind of weapons had vanished. 'Lee Enfields? Are you sure?' Then Mandelson was asked to explain where the armoury was situated in the college basement and who had the keys.

'It used to be Canon Williams. But now nobody's really in charge of the Rifle Corps. Dr. Bush asked Monsieur de Chirac the French master to keep an eye on things, but we all refused to have anything to do with him because he's a Frenchman. The Duke of Wellington would be turning in his grave.'

Adams asked some more questions and then leaned forward to the two boys. 'Can you two keep a secret? You must keep what I am going to tell you strictly between these four walls.'

Blair and Mandelson nodded silently.

'I have reason to believe that Fat Sam may have your rifles. If I were a betting man, I would say they're in the cellar of the Saracen's Head.'

Blair knew the sinister reputation of the Saracen's Head, the largest public house in Mesopotamia, though he had never been inside. It stood only a few yards from the school mission, and the rowdiness of its ill-favoured patrons during Sunday service regularly drove Dr. Bush to distraction. Blair recalled a sunny day in the Trinity term when he and the good doctor made their usual way in the trap to the mission hall. As they passed through the spacious suburbs of Coalhaven, gentlemen doffed their straw boaters and he raised his politely in return. But when they reached their destination they were greeted by a volley of jeers from the direction of the Saracen's Head. One youth with nothing better to do threw a firecracker at them, startling the horse. The public house appeared to be beyond the control of the Coalhaven constabulary, who rarely ventured into the dank neighbourhood that surrounded it. On Saturdays and Sundays a constant procession of small children, some of them barefoot, carried empty jugs to the off sales window and returned home with them filled to the brim. At the back of the building was a large room with a stage and curtains, which was reputedly the haunt of women of easy virtue and stevedores from the wharves. On summer days the noise of piano music and vulgar singing drowned out the hymns sung by the mission choir. No boy from St. Stephen's, not even a boastful day-boy, would admit to frequenting the Saracen's Head. Fat Sam himself was rarely seen, though his son Percy owned a motor cycle, on which he would race up the High Street with a deafening roar, sometimes at speeds of over twenty miles an hour. The police had more than once knocked on Fat Sam's door with a warrant to search the premises for stolen goods, but had found nothing and been forced to beat a humiliating retreat. The excise men had also been to call, looking for smuggled tobacco, but had gone away empty-handed.

'ON SATURDAYS AND SUNDAYS A CONSTANT PROCESSION OF SMALL CHILDREN,
SOME OF THEM BAREFOOT.'

'Can you get inside to have a look?' Blair asked. McGuinness laughed.

'Easier said than done, my lads. Fat Sam knows our faces too well. To tell the truth, he cannot abide honest Irishmen, and we once came to blows over a horse. We are sworn enemies.'

'We could offer you a share of the reward money,' Mandelson piped up. 'Would that make a difference?'

'It might indeed,' said Adams cautiously. 'There is one thing I can do for you, for no remuneration at all.'

'What's that?' asked Blair.

'If you can arrange for me to visit the school armoury on the quiet, I can have a good look at the remaining rifles. That will help me to identify the missing ones.'

Blair nodded, and was about to accept this generous offer, when he felt Mandelson's shoe connect painfully with his shin under the table. 'I'll have to see what I can do. How do we contact you?' he asked.

'Round the corner to the right, and you'll see the sign outside our yard saying Scrap Metal Bought, Good Prices Paid. We're also in the pawnbroking business, if you're ever short of a bob or two. Now, how about a quick game of billiards? It'll be a feather in our cap, to be sure, if we take on the boys from the college.'

Four cues were produced from behind the bar and soon the table was alive with the clicking sound of balls being struck. Each time Blair knocked a ball into a pocket, or came close, McGuinness would slap him on the back and exclaim: 'Good shot, sir!' Blair had only played twice before, when he had accompanied his father to the Constitutional Club. Ma Mowlam's table had seen better days, with cigarette burns on the mahogany and dirty brass fittings. The cloth was threadbare, with grease stains in one corner.

It was Blair's turn to try to pull off a particularly awkward shot, leaning across the table using a cue-rest and lifting one foot off the ground. But alas! Youthful overconfidence proved again to be his undoing, and he mistimed his shot. With a ripping sound, the cue bored into the green baize, leaving a six-inch gash. Blair turned crimson with embarrassment, and looked around to the sea of faces in the room. There was a murmur of 'Look over 'ere, Ma!' and the slovenly woman marched over to the table. Arms akimbo, she subjected Blair to a volley of imprecations and oaths, the like of which he had never heard before, and whose exact wording can thankfully be omitted from this narrative.

'Of course I'll pay for the damage,' he stuttered.

'Ten pounds, then. If you don't have it, you must leave a surety.'

Blair and Mandelson looked at each other in despair. Ten pounds was a sum that neither of them could hope to raise before the end of term. At that point, Adams intervened. 'Now, boys, that was a spot of bad luck, to be sure. What's the damage?'

He pulled two crisp five-pound notes from his pocket and gave them to the woman, who snorted and tucked them into the pocket of her apron. 'Thank you, sir,' said Blair. 'How can we repay your kindness?'

Adams looked the pair of boys up and down. 'That's a nice gold watch,' he said, looking at the timepiece and chain which Mandelson wore in his waistcoat.

'It was my father's,' Mandelson replied. 'When I took it to school I promised the mater never to let it out of my sight.'

'It'll be quite safe with us. We'll give you a regular broker's chit and it will be safe under lock and key. Safer than at that college of yours, I shouldn't wonder, where things go missing from one day to the next.'

Mandelson meekly handed over the watch, and the Irishman wrote out a receipt. Blair felt they had made a narrow escape. He shook hands warmly with his new friends, who clapped him on the shoulder and confessed that for them too, the encounter had been a real pleasure.

As they left Ma Mowlam's yard, the two boys registered an observant pair of eyes following their every move. They belonged to a sallow-faced boy with a cigarette in his mouth, who sat by the window mending a fishing rod.

Once safely on the road home, Blair turned to Mandelson and broke the silence. 'I think that worked out all right in the end. They seemed quite trustworthy fellows.'

Mandelson shook his head. 'Fancy inviting a couple of Fenians for a guided tour of the school armoury! Perhaps you'll arrange for them to take tea with the King at Buckingham Palace next? Sometimes, Anthony, I worry about you.'

Blair's brow furrowed. Perhaps his friend was right. He had always been brought up by his parents to believe the best of other people, but it was undeniable that not everybody's intentions were as innocent as his own. Nonetheless he felt that, for the time being, the Irishmen should be given the benefit of the doubt.

'I can't possibly go home for Christmas without my father's watch,' Mandelson continued. 'I shall have to find the money somewhere, or I shall die of shame.'

For several weeks Mandelson was reduced to looking up at the school clock tower to make sure he would not be late for lessons. Then one day, shortly before the start of the Christmas holidays, he appeared with the gold watch and chain attached to his waistcoat. Blair was the only one to notice the change, but something in Mandelson's distant look made him reluctant to enquire about how his friend had solved his financial dilemma.

It was on the evening of the same day that Brown opened the oak door of his study to a discreet visitor. It was the sallow-faced boy with the fishing rod, but this time he was dressed in an Eton collar and jacket. Only the tobacco stains on his fingers and a certain vulgarity in his speech marked him out from the hundreds of other boys hurrying along the corridors.

'Come in, Charlie,' said Brown. Then he closed the door, turned the key in the lock, and listened with great interest to what his visitor had to say.

CHAPTER XI

A FALL FROM GRACE

It was the day before the end of term and the boys were in high spirits as they prepared to head home for Christmas. The third and fourth forms had staged their traditional concert, attended by Blair and most of the other prefects. 'Not bad, but not as good as you were in your heyday,' said Matron Boothroyd to Blair as they applauded the performance. It was commonly accepted that Blair's incarnation of Henry V was on a level which future generations of St. Stephen's boys would find it hard to approach.

The search for the missing rifles had made no further progress and the reward was still unclaimed. Dr. Bush received several pressing letters from the War Office asking for details of the investigation into the theft, and insisting that extra precautions be taken to secure the school armoury at a time of social unrest. This was a reference to strikes and a lockout at the Coalhaven collieries, which were accompanied by disturbances in the docks. The Marquess and the town's other Justices of the Peace met the Watch Committee and the Inspector of Police at the Constitutional Club and agreed that while a full-scale insurrection was unlikely, the situation in the town was volatile. There was even a rumour that foreign agitators had been spotted.

None of this disturbed the end-of-term mood at St. Stephen's. Brown seemed particularly cheerful as he completed his accounts for the sports clubs and societies, ticking off long lists of names and totting up large piles of silver and coppers, which he stored in a japanned metal box. He gathered a sheaf of papers under his arm, and climbed the stairs to Blair's study. The door was open and he entered without knocking.

'Come in and take a pew, old chap,' said Blair, looking up to see that his guest was already installed in the best leather armchair. 'What's up?'

'There's a problem with the fifth form sports subs. Your little friend Mandelson seems to have collected them, but he hasn't handed them over. He sent me a note saying he's mislaid the envelope with the money, but he'll have it by the first day of next term.'

'What's so bad about that?'

'I happen to know he's not telling the truth. Mandelson is an embezzler. You have protected the little cad far too long.'

Blair felt a surge of blood. What right had Brown to accuse his friend of dishonesty?

'You'd better withdraw that remark immediately, or else!'

Brown smiled the kind of death's head smile that in most people requires an hour or two of practice in front of the mirror. 'Or else what?'

'Or else this!' Blair retorted, clenching his fist and waving it in Brown's face. It needed only a spark for the two of them to come to blows.

'Perhaps you should listen to what I have to say,' Brown continued. 'Or else you may find yourself being expelled as well as your friend.'

Blair hesitated, dropped his fist and fell silent. Brown began by making clear he knew all about Mandelson's unpaid debts to Thatcher and the other town tradesmen. He also knew about Mandelson's illicit visits to Ma Mowlam's yard and his meetings with the two Irishmen. He knew about the pawning of the gold watch and the exact day on which it had been redeemed, only a few hours after Mandelson, as fifth form monitor, had collected several pounds in sports subscriptions in a brown envelope.

Brown said nothing about Blair's involvement in the story, but there was a hint of menace in his voice which gave an unspoken reminder that he was in possession of further facts which he could reveal if necessary.

'Hadn't you better call Mandelson in and let him give his side of the story?' Blair asked.

'Very well.' A passing fag was commanded to take a message, and within a minute, Mandelson joined them.

At first he denied misappropriating the sports club money. 'I've just mislaid the envelope,' he explained, shrugging his shoulders in exaggerated fashion. 'The money's still in it.'

Brown drew a brown envelope from his pile of papers. 'Here it is, you snivelling little toad. You hid it behind the bookcase in your study!'

Mandelson looked as though a large boulder had fallen from a cliff and crushed him. He crumpled on to the sofa, put his head in his hands and wept. 'It's all over! I shall be expelled! What shall I tell my poor mother!' he exclaimed. Blair patted him on the arm.

'Come on, pull yourself together, old chap. That's not the way a St. Stephen's boy should behave. Here, have a handkerchief.'

Mandelson blew his nose, dried his eyes and began to tell the full story. 'I got a note asking me to come back to Ma Mowlam's. When I got there, Adams asked me again about the rifles and the armoury. I said the Famulus had been told to fit extra locks on the door. Then he became insistent. He gave me a tin of wax to copy the key and let him in to the school during the night. He promised to forgive the debt and give me the watch back with an extra five pounds. But if I didn't do what he said, he was going to write to Dr. Bush and tell him about the billiard table and the dog.'

Blair and Brown exchanged glances as Mandelson paused to blow his nose. 'What did you do?' Brown asked.

'I was going to agree, then I thought how terrible it would be for the school if the Fenians were to get into the armoury and take all the rifles. So I used the sports money to redeem the watch and get myself out of their clutches. I've been a terrible fool.'

Blair stood up. 'You've made a full and honest confession. I think we can rule out expulsion because neither of us is going to peach on you to Dr. Bush. But you're going to have to resign as fifth form monitor.'

Brown nodded. 'You must pay back the money you owe on the first day of next term. And I'm afraid we will have to explain to the fifth form why you resigned. *Sumptus censum ne superet.* Live within your means. Borrowing money from the sports kitty isn't a hanging offence, but it's not going to make you popular.'

'I'm not popular anyway. Everyone hates me here!' Mandelson sniffed.

The painful interview was terminated. Mandelson left school early on the last day of term, with a large empty wooden box in one hand and his portmanteau in the other. At the station, he took a cab in the direction of Mesopotamia, and was seen thirty minutes later returning. This time the box was no longer empty, for Oscar the terrier was inside, barking in protest at the sudden disruption to his previously serene existence in the boatyard. Oscar had planned to spend the afternoon stalking a particularly elusive rat around the riverbank, but now he found himself dumped in the guard's van of a railway train, boxed in on all sides with a label showing his destination. Life for dogs, he reflected as the train began to move, was full of unpleasant reversals of fortune. At that moment, however, the lid of the box was opened and he looked up to see a familiar face. Never did a canine tail wag so furiously as at that moment; never did a pink canine tongue lick its master's face with so much enthusiasm.

'Come here, Oscar,' said the familiar voice. 'At least you haven't left me in the lurch.'

The holiday season in the Blair household should have been full of good cheer, with the captain of school returning triumphant after his first term in office. But Blair was uneasy as he reflected on the course of events since half term. His sister Lizzie noticed his change in mood and bombarded her big brother with questions about life at St. Stephen's.

'Do you have ripping midnight feasts in the dorm?' she enquired.

'No, Lizzie. Unfortunately, I have to enforce the school rules now.'

'So all the others can have midnight feasts, but not you! That seems highly unfair.'

In her innocent way, Lizzie had put her finger on the nub of the issue, Blair reflected. Rules were all very well, and the school could not function without them, but like chocolate eclairs, they should not be an excuse for over-indulgence. Early on in his school career, he had technically infringed the rules by climbing out of the sanatorium to take part in a concert, but he had never regretted doing so. Of course there had to be rules on the rugby field, like the off-side law, which he had never quite mastered. But such rules depended entirely on the referee for their enforcement, and referees were always fallible. Off the pitch, life was more complicated. A boy cycling without a lamp after dark was breaking the law of the land, but what if he was on his way to prevent a burglary or catch a murderer? *Si finis bonus est, totum bonum erit*. Often there was a greater good to be pursued, in defiance of the letter of the law. The words of one of Dr. Bush's interminable sermons came into his mind. 'The laws we must obey first are the laws of God, not the laws of men.'

At the start of his reign as school captain, Blair had craved acceptance from his peers; he wanted to be liked and he used his natural charm to win over his enemies, especially in Salisbury's house. But from the bruising experiences of the past few weeks he had learned that in future he would have to harden his heart. Pursuing popularity for its own sake yielded diminishing returns, and he could never please all the people all of the time. Besides, a closer acquaintance with the boys who were his fellow prefects had bred in him a feeling of contempt for most of them. With the exception of Brown, who he secretly admitted was his intellectual superior, they were a disappointing lot. There was the sleepyheaded Hoon, the oafish Blunkett and a string of others, none of whom he trusted entirely. The only loyal one was his deputy Prescott, the poet with the flowing locks whose rough-hewn verses in the manner of Sir Henry Newbolt still graced the pages of the *Rocket* almost every week. With Mandelson now disgraced, Blair realised that he would have to find some other confidant to shield him from the slings and arrows of outrageous fortune when the new term began.

Blair's reverie was interrupted by Lizzie challenging him to a game of bagatelle. He had promised Lizzie long ago that her friend Peter, the inventor of 'shrimp cricket', would be coming to stay as soon as he had spent Christmas with his widowed mother. Then came the series of painful events which we have chronicled. Mandelson wrote just before Christmas, saying he no longer wished to force himself on the Blair household if his presence would cause embarrassment. Blair replied by return, saying he was still welcome, and suggested he bring Oscar the dog with him for New Year.

The Blair family Christmas came and went. After his introduction to grand society by the Marquess and his daughters, Blair looked on his own domestic arrangements with a newly critical eye. Fundamentally he was neither a swell nor a snob, so he was quick to feel a stab of remorse for finding his parents' social customs rather provincial and redolent of the nineteenth century. Why did his father have to serve cider cup rather than champagne? And why was he so slow to install a telephone and exchange the family pony and trap for a motor car? Why did the house still have gas lights when everybody knew that electricity was so much more modern?

The arrival of Mandelson and Oscar lightened the mood considerably. Despite his fall from grace, or perhaps because of it, Mandelson's biting wit on the subject of his fellow pupils was as sharp as ever. Lizzie listened wide-eyed to his account of how he and Campbell had collaborated in editing down one of Prescott's poems from five hundred lines to around fifty. 'Then he had the damned cheek to complain it didn't scan properly!' Mandelson explained, to general mirth around the table.

The next morning a telegram arrived. 'STAYING WITH RELATIVES NEARBY STOP WILL CALL NOON NEW YEARS DAY STOP CAMPBELL.' The day dawned icy cold and snowflakes were falling thick and fast all morning. Oscar skidded around on the frozen garden pond, barking furiously, and Blair wondered whether the weather might prevent Campbell's visit. Then he spied a tall figure wrapped in a football jersey and a colourful scarf loping up the road.

'I'm in training for the Arbuthnot-Jones trophy,' Campbell panted. 'Sorry I didn't bring my bagpipes.' The trophy was awarded annually for a cross-country race between St. Stephen's and two neighbouring schools. 'We're hosting the race next term, and I'm determined to win. So I've cut out ginger beer and pastry and all those rotten things.'

'You won't even have a mince pie?' Blair asked.

'Certainly not. Get thee behind me, Satan!'

After lunch the three boys went for a walk with Oscar, leaving behind Lizzie, who was told that important college matters would be under discussion that were not for her tender ears. As they set off across the fields, Mandelson was forced to sprint ahead to keep up with Oscar, who dived into the hedgerows and eventually vanished down a hole.

'How's the newspaper? I haven't seen Murdoch for a while,' Blair asked cautiously.

'That's what I wanted to talk about,' replied Campbell. 'He feels the *Rocket* has been giving you a rather easy ride recently. He asked me if you were a man or a milksop.'

Blair frowned. 'What does he mean by that?'

'He's not impressed by the way you handled the whole Rifle Corps business. To tell the truth, neither am I. You can't be a leader by just sitting back and waiting for things to happen, you know. You've got to show pluck and initiative – make people aware that you're in charge.'

'You mean like Nelson at Trafalgar?'

'That's right. He didn't wait for the French to attack our fleet. He attacked the enemy first.'

Blair was an expert on Admiral Nelson and had pored for hours over the big family atlas to trace his campaigns. He had often dreamed of dying a heroic death somewhere on a far-flung shore, of being wrapped in the Union Jack and posthumously receiving the homage of a grateful nation amid a volley of musket fire.

'You know what your problem is?' Campbell continued, jabbing a finger in Blair's direction. 'You need to be a bit more ruthless. Then people will respect you. Play the game to win. It's called leadership.'

Blair was a little taken aback by the frankness of this advice, but stayed his tongue. Campbell seemed to have his interests, and those of the school, very much at heart. His counsel was sharp and to the point, and his articles in the school newspaper demonstrated that his skill with the bagpipes was matched by his way with words. He understood why Campbell, like Murdoch, scorned the idea of being a prefect. Compared to the plodding nonentities who walked around the school wearing prefect's caps, Campbell was a great source of common sense.

'This business of the missing rifles,' Campbell went on. 'You can't go on dithering around. You must tell the school that you know where they are and you're going to do something about it. Where do you think they are?'

'I have it on good authority that they're being hidden at Fat Sam's. You know, the Saracen's Head.'

'That's a topping story. I shall write it up for the *Rocket* and say the forces of law and order are closing in. Detectives are on the trail, Scotland Yard is on the case, bloodhounds are sniffing around, the villain is cornered in his lair.'

'I don't know how much of that is actually true,' Blair interposed.

'If it isn't it soon will be,' Campbell retorted. 'Never underestimate the power of the press.'

At that moment Oscar came bounding towards them across the field. In his jaws the dog held what appeared to be a dark lump of earth, but as it came closer, Blair could see a long tail hanging down. A trickle of blood spattered on the snow as the dog stood there, panting with pride.

'He's caught Fat Sam the rat!' shouted Campbell. 'Hurrah for Oscar!'

The three boys returned home and ate a hearty tea, though Campbell refused all offers of cake and pastries. 'There's no point in entering a race unless you win it,' he announced with an obsessive gleam in his eye. Blair and Mandelson watched as their visitor ran away into the gathering dusk.

When term began in January at St. Stephen's Mandelson, whose downfall from the lofty post of monitor was greeted with ill-concealed glee by most of the fifth form, kept himself to himself. Blair, whose accident at the

'A TRICKLE OF BLOOD SPATTERED ON THE SNOW.'

billiard table lay at the origin of his misfortunes, helped him to repay to Brown all the money owing for the sports subscriptions. Mandelson let it be known to anyone who enquired that no matter what had happened, he and Blair were still on close terms. Coalhaven was still out of bounds, and there was no question of further visits to Ma Mowlam's house of ill repute, but on one Sunday afternoon Blair and Mandelson made another trip into town together as far as Berlusconi's café.

'Delighted to see you gentlemen,' the Italian said. 'Icecreams are on-a the house!'

'We were thinking of a hot chocolate, actually,' said Blair.

'Hot chocolate is on-a the house!' Berlusconi exclaimed. 'Business is not-a so good these days with no St. Stephen's boys coming to town.'

Blair explained why the town was still out of bounds and told Berlusconi in confidence that there was evidence linking the Saracen's Head to the missing rifles. The Italian nodded.

'Is a bad place, Mesopotamia. The hooligans are in the High Street every night. The police, they do-a nothing!'

Blair promised to speak to Dr. Bush to see what might be done to relax the rule keeping boys out of Coalhaven. As he and Mandelson trudged back up the hill to the College in the winter twilight, a mufflered figure sped past in the distance, wrapped in a cricket jersey.

'It's Campbell, practising for the cross-country race,' Mandelson said. 'He's a cert to win if he carries on like this.'

Campbell was as good as his word. The *Rocket* reported in dramatic terms how Blair was resolutely facing up to the potential danger posed by the missing rifles, and how the police were investigating links between the Saracen's Head public house and the foreign agitators responsible for the recent trouble in the docks. After a quiet period during which sales of the school newspaper had been sluggish, the front page story headlined 'Armed Threat to College?' ensured that it was read in every day-room. Inside, the newspaper carried the first of a special series on Great British Battles, beginning with Agincourt. The series, for which Blair penned an introduction, promised heroic tales of Blenheim, Waterloo, Trafalgar, the Crimea and the South African war. Prescott promised to write a patriotic poem about the relief of Mafeking to round off the series.

Blair proudly showed a copy of the newspaper to 'Flogger' Williams, whose own military exploits in the Soudan and South Africa were well known. But the padre gave him a peculiar look.

'Listen to me, Blair. A lot of boys seem to think that war is rather jolly. You imagine it's a fine sort of game that you sign up for, like cricket or rugger. I have been a soldier and I can promise you it is nothing of the sort. *Dulce bellum inexpertis.* War is sweet to those who know it not.' The padre folded up the supplement, pushed it back into Blair's hand, and looked him in the eye. 'The next war will not be like the ones I fought in. You and your friends won't be making cavalry charges against the fuzzy-wuzzies.'

'You mean we'll have dreadnoughts and aeroplanes, sir?' he asked.

'If the next war is against Germany it will be fought in trenches with Maxim guns and high explosive. You will go to the slaughter like rats. You will die face down in the mud, calling for your mothers. The best thing you can do with your newspaper is burn it.' The padre's beard was quivering as he spat out the words.

With that he was gone. Blair watched the tall figure of the school chaplain limping away down the corridor, shaking his head.

'I wonder what's biting the old fellow now?' he thought.

CHAPTER XII

AN ALIEN INTRUDER

Snow blanketed the countryside as far as the eye could see. The winter gales roared over the clifftop, blowing the seagulls off course as they swooped over the great clock tower, their cries snatched away by the wind. The boys of St. Stephen's College quietly abandoned the unofficial rule that overcoats were only worn by milksops and mother's pets and went to the other extreme, competing to add layers of flannel and woollen socks as if they were polar explorers. Apart from skating on ponds, outdoor sporting activities were cancelled. Few complained that the town was out of bounds, for the walk to and from Coalhaven was now only for the intrepid. Only Campbell and a few other energetic souls continued with their training for the Arbuthnot-Jones trophy race, pounding along the clifftop path, their boots skidding on the ice and their faces hidden by scarves.

In Coalhaven itself the canal froze over, though the River Smeath still flowed industrial brown past Ma Mowlam's yard down to the docks. The women's clogs were muffled on the cobblestones and the horses picked their way over the rutted ice. To a casual visitor the town seemed quiet enough, but the *Coalhaven Gazette* recorded a number of worrying incidents. Twenty miles away, the miners were still locked out of the collieries in the harshest winter that any of them could remember; extra police were drafted in from Coalhaven, leaving the constabulary in the town seriously under strength. Windows were broken, burning rags were pushed into pillar-boxes, and these outrages were blamed on the suffragettes. In the docks there was fighting every Saturday, and respectable citizens gave Mesopotamia a wider berth than usual after the Marquess of Coalhaven's Rolls-Royce was stoned by a mob as he returned from a meeting of the Board of Guardians. After a number of incidents of poaching on his estate, the Marquess ordered his keepers to patrol with their shotguns loaded at all times.

The school was also witness to a number of puzzling crimes. A glass cabinet was found with its door open and a silver cup was reported missing. Luckily, the Arbuthnot-Jones trophy was in safe storage at Rossworth School, which had retained it for the past three years. A week later, the rope on the school flagpole was cut in three places, leaving the Union Jack lying in the snow. These matters were reported to Dr. Bush by the Famulus, but the headmaster shrugged his shoulders. One Sunday, as he returned from his weekly visit to the mission, he called as usual for Horatio, to be greeted by silence instead of a friendly bark. Dr. Bush looked inside the corridor running to the school kitchens, where Horatio was mostly to be found in bad weather, to find the dog prostrate on the stone flags. His mouth was open, his body was stiff and, though Dr. Bush examined the old black labrador carefully, there were no signs of external injury. News of the death of Horatio travelled round the school within minutes and there were immediate suspicions that he had been poisoned. Dr. Bush overcame his habitual detestation of the telephone to make contact with the Coalhaven police, only to be told by a constable that he was 'alone manning the fort' and could not be spared to come to the school and investigate the demise of a dog, however suspicious.

That very afternoon, there was a knock on the door of Blair's study. It was Campbell, panting furiously after his run. 'I just thought you should take a look at this,' he said, opening a small tin. 'I found it on the cliff path, just by the back gate to the school.'

'It's a cigarette end,' said Blair. 'What's so jolly special about that?'

Campbell sighed theatrically in the manner of a mathematics master faced with a boy unable to work out a simple fraction. 'Can't you see it's foreign?'

Blair's imagination immediately took wing to 221B Baker Street, where Holmes and Watson were examining the foreign cigarette end with great interest. It was a three-pipe problem. He had always thought of himself as Holmes, but now the tables were turned. Campbell seemed to be assuming the role of the great detective, while placing him in the position of the slow-witted Watson, or even the imbecile Lestrade of Scotland Yard. He wondered if the College library had a copy of Holmes' famous monograph on the ashes of 140 different varieties of tobacco.

The cigarette end was of a strange type. It was composed of a cardboard tube about two inches long, with a little tobacco encased in paper at one end. There was strange writing on the tube. Blair could make out an A, a K, and what looked like an R written backwards.

'By jiminy!' Blair exclaimed. 'Nobody uses that path except boys from school.'

The two boys agreed they should keep their discovery a secret, and carry out further investigations the next day. Then Blair had a brainwave.

'We'll get Ashdown in on this. He knows all about tracking and signs and so on.'

Ashdown was the captain of Gladstone's house and the leader of the school's Boy Scout patrol, which he christened the Beavers. Ashdown had been to camp on Brownsea Island with the great Baden-Powell himself and had learned the secrets of 'spooring' and how to survive in the wild. 'Fried snake is not half bad,' he remarked at breakfast one morning. Following the precepts of Baden-Powell, the Beaver patrol spent their breaks practising the Clove Hitch, the Bowline and the Sheet Bend, looking for the opportunity to do good turns and making plans for their summer camp. Once a week they donned their uniform with its khaki-coloured flat-brimmed hat, shirt, neckerchief and belt, and practised finding their way by the stars.

When Blair and Campbell arrived at the back gate to the school at the appointed time, wrapped against the cold, they were amazed to see Ashdown wearing his Scout uniform, consisting of just a flannel shirt and short blue trousers. He carried an assegai which he had won in a tracking contest at Brownsea island.

'Won't your knees get frozen?' asked Blair.

'Not at all. We shall set a brisk pace,' Ashdown retorted.

The three boys set off, with Ashdown leading the way, scanning the snow for footprints. After a few hundred yards, just as the clifftop path crossed some gorse bushes, he stopped and bent down to the ground. 'I thought so.

It's a man with a hole in his boot, dragging something heavy. He's left the path.'

Carefully and quietly, the three boys followed the tracks to the very edge of the cliff, where the path seemed to come to an end. Then they saw rough steps leading down the cliff-face. Hanging on to the gorse bushes, they scrambled downwards.

'There's a cave!' Ashdown whispered. He tossed a pebble at the cave entrance and waited. But nobody emerged and in a moment or two the boys were inside, trying to penetrate the darkness. Ashdown produced an electric bicycle lamp, and they looked around.

There was a makeshift bed with a blanket, a cooking pot and traces of a fire. A small tin trunk, some candles and matches and a sack of vegetables completed the inventory.

'Poor devil. Fancy sleeping rough in this weather!' Blair exclaimed.

'He's probably an escaped prisoner,' Campbell countered. Meanwhile Ashdown was poking the fire with his assegai.

'It's warm. That means he's not far away. Look, here's more of those funny smokes.'

Inside the tin trunk was a packet of the strange foreign cigarettes and some papers and books with the same peculiar writing. Ashdown picked up a newspaper.

'Can either of you make head or tail of this?'

'*Hamburger Abendblatt*,' said Campbell. 'It says *Fussball* – that's German for football, I shouldn't wonder. But the other papers are in another language.'

Ashdown picked up a spoon and fork and squinted at the handle. 'These are from a steamship,' he declared. 'This man has come here from the port. He may be some kind of stowaway.'

'A German spy!' said Campbell. '*Ein Deutscher Spion.* This is an ideal spot for signalling to ships at sea. He's probably going to be picked up by submarine. What shall we do?'

Blair realised that the other two were looking to him to take the lead. 'I think we should wait here,' he said. 'Then we can question him. There's no point in trying to get the police all the way from Coalhaven. He's bound to come back in daylight, because he won't risk that path in the dark.'

The three boys crouched down in the darkness at the back of the cave. Ashdown rubbed his bare knees, which had turned a bluish colour, but otherwise they did not make a sound. Half an hour later they heard steps at the entrance and saw the silhouette of a man step slowly towards the bed and lie down with a groan.

Within a second, the boys were on him. Blair and Campbell sat on his legs, while Ashdown shone the lamp into his face. The man was a swarthy Continental type, with a long black beard and a blue cap with a short brim. He wore a dirty padded tunic and trousers tucked into knee-length leather boots.

A torrent of incomprehensible phrases escaped his lips. 'Speak English, damn you!' the boys shouted. Blair tried a few words of French, but to no avail. When Campbell tried German, the man became more animated. '*Nix polizei!*' he stuttered.

Campbell hit the man in the face and a trickle of blood oozed from his mouth. 'It's no good, he doesn't speak proper German at all,' he said.

'Let me have a go,' said Blair. He let the man sit up and gave him a piece of chocolate. 'Who are you?' Somehow the sense of the question became clear and the man realised he was being asked his name.

'Mandelbaum, Lev Davidovich.'

Blair turned to the others. 'He's Russian, with a name like that. Has to be.'

The man nodded vigorously. *'Rossiya, Rossiya. Vilno.'* Then he drew a finger across his throat. *'Pogrom,'* he added.

Blair recalled the novel he had enjoyed so much about the two English boys saving the Tsar's life, and stood up. 'I think I know who this man is. He's a Russian anarchist.'

'You mean a nihilist?' said Campbell, not to be outdone.

'Same thing. We'd better make sure he's kept under lock and key.'

Ashdown was about to use the lanyard on his uniform to tie the man's hands, when he spotted a coil of rope on the floor of the cave. 'If I'm not mistaken, that's the rope that went missing from the flagpole!'

Half an hour later, the man was safely in a basement room at the school, with his hands untied. Blair and Campbell brought him some biscuits and a mug of tea, and found him an old bed and a mattress. Ashdown took Blair to one side. 'What are you going to do with him? We can't just keep him here. It may not be legal.'

Blair hesitated for a moment. He knew he was doing the right thing in the circumstances, for it would quite plainly be wrong to let the anarchist free to roam the streets and throw bombs at people. 'I'm sure it's legal,' he said. 'If you're worried, we can look it up later.'

Blair's father, hoping his son would follow him into a career in the law, had presented him at Christmas with a slim volume entitled *Introduction to the Law of England,* which was lying on the bookshelf in his study underneath a jar of marmalade. He had not opened it.

Mandelbaum was warming himself next to an iron stove, clutching the mug of tea. He turned round and threw himself to his knees at Blair's feet. '*Spasibo! Danke!*' he mumbled. '*Bitte, nix polizei!*'

'He wants you to promise you won't hand him over to the police,' Campbell said.

'That's fine,' said Blair. 'We'll get Blunkett to look after him here for a while.' He pulled Mandelbaum to his feet, clasped him by both hands and looked him in the eye.

'You can trust me. *Nix polizei, nix polizei,*' he repeated. Mandelbaum flung his arms around Blair and kissed him on the cheek in gratitude.

News of the capture of Mandelbaum, the notorious Russian anarchist who had plotted to kill the Tsar, spread like wildfire around the school. Boys queued up in the courtyard to squint through the narrow window into the cellar where he was confined. Some were convinced that he had been caught red-handed making a bomb, while others argued that he had been captured with a bottle of arsenic, with which he had laced Horatio's food. It was agreed that it would be unwise for the *Rocket* to publicise what had happened, in case Mandelbaum was part of a larger gang of aliens who might attempt to rescue him.

'We're putting Blunkett in charge,' Blair told Dr. Bush, who nodded gravely to indicate his consent. 'He won't get away. And he might be able to give us some useful information about the missing rifles.'

Blunkett, one of Blair's prefects from Hardie's, was delighted to be looking after the prisoner. 'Here, you might need to consult this,' said Blair, handing him his book on the law of England.

'I doubt it,' said Blunkett. 'Just leave him to me.'

Blunkett proved a conscientious gaoler. Mandelbaum was brought food three times a day, soap and water and a toothbrush, and a set of workman's clothes to replace his own. But he was not allowed out of his cell for exercise, for fear he might escape.

Blunkett's goal was to extract a confession from Mandelbaum of his past crimes, or failing that, an indication of the future outrages which he intended to commit on British soil. When classes were over for the day, he would make his way to the basement, undo the padlock and shake the sleeping prisoner awake. But with no common language, the interrogation made little progress.

'We know he's hiding something,' Blunkett told Blair.

'You do what you think is necessary,' Blair replied. 'I don't want to know the details.'

Blunkett then tried out some of the rich arsenal of methods which had been used at St. Stephen's since time immemorial to keep rebellious fags in line. He waved a red-hot poker in Mandelbaum's face, poured cold water over his bed, tied him up with rope and put a sack over his head. But the man either remained silent, or spoke in a mixture of Russian and German which nobody could understand.

After two weeks, Mandelbaum used signs to request a pen and paper, which Blunkett brought him with his evening meal. The next morning, the paper was covered in a childlike scrawl, with pictures of steamships and a crude map, and some short sentences in German. Blair and Blunkett took the paper to Dr. Bush, having re-membered that the headmaster had once spent a year in Heidelberg.

'He says he came on a ship from Riga to Hamburg,

then another ship to Coalhaven, on his way to Liverpool and New York,' said Dr. Bush. 'He has a brother in New York. But the police refused to let him disembark in Coalhaven, so he was taken back on board. Then he paid all his money to a seaman to help him ashore at night and found his way to the cave in the cliffs.'

Blair and Blunkett looked at each other.

'All that's very well if it's true. But we don't know that,' Blunkett said.

'That's right. He can't prove any of it,' Blair added. 'And even if it is true, he's committed several crimes. He landed here as an illegal alien, and he trespassed and stole the rope from the flagpole.'

Dr. Bush frowned. 'Did you manage to inspect his belongings?'

'No, sir, I imagine they're still in the cave.'

'Leave it to me,' interjected Blunkett. 'I shall see that we go through everything with a fine toothcomb.'

Within a few hours, Blunkett knocked on the door of Blair's study with a triumphant look. 'See what we've found?'

There was a pile of papers in German and Russian, a family photograph with the imprint of a studio in Vilno and a hand-drawn map of the road leading from the Coalhaven docks to Mesopotamia. At the end of the road was a cross and by it the artist had written in capital letters 'The Saracen's Head'.

'Very good,' said Blair. 'Now I think we know where we are.'

After several weeks of incarceration, Mandelbaum lay listlessly on his bed, refusing meals. The buzz of interest which his arrival had excited in the school had fallen away and boys no longer peered through his window. There had been a general expectation that the dangerous anarchist would be led away in handcuffs to be charged and put on trial. The *Rocket* referred in general terms to the danger of foreigners conspiring to evade the provisions of the Aliens Act and infiltrate themselves into Britain. Several boys with foreign-sounding names found themselves subjected to a degree of persecution by their fellows that seemed to go beyond the limits of British fair play.

One afternoon, Blair was sitting in his study with his Latin prep and his latest adventure novel *In the Sands of the Kalahari* open on his desk, when the door burst open and in stalked Mandelson, in a state of extreme agitation.

'I really won't stand for it!' he exclaimed. 'I shall get even with them, Anthony, you see if I don't!'

'*Nil desperandum,* Peter,' said Blair, who was used by now to these emotional outbursts. 'What's the matter?'

'They pinned this to my back during class without me noticing,' came the reply. He thrust forward a square white card with a bull's eye traced on it and the words 'Send me back to Russia'.

'But you're as British as I am!' said Blair. 'As near as makes no difference.'

'They're all calling me Mandelbaum to my face. You're going to have to get rid of him. Either he goes, or I go!'

'That's jolly beastly,' Blair replied. 'All right, I shall see what I can do.'

Blair, Blunkett and Campbell could be seen later that evening descending the stairs to the editorial office of the *Rocket*, where Murdoch offered them the chance to discuss the forthcoming issue.

'I've been keeping a whole page free for the day when you make up your mind what to do with this anarchist.

The best thing will be to hand him over to the police. If they let him go, you can complain they're mollycoddling criminals. If he's put on trial and sentenced to penal servitude, you can take the credit.'

Blunkett was unhappy about losing his prisoner, but agreed that Mandelbaum's health and morale appeared to be weakening, and it would be better to hand him over to some other authority before he did serious harm to himself.

'We're agreed, then,' said Blair. Arrangements were put in place and on the following afternoon two police constables called at the school, to find a reporter and a photographer from the *Coalhaven Gazette* already in position.

Mandelbaum was brought up from the cellar and handcuffed to one of the policemen as a mixture of cheers and jeers rang out from the crowd of boys.

'Dangerous anarchist apprehended,' said the *Gazette* headline next day. 'Plot to kill Tsar foiled in Coalhaven. Police on alert for further suspects.' The *Rocket* carried an exhaustive account of the whole affair, highlighting Blair's personal courage and decisive leadership. The story filled several pages, with a special feature on the arrested anarchist's clifftop lair and a reproduction of the map showing the Saracen's Head. An editorial comment under the headline 'Britain for the Britishers', written by Murdoch himself, referred to the need for vigilance against 'foreign flotsam and jetsam'.

The dangerous anarchist spent the best part of a month in police cells, where he taught chess to the custody sergeant and learned several useful English phrases. At his third appearance before Coalhaven magistrates, Mandelbaum was bound over to keep the peace and fined five shillings for damaging a flagpole. The fine was paid by the representative of a Hebrew charitable organisation, who undertook to buy him a third class train ticket to Liverpool and an onward berth to New York.

His departure from Coalhaven was as unnoticed and unchronicled as his arrival. For by the time the snows melted and the ice on the canal thawed, a series of events was in train at St. Stephen's so momentous that the name of Mandelbaum was quickly forgotten.

CHAPTER XIII

WINNERS AND LOSERS

The Arbuthnot-Jones trophy race always took place on the Saturday before the Easter holidays. The large silver cup had been presented by General Arbuthnot-Jones, an old boy of St. Stephen's, so it was painful to know that the 'Rossers', the boys of Rossworth School, were in proud possession of it. A large empty space in the trophy cabinet reminded the boys that it was four years since the school had won it. In the previous year's race, run at Rossworth, the home team had romped home, with Northcaster College in second place and St. Stephen's a poor third.

So there was more than usual excitement when Campbell announced his determination to bring the trophy back to St. Stephen's and win the race on home soil. After pounding the clifftop path in all weathers through the winter, he was universally acknowledged to be the favourite. When the Rossworth and Northcaster boys arrived at Coalhaven station on the day of the race, they were quickly informed that this year they would face a real contest. After lunch, at which the St. Stephen's boys did their best to ply the visiting teams with pastry and jam roll, and the visitors politely declined, the teams assembled at the start and finish line underneath the clock tower.

'Good luck, old chap,' shouted Blair, taking Campbell's blazer and scarf. The snow had melted, leaving the roads and paths covered in brown mud. The thermometer showed only a degree or two above freezing and a sea mist hung over the countryside as Hetty and Clemmie, deputising for their father the Marquess, prepared to drop a white handkerchief to signal the start of the race. There were twelve runners from each school and the course was a punishing ten miles. Only the times of the first six runners would be counted. Rossworth's team was led by Gilligan, the winner of the previous year's race, while the Northcastrians were an unknown quantity.

'The mist should help us,' Campbell whispered to his team-mates. 'Make sure you follow the signs and don't take any wrong turnings.' The runners lined up and, as the great clock chimed three, the handkerchief fluttered to the ground. Boys lined the school drive to cheer as the runners faded into the mist.

Readers unfamiliar with the technical aspects of organising a modern cross-country race should understand that unlike the traditional 'Hare and Hounds', the route is always fixed in advance. For the Arbuthnot-Jones trophy, an army of small boys was deployed at points on the course to make sure the athletes took the correct turnings. The easiest task belonged to the boy stationed at the school gates, whose firm semaphore direction told the runners to take the clifftop path. This continued for some distance before leaving the shore and turning inland down a muddy path that ran close to the Fairhaven home farm. At the halfway point by a church, the course turned to the right around an orchard before looping back across the Fairhaven estate. Then the route wound its way through woods and fields on to the Coalhaven road, where the runners faced the steep final climb up to the school.

Most of the boys chosen to mark the route were the ones usually accused of 'funking at games'. They lacked the manly demeanour of true St. Stephen's boys through indolence, mollycoddling or a weak constitution. Some had the reputation of 'swots' and were aces at Greek and Latin; others simply preferred spending the afternoons with their books. One of these was Kelly, whose diminutive stature quickly earned him the nickname 'Pygmy'. Because their allotted stations were several miles from the school, Kelly and four other boys were given the unexpected treat of a motor car ride. 'Hop in, you lot,' said the young maths master as soon as lunch was over. 'I'll be back to pick you up as soon as the last runners go past.'

As he watched the motor car depart into the distance, Kelly felt rather like Robinson Crusoe, with a knot of uncertainty in his stomach. Would he ever be rescued? It was only half past one by the church clock and the race did not even start until three. He estimated that he had at least two hours to kill and thanked his lucky stars he had remembered to bring his pocket guide to British birds. St. Stephen's was a rough place for a bookish boy and he welcomed the chance to disappear into quiet corners where he would not be noticed. His worst nightmare was to be the centre of attention and it had taken him all of his first term at school to overcome his shyness at morning and evening callover. Eventually he learned to shout *Adsum* loudly enough to be heard, so he could scurry back to his collection of bird eggs and feathers. It is fair to say that none of the sixth formers at St. Stephen's had any idea who he was. Unfortunately for Kelly, his days of pleasant obscurity were about to end.

As they left the road for the narrow cliff path, the runners jostled for position and settled into single file. It was almost impossible to overtake and the first two miles were on the flat. Campbell, Gilligan and the other fancied contenders kept to the middle of the field, eying each other carefully. None of the three teams secured an advantage until the path turned into a switchback, with a series of sharp ascents and descents that began to separate the contenders. Campbell and Gilligan were neck and neck as they entered the muddy track leading inland, but here the St. Stephen's man began to gain the upper hand. Gilligan, who had been training on metalled roads, found his shoes slipping in the mud and measured his length as he crossed a stile. He looked up and saw Campbell sprinting away from him into the mist. Desperate to remain in sight of the leader, he redoubled his efforts to keep within range as his target slipped in and out of the fog. He estimated Campbell's lead at around a hundred yards, little enough in a ten-mile race lasting over an hour. And he knew that the last section would be on a road, giving him the chance to unleash a final sprint.

Campbell sneaked a look behind him as he approached the church; his pursuer was nowhere to be seen, but he knew that to slacken off would be fatal. He looked up at the church clock, showing twenty-five minutes past three, then peered forward into the mist, looking for directions. Was it left, or right, or straight on? Where was the boy who was supposed to be showing him the route?

Kelly was at that exact moment sitting on a bench at the entrance to the churchyard, deeply engrossed in reading about the reed-warbler, and wondering whether he might spot one. Suddenly he was aware of feet pounding towards him and jumped up. 'That way!' he shouted, as Campbell pounded past. A few seconds elapsed, and he shouted 'Round the orchard!' at the disappearing figure.

By the time Gilligan hove into view, Kelly was fully alert. 'Round the churchyard, then keep right round the orchard,' he shouted. The mist appeared to be clearing a little, and Kelly watched Campbell stop, hesitate for a second, then climb over the stile and into the orchard, where he vanished from view. A few seconds later, Gilligan reached the stile and continued in a long loop to the right. He noticed that Campbell was no longer in sight. 'That's a deuced odd thing!' he thought to himself. When he emerged from the other side of the wood fifteen minutes later, his quarry had well and truly shown him a clean pair of heels.

The St. Stephen's boys were lining the road from Coalhaven to the school and a huge cheer went up as Campbell emerged in the lead. Some boys carried watches and worked out that Gilligan was a full minute behind. 'He'll never catch him now!' they shouted, dancing up and down as their hero approached the school gates. As the clock struck four, Campbell breasted the winning tape and collapsed on the grass, his body heaving. He had done it! Within a few minutes, the rest of the runners, led by Gilligan, were lying and sitting beside him, shaking each other by the hand. Campbell was waiting for Gilligan to congratulate him as a sportsman should, but the Rossworth boy ignored him. Instead, Gilligan drew aside a Rossworth master and the two held an animated conversation.

The result of the race was close, according to unofficial

'A HUGE CHEER WENT UP AS CAMPBELL EMERGED IN THE LEAD.'

calculations. With the first six runners home from each team, it was clear that Northcaster would carry home the wooden spoon. The top dozen places were almost evenly divided between St. Stephen's and Rossworth, but Campbell's first place would guarantee a historic victory for the home team. Blair led the congratulations, clapping his friend on the back.

It was at this point in the proceedings that young Kelly was spotted, emerging from the maths master's motor car with his bird book under his arm. Happy to be rescued from his vigil outside the church, and wondering whether he would rather have crumpets or hot buttered toast with his tea, Kelly was about to wander away, when he was summoned abruptly by the race referee.

'Come here, boy. You were the marker by the church?'

'Yes, sir.'

'Did you see the leading two runners pass you?'

'Yes, sir.'

'Did they both follow the course as far as you could see?'

An older and more experienced boy might have temporised at this juncture, realising the implications of his answer. But Kelly was often accused of mumbling, and so on this occasion, facing not just one master but a panel of three with stopwatches and papers in their hands, he was determined to speak out loud and clear.

'No, sir. Campbell went through the orchard, rather than round it.'

A collective gasp went up. Kelly tried to explain that it looked to him like an honest mistake. 'It was really all my fault,' he exclaimed, looking round in vain for a sympathetic face. But by now, nobody was listening. The three masters were huddled over their results, with paper and pencils. At last they stepped up to the table on which the silver cup was standing.

'The first runner to cross the finishing line, Campbell of St. Stephen's, has been disqualified. The winner is therefore Gilligan of Rossworth and Rossworth School retains the Arbuthnot-Jones trophy.'

Pandemonium broke out. There were scattered cheers from the Rossworth contingent and howls of fury from the St. Stephen's boys. Kelly realised that he had done a terrible, terrible thing for which he would never be forgiven. Forgetting all about the hot buttered toast and crumpets, he fled as fast as his legs could carry him.

Blair was speechless for a moment, as he looked at the pain and fury etched on Campbell's face. He put his friend's blazer round his shoulders, but Campbell remained with his head in his hands, unable to comprehend the enormity of what had happened. Disqualified! It was like a stain he would never be able to wash away.

'That little sneak!' Campbell groaned. Then he sprang to his feet. 'I shall get him sent to Coventry. We'll see how he likes that!'

Kelly's scandalous conduct in 'peaching' on Campbell quickly became the talk of the school. He was not a boy with many friends and those few he had were afraid to speak up for him. So there was no resistance in the day-rooms when resolutions were passed sending the small third former to Coventry until further notice.

'He needs to understand that he's not only let himself down, but the whole school!' said Blair, who was secretly hoping that Campbell's furious mood would calm down. He was afraid that his friend might wreak some terrible vengeance of his own on the boy who had dashed his hopes.

Kelly was still in his hiding place halfway up the staircase of the clock-tower several hours later, when he looked at his watch and found it was nearly time for callover. The staircase was strictly out of bounds, but he had discovered that the iron grille at the bottom was never locked and it was easy to climb the echoing spiral stairs. Halfway up was a window niche which he had made his own, where he could sit and gaze out at the seagulls and pretend that he was back in the Middle Ages.

He descended the stairs and made his way back to the third form day-room, known to generations of St. Stephen's boys as the Tadpole Room. As he opened the door, the hubbub fell silent. A dozen eyes met his gaze, then turned away.

'I say, what's the matter, you chaps?' he asked.

Answer came there none. He made his way to a corner chair and was about to sit down, when a school cap was thrown on to it. There was a loud hissing sound.

'This little sneak is trying to bag a chair when it's already taken. Just fancy that!' said one of the bigger boys.

At that point a bell rang, and Kelly was caught up in the rush of boys to evening callover and prayers. Normally he found himself standing tightly packed in a gaggle of other third formers, but tonight he was alone in his shame. No other boy approached within five yards of him, none looked in his direction and none spoke.

In the dormitory Kelly found his bedclothes soaked with water. When the gaslight was extinguished, there was a whisper of 'sneak, sneak' which he knew was directed at him. Eventually, when all the others were asleep, he crawled out of bed and found a towel to mop up the worst of the flooding. He heard the clock strike two before he finally fell asleep.

The next morning was no better. Sending someone to Coventry, like cross-country and rugger, is an adult game which schoolboys play with a rare kind of fanaticism born of inexperience. The sixth form, for whom Kelly was a complete unknown, might perhaps shrug their shoulders and abandon the game after a day or two. But for the third form, the humiliation of 'Pygmy' Kelly became a matter of honour. At breakfast, somebody pushed him in the back, forcing him to spill milk down his jacket. When he sat down, the boys on either side immediately got up and moved elsewhere. At morning prayers, the moment he had most been dreading arrived. The third form was traditionally placed in the front of Big School, with the prefects facing them. For some reason which Kelly could not fathom, Campbell was seated with the prefects when Dr. Bush walked in. After prayers, Blair rose and proposed three cheers for Campbell, describing him as the best runner in the school's long history. Kelly looked up, to see Campbell's eyes glaring straight at him, while all the others were turned away. 'Hip hip hooray!' echoed to the rafters. Kelly's mouth opened, but no sound came out.

In class, the isolation was less intense because the masters sometimes spoke to him. Kelly felt like a small shrimp in the depths of the ocean, in danger of being swallowed by sharp-toothed predators. The masters splashed about on the surface, oblivious of the deeper currents flowing all around them. 'Stop daydreaming, Kelly!' said the young maths master who had driven him on that fateful afternoon. Kelly gazed out of the window and wondered what he could have done differently. Was he really a sneak? His parents had always told him to speak up and tell the truth, and at the age of thirteen this seemed a simple enough code to follow. But here at St.

Stephen's telling the truth appeared to be the wrong thing to do. Why had he been accused of 'letting down the school'?

The pain of his situation was made worse by a feeling of betrayal. For the lowly third former, the captain of school was a remote, God-like figure. Some boys are born cynics, but he was not one of them, and he had always trusted in 'Good old Sooty' to be the friend and protector of the weak. He had wondered if he might one day be chosen for the ultimate honour of fagging for Blair. As he lay half asleep under his damp bedclothes, he dreamed he was a tiny fledgling, tossed out of the nest by its parents.

He avoided mealtimes with the other boys, restricting himself to the occasional piece of chocolate. Only three days remained until the end of term and Kelly wondered how he would be able to face his parents. He could not lie to them, but the idea of telling them that he had been sent to Coventry by the entire school was unthinkable. In every corridor and classroom, eyes were averted and backs were turned when he approached. Should he fall sick and throw himself on the mercy of Matron Boothroyd? But that would provide only temporary relief. He had been given what amounted to a life sentence and in the summer term his ordeal would continue.

On the third day he saw the latest edition of the *Rocket*. There on the front page was an account of the race and an attack on the unnamed boy who had disgraced St. Stephen's College by making false allegations against the winner. 'A stab in the back' said the headline. Suddenly he felt very angry. He was overcome by a fierce desire to make sure that those responsible for his suffering should suffer in return. And the masters who were turning a blind eye to what was going on would be forced to sit up and take notice.

Kelly dragged himself through the day until the bell sounded for the end of school. When nobody was looking, he donned his overcoat and slipped out into the dusk with his bird book, a bar of chocolate and a packet of biscuits.

Experienced readers of school stories will at this point be able to anticipate the climax of our narrative. The missing boy's absence is detected; our hero is determined to find him and risks expulsion by breaking out of school to follow his tracks; he suspects that the despairing runaway has headed for the railway station to catch the early morning milk train; he intercepts the fugitive and brings him back to school, where dramatic new evidence is revealed in the case of the missing postal order; the firm but kindly headmaster declares the fugitive to be without a stain on his character, while the real villain is unmasked and expelled. Cheeks turn crimson, tears are wiped away, hands are clasped in manly fashion, and the school song is sung with gusto.

Unfortunately, real life does not follow the conventions of the school story. At evening callover there was no reply when Kelly's name was called, but one of the third form boys shouted: 'I saw him ten minutes ago, sir. He was looking a bit green about the gills.' The duty master, who still had a pile of examination papers to mark, ticked Kelly's name and closed the register.

Kelly's body was found floating in the Coalhaven canal at first light the next morning by a milkman doing his rounds. The chocolate and the biscuits were still in his pocket, though spoiled by the water. There was no trace of the bird book.

Dr. Bush was deeply shocked by the tragedy and

penned a letter to Kelly's parents telling them so. A special service was held in the chapel the next day, conducted by the padre. Blair read the lesson and gave a short address with a catch in his voice that many considered to be genuine.

'This is a sad day for all of us. Our friend Kelly has been taken prematurely. Who knows what he might have achieved in the classroom and on the sports field? Our thoughts today must be with his family, who have lost a dear son. St. Stephen's has lost a promising scholar, popular among his classmates. We all knew Kelly and shall remember his contribution to school life. Some of you may be tempted to blame yourselves for his untimely death. We all ask ourselves the question, could we have done more? If only we had known! But I say unto you, the Lord giveth and the Lord taketh away. Thy will be done.'

After the service, Blair was ushered into Dr. Bush's study, where a tall uniformed figure was standing on the Persian rug where Horatio had once slept.

'Come in, Blair,' said the headmaster. 'This is Police Constable Hutton. He has come to inform us of the latest state of the investigation.'

The policeman opened his notebook and began to read.

'The boy died of drowning. No signs of foul play, though of course in that area of town, nothing can be ruled out. We don't know what he was doing there in Mesopotamia, down by the canal. Was he worried about anything, that you know of?'

Blair looked straight at the police constable. 'Nothing that I am aware of. I think he was looking forward to the end of term, like the rest of us.'

The constable nodded and put away his notebook. 'There are no gas lamps or railings by the canal and it was a moonless night with cloud and rain. Unless evidence emerges to the contrary, it is my conclusion that the boy must have tripped and fallen in. Very sad.'

Blair looked at Dr. Bush, who walked over and shook the constable by the hand.

'A tragedy. But an accidental one. Thank you, Constable Hutton. The College is much obliged to you.'

CHAPTER XIV

UP IN THE CLOUDS

The Easter holiday was nearly over. Blair decided not to mention the death of Kelly to his father and mother out of respect for the dead boy. His own conscience was clear and he looked forward to testifying at the inquest, which Constable Hutton had told Dr. Bush was a necessary formality in such cases. Each time he thought about the forthcoming summer term, his last at St. Stephen's, he felt a strange mixture of emotions. On the one hand, he was looking forward to seeing the old College again. At the end of term he would throw his straw boater over the cliffs in a ritual hallowed by tradition, and his name would be traced in gold lettering on the board that listed the captains of school. Then he would make his way in the wider world – but how? His father kept dropping hints about the legal profession, but he found hairsplitting legal arguments dry and unattractive. He recalled Dr. Bush's distinction between the laws of men and the laws of God. Should he take holy orders? The choice was one he did not wish to dismiss lightly, for he had often imagined himself preaching from the pulpit. Or he might go into business and become a self-made man with his own joint-stock company, or even several joint-stock companies, like Horatio Bottomley, the publisher of his favourite magazine *John Bull.* He looked at his bookshelf and sighed. Six months ago, he would have fallen on the books he had been given for his eighteenth birthday and devoured them at one sitting. But now *A Boy's Adventure in Bechuanaland* and *Among the Pirates of the China Sea* lay unread. The truth was, he was sloughing off boyhood pastimes and pleasures. Adulthood was beckoning to him, like a faraway candle behind a windowpane. When he thought of St. Stephen's, he felt 'cabin'd, cribbed, confined'. He knew that destiny was calling him forth to play his part upon a wider stage, but did not know where.

Such was his mood when the postman delivered an envelope with a familiar crest. It was from Hetty.

Dear Anthony

What a turnup! Our big bro. Ernest has returned from Canada and is here at Fairhaven. What is more, he has learned to fly and is testing a new two-seater aeroplane for Mr. Rolls! We have told him all about you and he wants to invite you to loop the loop. Come and stay with us again before term starts – you will be quite safe as the hunting season is over. Father is still v. preoccupied with the colliery strike and is away most of the time.

Please reply by return.

Hetty (and Clemmie)

Blair rushed upstairs to consult the railway timetable

and pen a swift reply. Two days later, he was standing in the same large field where once the ill-fated Rifle Corps camp had taken place. The central strip had been neatly mown and there at one end was a biplane of the kind he had often seen in illustrated magazines. Hattersley the gamekeeper, recovered from his injuries, was standing by the wooden propeller and Ernie was holding out a leather flying helmet and goggles.

'Left foot first, swing the right one over and sit down carefully. Don't put your foot through the canvas!' Ernie admonished him. 'Once we get up there, we won't be able to talk, so ask me any questions now.'

Blair was too excited to ask anything at all. He clambered into the seat and Ernie turned round with a grin. 'Hang on tight. Don't worry, we're not looping the loop! We leave that to the Frenchmen.' Hetty and Clemmie were waving from the edge of the field and he waved back. Ernie gave the 'thumbs up' sign to Hattersley, who pulled the propeller down and jumped smartly backwards. There was a throaty roar from the engine and the machine began to move. Before he knew it, they were shaking and bumping along the turf at an astonishing speed. Hetty and Clemmie became two shrinking figures and the hedge ahead loomed larger. Suddenly after only a hundred yards or so the bumping stopped. The wind blew fiercely on his face as the flimsy craft gained height. Blair imagined himself an air scout in some future armed conflict, sent aloft to spy out the enemy's dispositions. Ernie turned round silently with a grin and banked the plane slowly to the right. They were now flying parallel to the cliffs, high above the path, with yellow gorse bushes dotting the landscape beneath them. And there was St. Stephen's! The clocktower, normally so imposing, now looked like a cardboard model. How fast were they travelling? Fifty miles per hour? Seventy? Perhaps one hundred? This was even better than the Rolls-Royce. Anybody could drive a Rolls-Royce, but an aeroplane was for the few, not the many! There was the metalled road snaking down the hill between the school and Coalhaven. What a shame that with two days to go before term began, there were no other boys around to witness his flight! They were soaring among the seagulls with wisps of cloud on either side. Again Ernie banked the plane and Blair could see Coalhaven spread out beneath him, beginning with the docks. The ships were tiny, and he could just see some upturned faces. He felt like the archangel Gabriel in the chapel window, swooping freely through the air while the rest of the town was pinioned to earth. Ernie stretched out a hand to indicate that they were going to fly lower and turned off the petrol tap, allowing the machine to glide downwards. The wind whistled past the struts and wires as the centre of Coalhaven rose to meet them. The engine roared back into life and Blair could see faces craning skywards on the High Street. There was Thatcher's grocery store, and Berlusconi's café! And there, between the river and the canal, he saw the shabby streets of Mesopotamia with their dirty back-to-back houses. He could see a group of urchins kicking a football against a wall. There was Ma Mowlam's yard, and the school mission, and the sinister shape of the Saracen's Head public house. Somewhere inside that building, he was certain, lay the stolen rifles. Who could tell what nefarious plans Fat Sam and his son were hatching? As the aeroplane swooped low, he thought he saw a middle-aged man's face at an upstairs window. He was close enough to throw a penny on to the slate roof, or even a

'HOW FAST WERE THEY TRAVELLING? FIFTY MILES PER HOUR?'

grenade, as Italian aviators had recently done against rebellious native tribes in North Africa. There was something intoxicating about the power conferred on him by the gift of flight. As the machine swung gloriously upwards again, he raised his eyes to the horizon, where the river twisted away between fields dotted with sheep and tiny lambs.

Before he knew it, they were coming in to land. He hung on tightly as Ernie cut off the engine and they glided down to the grassy strip. When the aeroplane bumped to a stop, he ripped off his goggles and helmet and clambered down. Ernie grinned back, sharing his exhilaration. 'It's all worth fighting for, isn't it?' the young pilot exclaimed.

'You mean England? Oh yes! Even Coalhaven looks beautiful when you fly over it.'

At dinner their euphoria was dampened by the arrival of the Marquess, who looked gloomy. The labour unrest in the collieries was continuing and a strike of seamen and dockers was paralysing the port, leaving the giant cranes standing idle. A lorry load of whisky destined for the Black Pig Brewery had vanished without trace from the Britannia wharf. Ernie was full of suggestions for volunteer detachments of young men to take the place of the strikers. 'I'm sure St. Stephen's could do something,' Blair added. 'Just say the word, and lots of us will stand up and be counted. I give you my word, we know how to use our fists if we have to.' These martial words were directed at the Marquess, but Blair could not help noticing out of the corner of his eye that they produced an admiring exchange of glances between Hetty and Clemmie.

The short stay at Fairhaven and the aeroplane flight renewed Blair's optimism about the summer term; as the Rolls-Royce drove him through the school gates he felt he was approaching a tryst with destiny. He felt more than usually humbled by the secret certainty that he would have to meet a challenge which the other boys would not face. When the moment came, he would be ready.

But the first few days of routine school business sapped his morale. How petty and provincial school life seemed after his glimpse of the world of aviation! The death of Kelly was not forgotten, especially in the third form, where the idea of sending boys to Coventry fell suddenly out of fashion. Matron came in tears to collect the dead boy's collection of bird eggs from his study, a task which had been forgotten at the end of the spring term. There was talk of taking up a collection for a memorial of some kind to Kelly, but it came to nothing. Blair sensed the changed mood when he approached a group of Hardie's fifth formers with a friendly grin, only to see them turn their backs and walk away with a hissing noise. It was more important to be right than to be popular, he decided. Being captain of school was of necessity a lonely, thankless role. At dinner he watched with a feeling of distaste as Brown moved around the tables, shaking boys by the hand and asking them about their holidays. Such shameless courting of popularity! Blair returned to his study alone and closed the door.

One May morning he was passed an urgent message to call on Dr. Bush. When he entered the study he found the headmaster pacing up and down in a state of agitation. Lying on the chaise-longue was the prostrate figure of the French master, Monsieur de Chirac, with a bandage round his head and his arm in a sling. 'Our local constabulary has failed again,' Dr. Bush began. 'The school mission has been attacked during the night by hooligans. I am told that every single window has been broken by a mob. Then they invaded the High Street and smashed the windows of Signor Berlusconi's café. He was accused of being a foreigner. Monsieur de Chirac was beaten within an inch of his life.'

'I 'ad to run for my life. Eet eez an outrage!' the Frenchman stammered.

Dr. Bush patted him on the shoulder. 'I have spoken to the police, but as usual they claim they are short of men. I wish there was something we could do.'

'But sir, I think there is something we can do.' Dr. Bush looked at Blair with rapt attention.

'You remember, sir, that Coalhaven has been out of bounds all winter. I am sure that is one of the reasons for the disturbances. Without the College boys walking the streets, sir, the town has started to go rather downhill. There is a general lack of respect. All the natives say so.'

'Natives?'

'I mean the day-boys, sir. What we have to do is mount patrols – not just up and down the High Street, but in Mesopotamia as well. That's where the problem lies. *Radix omnium malorum in Mesopotamia est.*'

Dr. Bush, as has already been explained, was an unworldly man. Apart from his beloved mission, he knew nothing of Coalhaven and its people. He had never bought a special strawberry ice-cream in Berlusconi's café, never sniffed the cheese at Thatcher's nor entered a public house.

'You see, sir, I've been investigating the missing rifles and I have reason to believe they're being kept in a public house called the Saracen's Head. It's the one just opposite the mission. And it's my firm belief that the landlord and his son are mixed up in this whole affair. They probably organised the mob.'

Dr. Bush paused in his perambulation. 'We must never forget that the evildoers are among us. *There shall be a fountain opened to the house of David and to the inhabitants of Jerusalem for sin and for uncleanness. And it shall come to pass in that day, said the Lord of hosts, that I will cut off the names of the idols out of the land, and they shall no more be remembered. And also I will cause the prophets and the unclean spirit to pass out of the land.* Are you familiar with the prophet Zechariah?'

Blair shook his head.

'Well, we must build that fountain. We must cast out the idols and drive out the unclean spirits.'

'Yes, sir.'

'Blair, Coalhaven will no longer be out of bounds. I leave it to you to organise the volunteer patrols.'

'I shall ask the College scout troop, sir. We will use the mission building as a base.'

Blair left the headmaster's study with a spring in his step. When lessons were over for the day, he lost no time in seeking out the study reserved for the head of Gladstone's house, where he knocked on the oak door.

'Come in at your own risk. I'm doing my exercises,' came a voice. Crossing the threshold, Blair was confronted by the sight of Ashdown, the captain of Gladstone's, wearing only a pair of blue knickers. He was sweating profusely and waving a pair of Indian clubs around his head.

'Watch out! Don't stand too close, old fellow! You could get a nasty knock,' his host proclaimed. The clubs swung faster and faster, narrowly missing the gaslights on the wall. Ashdown was counting under his breath, and when he reached one hundred, he tossed the clubs into a corner of the room and sat down.

'What can I do for you?'

'There's a chance for your Scout patrol to do something more exciting than tying knots. The school mission down in Mesopotamia has been attacked by a mob. We need to get down there and get on the trail of who did it. Then we can think about giving the blighters a lesson they won't forget in a hurry.'

Ashdown did not hesitate. 'That sounds a capital idea. If you can get us all excused from games and extra-tew, we'll mount a special patrol on Saturday afternoon. *Zing-a-zing! Bom-bom!*'

'I beg your pardon?'

Ashdown chuckled. 'I can see you've never read *Scouting for Boys*, old chap. You come with us and make the tea and we'll teach you all about scout lore.'

On Saturday the Beaver patrol paraded, clutching their staves and bedrolls and haversacks with supplies. They wore their flat-brimmed felt hats, their red neckerchiefs, their belts and knives, their stout boots, and their dark blue short trousers. One boy carried the scout flag, while Ashdown as patrol leader had a whistle round his neck and carried his assegai. Blair felt a little under-dressed in his school clothes.

The boys varied in height from some six feet tall to the smallest, a ginger-haired little chap with bright pink cheeks and knees named Kennedy. The patrol performed the scout salute, gave three cheers for the captain of school and turned sharply to the right. Ashdown inspected their handcart, on which the cooking billies, frying pans, coils of rope and other supplies were packed. Whatever else might transpire that night, it was certain that the Beaver patrol did not plan to go hungry. There was flour, tea, cocoa, bacon, butter and milk from the school kitchens, a box of candles and a sack of potatoes. As they marched, they broke into repeated renderings of what sounded to Blair like a strange African chant. *'Een gonyama – gonyama! Invooboo! Yah bobo! Yah bo! Invooboo!'*

'What's all that about?' Blair enquired of the nearest scout.

'It means something like "He is a lion! Yes! He is better than that – he is a hippopotamus." At least, that's what Ashdown says.'

The patrol halted at Berlusconi's café, where the proprietor served them tea and cocoa 'on-a the house' and insisted they take a tray of jam puffs with them. Only a smell of putty and fresh paint betrayed the fact that the two windows facing the street had been replaced. But when they crossed into Mesopotamia and reached the mission, a dismal sight met their eyes. The low wall surrounding the forecourt had been demolished and the bricks used as missiles to smash the windows. Though the stoutly locked front door had resisted the mob, the back door to the scullery was smashed wide open. The intruders had scattered prayer books and hymnals all over the floor. The scouts immediately set to with a will and after an hour of hard work the debris was removed.

'Let's stop for a brew,' Ashdown called out. The boys made for the scullery, where Blair made tea in a large brown enamel pot and distributed the jam puffs. When the boys were all seated, Blair began to address them on their tasks.

'Just a minute. Where's Kennedy got to?' asked Ashdown. 'I bet he's puffing on a cigarette!' The suspicion proved correct, for the small ginger-haired boy was apprehended behind the scullery door, a cigarette clamped between his little pink fingers. When the miscreant returned to the fold, Blair gave him a round of applause which made him blush to the roots.

'What I want you brave lads to do is to keep an eye on the mission tonight and stand sentry duty. But the most important thing is to find out what is going on at the Saracen's Head. We need to mount a night patrol to spy out the premises.'

'But we don't understand,' asked one of the scouts. 'What's this all about?'

'Fat Sam the landlord is a notorious villain,' Blair replied. 'There's a good deal of firm evidence linking him with the missing silver cup, and the poisoning of Horatio, and the beastly attack on our good friend Berlusconi. If we don't nip this sort of thing in the bud, honest citizens won't be able to walk the streets of Coalhaven unmolested. You've seen his son riding his motor cycle up and down the High Street as if he owned it, scaring every cat and dog within fifty paces?'

The boys nodded. Blair lowered his voice to a whisper and they bent forward to hear what he had to say.

'You remember the missing rifles from the corps camp? Well, I have proof that they're somewhere in the Saracen's Head, probably in a storeroom or a cellar. It's your task to climb in and find them while everyone's asleep.'

'But isn't that burglary?' asked one boy whose father was a barrister-at-law and who was often taken to sit in the public seats of the county sessions during school holidays.

'Not under the law of England,' said Blair. 'Not if you're apprehending a dangerous criminal. Are you all game for an adventure?'

'By golly, yes!' came the chorus of replies. All the scouts volunteered to spy on the Saracen's Head, while nobody was keen to stand sentry duty. 'Can I go, please?' asked Kennedy, anxious to make amends for the incident with the cigarette. 'I'm small, so I may be able to squeeze through a window.'

'Very well,' said Blair, before adding hastily: 'If your patrol leader agrees, of course.'

The boys spent the evening cooking a hearty meal on the gas ring in the scullery and then washed up all the knives and forks and plates with great enthusiasm. Then they paraded in a line and Ashdown led the Scout's war dance, in which one boy acted out the killing of a wild buffalo while the others chanted and banged on the floor with their staves. Ashdown shouted 'Be Prepared!' three times and the scouts danced around in a circle, chanting and stamping. Blair found it all very impressive.

By the time they finished, darkness had enveloped Mesopotamia. There were no street lights and only the two gaslamps burning over the door of the Saracen's Head cast a glow on the pavement. Working men in large cloth caps thronged the public bar. Every time the door swung open, a roar of noise and light spilled outwards for a second. Wrapped in their mufflers behind the broken windows of the mission, the boys caught the sound of piano music from the big room at the back of the building. Occasionally there was the shriek of a female voice and the sound of a music hall melody. This was not the kind of spying operation which Baden-Powell had envisaged when he wrote *Scouting for Boys*. It had little in common with tracking the spoor of lions in Bechuanaland. However Blair was a keen reader of the *Police Illustrated News* and knew all about low dives and opium dens. He knew that like Whitechapel in the East End of London, Mesopotamia was the kind of place where white slavers were ten a penny, where honest sailors were 'shanghaied' and relieved of their pay, where smugglers and coiners and cardsharps flourished. The thrilling element for all the boys was that this was no longer a story from the *BOP* or *Chums*. This time, the adventure was real and they were in it.

It was well after midnight when the noise and lights began to fade. The front door of the public house was bolted and the last shouting died away. After exchanging their boots for rubber-soled shoes, the boys crept silently out of the back door of the mission, crossed the street in Indian file and took up their positions, leaving two of their number to keep lookout and guard their retreat. Blair stayed with them, carrying an axe and a coil of rope in case of emergencies.

The scouts were crouched at the back gate of the Saracen's Head, wondering whether to force it open or to climb over, when they heard two male voices. 'Hop on the pillion seat, lad,' said one. 'I'll have thee home in no time.' Then the gate swung open and the boys pressed themselves silently into the darkness at the foot of the wall. There was the noise of a motor cycle engine starting and a voice saying 'Hold tight!'; then the roar of the engine drowned out the voices as the machine sped away across the cobblestones. Blair motioned to his two fellow sentries to seize the coil of rope. 'Tie it across the street. He'll be back in ten minutes, and we'll catch him. He'll never see it in the dark.'

Meanwhile, the rest of the scout patrol, profiting by the open gate, crept into the yard at the back of the building. The ground floor doors and windows of the inn were firmly locked, but a small casement on the first floor was open. 'Let me go!' said Kennedy. The rest of the patrol lifted him on to a low sloping roof and he inched his way towards the casement. It was a tight squeeze, but the boy managed to push first his feet and legs and then his head and arms through the narrow opening.

Kennedy found himself in an upstairs bathroom. He tiptoed to the door, and turned the handle gently. He entered a long corridor, with bedrooms to his left and an open landing with a balustrade to his right. From below came the sound of voices and the dim light of an oil lamp. Desperately trying to avoid making the wooden boards creak, he squatted behind the balustrade in the dark, trying to make out what the men were saying. His heart thumped inside his chest.

'Lookee here, Sam. You're trying to kill the goose what lays the golden egg. There's a notice up about pilfering. I can't take another lorry load. There's police crawling all over the docks and extra men on the bonded store at the wharf, and I can't rely on not being stopped no more.'

Kennedy's heart leapt into his mouth. There was dirty business under discussion, that much was clear. He swallowed hard and tried to follow the rest of the conversation.

Meanwhile, outside in the street, the put-put of an approaching petrol engine broke the silence. Blair and the two sentries gave a final tug to the rope they had suspended across the street, then ducked out of sight. Around the corner came the motor cycle. The rope caught the rider at chest height and he fell awkwardly in the gutter, hitting his head on the cobblestones. The riderless machine skidded sideways, crashing to a halt outside the public bar with a noise of tearing metal.

'What was that noise?' came the voice from below the balustrade. Kennedy caught his breath and froze, and found himself battling against an uncontrollable coughing fit. If only he had read Baden-Powell's advice against tobacco earlier, before acquiring a taste for 'gaspers'! He stuffed a handkerchief in front of his mouth and tried to breathe through his nose as Baden-Powell recommended, but it was too late. The unmistakable hacking sound of a smoker's cough betrayed his presence. Two men came bounding up the stairs and, before Kennedy knew it, his arms were locked painfully behind his back.

Dragged down the stairs, he caught a glimpse of coarse-featured and swarthy faces, all staring at him. Seated at the head of the table was a man almost as wide as he was tall, who was giving orders to the others. 'Blindfold him!' the man said, and Kennedy felt his red scout kerchief being bound tightly around his eyes. A fist hit him in the face and he fell sideways to the floor.

'Young man, we're going to ask you a few questions,' said the voice. 'You'd better 'ave some good answers.'

CHAPTER XV

IN FAT SAM'S LAIR

The man lying in the gutter moaned slightly, then lay still. There was a strong smell of petrol from the damaged motor cycle. 'You'd better carry him inside the mission,' said Blair. 'We can ask him a few questions.' Silently, Blair helped the two boy scouts to drag the unconscious figure into the scullery and lay him on the floor. By the light of a candle they could see the man wore a leather jacket, breeches and leggings over heavy boots. His face was pale and there was an ugly cut on his temple where his head had hit the pavement. Blair ran a cloth under the tap and mopped the mixture of blood and dirt off the man's face with a shudder. The prostrate figure moaned and opened his eyes. Blair remembered how Boer agents had been interrogated during the South African war and ordered that the prisoner be blindfolded. 'Here, take off that red kerchief thing and tie it round his eyes,' he said.

The motor cyclist groaned and rose to his knees. The two scouts, after a brief argument about reef knots and clove hitches, tied his hands together behind his back.

'Tell me your name,' Blair began.

'I'm Percy Jenkins. Are you the police? I know my rights!'

'Never you mind who we are. We're on the trail of a criminal gang at the Saracen's Head. We believe you can help us.'

'Damned if I will. You have no right to throw me off my bike and tie me up.'

'Tell us where the missing rifles are and we'll let you go.'

'I don't know nothing about no missing rifles.'

'Don't give me any of that nonsense. I know Fat Sam has got them somewhere. You're his son?'

'I am Sam Jenkins' son and proud to be,' the man replied. The repetition of the name Jenkins caused Blair to hesitate. Where had he heard that name before?

The man, by now fully conscious, sensed Blair's hesitation.

'You're working for Billy, aren't you?'

'Who?' asked Blair, not expecting to be questioned in his turn.

'Billy Jenkins, Marquess of Coalhaven to you. Bastard Billy to us. He and my old man are cousins, but Billy married into money and won't speak to the rest of us no more. Now he's a peer of the realm and a wealthy man, he don't want to be reminded of the fact that his mother served behind the bar at the Saracen's Head.'

Blair took a second to digest this information. 'The Marquess of Coalhaven is a gentleman and I am proud to count him my friend,' he retorted. 'In fact we had dinner together before the beginning of term.'

Percy interrupted him. 'The beginning of term? You're from St. Stephen's College, aren't you?' There was no reply from Blair. 'I'd know your voice anywhere. I've heard you taking Sunday school at the mission across the road.'

The interrogation of the prisoner was no longer going to plan. The two young scouts began shifting uneasily from one foot to the other. Percy Jenkins struggled to his feet.

'You had better leave off this nonsense, or I shall report you to your headmaster.'

'Our headmaster knows we are here,' said Blair. 'We are on patrol and keeping His Majesty's peace.'

'I don't suppose your headmaster knows you're going around pulling law-abidin' citizens off their motor cycles,' Percy exclaimed. 'Look sharp and untie that rope, or you boys will be in trouble.'

At this point the plucky hero of a schoolboy story would have punched Percy sharply in the solar plexus, or dealt him a crisp blow to the jaw to reinforce the importance of keeping His Majesty's peace. But Blair was squeamish about using his fists on a helpless opponent and his hesitation proved fatal. The two scouts untied Percy's arms and the prisoner tore off his blindfold.

'Let me get a good look at you! That's right. I'll know your face next time,' he said with a menacing leer in Blair's direction. He was about to leave when the door of the scullery opened and in came Ashdown, with anxiety written all over his face.

'Kennedy hasn't come back. I think they've captured him,' he muttered. 'Time we held a little council of war. Who's that?'

Percy turned, glared sharply at Ashdown, and stalked out.

'That's Percy Jenkins. He's Fat Sam's son.'

'And you're letting him walk out? We need him as a hostage!'

Blair grinned sheepishly. 'I'm sorry, old fellow. I had no idea.'

Ashdown banged his scout's stave on the floor and looked at Blair with barely concealed contempt. 'We've got to rescue Kennedy. This isn't just a game any longer.'

Inside the Saracen's Head, Kennedy was sitting upright, tied to a chair and blindfolded. His jaw ached and he had a terrible feeling that he had let down the Beaver patrol, the Scout movement, the Chief Scout and of course the whole school. He had volunteered with alacrity for the night patrol because he was keen to win his scout's badge and stop being a 'tenderfoot'. He had failed the qualification once already, having hoisted the Union Jack upside down, muddled up his reef knot and been unable to answer a question about the Beefeaters and the ravens in the Tower of London. Now he had failed again, in miserable fashion. If only he had not become addicted to cigarettes! What would his hero Ashdown have done in the circumstances? No doubt he would have jumped over the balustrade with an Indian club in one hand and his assegai in the other and scattered Fat Sam's criminal gang single-handed.

'What are you doing here, you young whippersnapper?' The voice seemed to come from a few inches away and he could smell what he assumed to be the unpleasant odour of whisky on his interrogator's breath. 'Out with it! Or we shall have you sent down for penal servitude as a burglar!'

He felt another blow to the jaw, which left him reeling. Then there was a sharp pain in his side, which could only come from the blade of a knife. 'What are you doing here? Why did you climb in that window?'

Kennedy was not totally sure in his own mind why he

was there. He knew he was on a scouting adventure with his patrol, but the finer details of the mission had been beyond him. He knew that a good scout did not question his orders. Then he remembered.

'It's the missing rifles. We're looking for the missing rifles, to stop them falling into dangerous hands. And there are foreign agitators meeting here.'

The response was a cynical laugh.

Kennedy bristled. 'I am a British subject and I demand to be released!'

'That's a funny one and no mistake!' said a second voice. 'Let's leave him in the cellar for now and see if he's got any better jokes tomorrow.' Kennedy found himself manhandled roughly by two men, who opened a door and forced him down some stone steps. The air was cold in the cellar, and when the men took off his blindfold he could see almost nothing. He heard them climbing back up the steps and bolting the door behind them. Nobody knew where he was, although Ashdown would be sure to raise the alarm. Meanwhile he was trapped and in the hands of the Almighty. He had always imagined Him not as an English gentleman, but as a kilted patriarch living on a mountain-top somewhere in the Highlands, watching tirelessly over the interests of His fellow Scots. He vowed that if he ever escaped from his dungeon, he would never touch tobacco again.

By the time dawn broke over Mesopotamia, Kennedy was asleep. So were Fat Sam, his henchmen and his son Percy, who told his father he had been waylaid by a gang of at least thirty armed ruffians from St. Stephen's College. Percy unlocked a drawer by his bed, took out a revolver, loaded it and placed it under his pillow before his eyes closed.

Blair agreed to return to the school for reinforcements, leaving Ashdown and his scout patrol to mount guard over the mission. The captain of school trudged uphill in the teeth of a gusty wind. By the time he knocked on Dr. Bush's study door after breakfast, he had worked out a plan of action.

The good Doctor was in a receptive mood. Blair told him the story of the night's adventures in full, though he tiptoed diplomatically around his own role in allowing Percy to escape from custody.

'It seems to me, sir, that Fat Sam and his chums have been making problems not just for St. Stephen's and for the town of Coalhaven, but also for the Marquess. I'm sure he'll be jolly grateful if we put the Saracen's Head out of business for good.'

'But how can we do that?'

'I think we should get the corps down there without delay,' Blair replied. 'The chaps will be keen as mustard to see what they can do.'

'An excellent idea,' said Dr. Bush. 'By the way, I have asked Brown to bring the Rifle Corps accounts up to date. They appear to have been neglected since Canon Williams handed them to me. Brown tells me there is a file of correspondence with the War Office about the missing rifles. Let us hope the matter will be successfully resolved.'

'You can count on me, sir.'

Dr. Bush walked over to his desk and thumbed through his copy of the Bible. 'I shall certainly count on you, Blair. But can God count on you? That is far more important. Here, read this.'

Blair began to read aloud. He loved the cadences of the Old Testament, though he sometimes found their meaning obscure. *'Put yourselves in array against Babylon round about: all ye that bend the bow, shoot at her, spare no arrows: for she hath sinned against the Lord. Shout against her round about: she hath given her hand: Her walls are thrown down: for it is the vengeance of the Lord: take vengeance upon her; as she has done, do unto her.'* As he read, he looked at Dr. Bush, who was mouthing the words. He realised that the headmaster knew the book of Jeremiah by heart.

Dr. Bush fell to his knees, motioning him to follow. *'Thus saith the Lord of Hosts; the children of Israel and the children of Judah were oppressed together: and all that took them captives held them fast; they refused to let them go. Their Redeemer is strong; the Lord of Hosts is his name; he shall thoroughly plead their cause, that he may give rest to the land, and disquiet the inhabitants of Babylon.'*

Dr. Bush made the sign of the cross and rose to his feet, patting Blair on the shoulder with a smile. *'The Lord hath brought forth our righteousness: come, and let us declare in Zion the work of the Lord our God.'*

'Very good, sir,' said Blair. 'I shall get Hoon to parade the corps in time for chapel. Then we shall deploy our forces.'

'Do what you think is necessary, Blair. But don't discuss it with Canon Williams. I have a feeling he may not entirely agree with what we are doing.'

The news that the corps was to be deployed to Coalhaven spread around St. Stephen's like a fire on the tinder-dry veld. Boys who were enjoying an idle Sunday threw aside their pastimes and rushed to find their uniforms. Corps parades once a week were normally regarded as a chore, but this time there was the promise of some real action. 'Are you volunteering?' normally indolent sixth formers asked each other. 'Rather! It sounds like a chance for a rag. Wouldn't miss it for the world.'

Hoon ordered the loading of military supplies onto handcarts and the unlocking of the armoury. Rifles were issued and boxes of blank ammunition were carried in a human chain up from the cellars. Reports of the fate of young Kennedy, trapped and held prisoner in Mesopotamia by evil forces, galvanised even the most pacific boys into offering to 'do their bit'.

Blair and Hoon met in Blair's study to set up what they described as the HQ. Subsequent police investigations into the events of that night were to reveal that the lack of proper supervision over the loading of the armoury supplies was to have fatal consequences. Witnesses testified that the boxes of blank and the live ammunition were stored together and were hard to tell apart in the dark.

When he arrived to take Sunday evensong 'Flogger' Williams was puzzled to see most of the school dressed in khaki. He refrained from comment, assuming that the boys had just returned from an afternoon route march. He noted that they sang 'Onward Christian Soldiers' with special relish, but thought no more of it.

The light was already fading when the boys paraded with their rifles beneath the clock tower. Blair was still on his knees in a quiet corner of the chapel, seeking divine guidance. He knew his moment of destiny had come; all the tests and trials of his life at St. Stephen's were but a preparation for the challenge ahead of him. *Alea iacta est,* he thought. He was crossing the Rubicon. Would he stand firm, like tempered steel in the furnace, or would his resolution crumble? He looked straight ahead, and saw behind a pillar a small stone plaque dedicated to the memory of Smith, his predecessor. Originally there was wide support for a stained glass window to Smith, and

Blair himself had been in charge of raising a subscription, but the idea had somehow petered out. Less than a year had gone by since Smith's untimely death and the former captain of Hardie's house was all but forgotten. How much water had flowed under the bridge since the accident! Blair remembered as if it were yesterday how he had launched himself into the air and brought the runaway horse to a halt. *Fortes fortuna iuvat.* Fortune, he reflected, favoured the bold. Smith had lagged behind and paid the price. For all his virtues, Smith would probably have left the evildoers of Mesopotamia in peace.

His prayers were interrupted by a cough. It was Brown, holding a sheaf of papers. 'Before you burn your boats there's something here you ought to look at. Those rifles you're looking for may not exist at all.'

Blair looked him straight in the eye. 'Of course they exist. We've known that for six months. And we're about to find them.'

'I wouldn't be so sure, if I were you. How many rifles were reported missing after the half-term camp?'

'Twelve.'

'I've found a letter in this file from two years ago. Twelve of the Lee Enfields delivered to the school were found to be faulty and the War Office asked for them to be sent back.'

'That proves nothing at all. I know Fat Sam has got them. I have sources of information that you don't know about.'

The two former friends glared at each other. As so often in their conversations it was clear they would not agree, and the only question was who would end it first.

'So do I, Sooty, so do I,' said Brown, and stalked out of the chapel.

Blair bent his head to pray for Brown to repent of his many errors. As he rose to his feet and left the chapel he felt more than usually humble.

The Rifle Corps was waiting for him. Hoon brought them to attention and ordered them to present arms. Then he drew his ceremonial sword and marched up to Dr. Bush. With a strangulated cry he announced that the corps was ready for inspection. Blair followed the headmaster through the ranks, suppressing his normal smile and looking serious. He had only one regret: the light had already faded, and it was too dark for any photograph of the event to be taken for the next edition of the *Rocket*. Still, he thought, Henry V had managed at Agincourt without a photographer, and he would do the same.

The boys were stood at ease, and Blair moved forward to address them.

'You go forth today in a just cause. You all know what has happened at the Saracen's Head. The college mission has been sacked by hooligans; and now a member of the Scout troop has been captured and is in mortal danger. I vow here to you with every breath in my body that no effort will be spared to rescue young Kennedy and bring him back safe and sound. No boy at St. Stephen's College will sleep easily, and no resident of Coalhaven will breathe freely, until the threat posed by Fat Sam is dealt with. You all know about the missing rifles. Our information is that the cellar of that infamous public house is also a poisoner's den. None of you has forgotten the painful death of Horatio. If this man is capable of stooping low enough to deliberately poison man's best friend, who knows what he might not do to the rest of us? Let me tell you something else in confidence. We have uncovered evidence linking the Saracen's Head to Mandelbaum, the foreign anarchist who tried to assassinate the Tsar. He was a courier for the network of agitators which my good friend the Marquess of Coalhaven has told me is fomenting the strikes in the collieries and the unrest in the docks. Boys of St. Stephen's! The poor people of Mesopotamia deserve a better life. By dealing with Sam once and for all, you can turn their despair into hope.'

Blair paused, turned to his right and raised the Union Jack to his lips. It was a gesture which he had practised earlier with a bathtowel before a mirror in his study.

'And now God speed you on your way! Whatever you do, uphold the honour of the school and behave like true patriots and true Britons!'

Hoon called for three cheers for St. Stephen's College and three cheers for the captain of school. The corps band, consisting of younger boys who were deemed too young to carry rifles, played the only tune they knew, 'The British Grenadiers', as the boys shouldered arms and marched down the drive towards the school gates. Campbell, wearing full Highland dress, led the way playing his bagpipes.

Blair watched proudly as the marching platoons disappeared into the distance, escorted at front and rear, as army regulations required, by boys carrying lanterns. He turned to find a familiar figure barring his path. It was wee Cookie, carrying his prefect's cap.

'Don't you think you might have called a prefects' meeting to discuss this whole affair? We haven't had one for ages.'

'You can't get bogged down in endless discussions when there's action to be taken,' Blair retorted. 'I know I shall be unpopular over this, but I really don't care about that. I'm doing the right thing.'

'I don't think you have any right to take the law into your own hands like this. Fat Sam may be a bounder but he's a British subject like you and me and you can't just barge in through his front door.'

Blair looked at him coldly. 'If you feel that way, then perhaps you should consider your position as a prefect,' he declared.

'That's exactly it,' said Cook. 'You can keep my prefect's cap. I'm resigning.'

With that, the Scottish boy stalked off. By the gaslight illuminating the school entrance, Blair could see him deep in conversation with 'Flogger' Williams. How could a boy in whom he had placed so much trust let the school down so badly? The boys of Hardie's house always had an unreliable streak compared to Salisbury's, he reflected. What did it matter in the long run if wee Cookie was a prefect or not?

Blair's confidence in the Salisburians' enthusiasm for the expedition was well founded. His speech had been calculated to appeal to their martial instincts. As the rifle corps marched down the hill towards Coalhaven, the boys of Salisbury's house were in buoyant mood. When the column halted after fifteen minutes to change the crews pulling the handcarts with ammunition, they persuaded Campbell to pause in his bagpiping.

'We'll sing that new John McCormack song,' said Soames, one of four senior boys in Salisbury's who had clubbed together at the start of the summer term to buy a gramophone. Soames, Duncan Smith, Ancram and Howard, a Welsh boy with a fine tenor voice, formed a barber shop quartet.

'Should be a good rag tonight,' said Duncan Smith. 'We haven't had a proper scrap for ages.'

'Better than another boring Sunday evening swotting,' said Ancram. 'I suppose we'll be back in time for breakfast.'

'I packed a couple of kippers just in case,' said Soames. 'But it'll all be over by midnight, you wait and see.'

As Blair hurried down the hill after his troops, he could hear on the wind ahead of him the sound of Howard leading the singing, and his heart began to beat faster.

> *Up to mighty London came*
> *An Irish lad one day,*
> *All the streets were paved with gold,*
> *So everyone was gay!*
> *Singing songs of Piccadilly,*
> *Strand and Leicester Square,*
> *Till Paddy got excited and*
> *He shouted to them there:*
>
> *It's a long way to Tipperary,*
> *It's a long way to go.*
> *It's a long way to Tipperary*
> *To the sweetest girl I know!*
> *Goodbye Piccadilly*
> *Farewell Leicester Square!*
> *It's a long long way to Tipperary,*
> *But my heart's right there!*

CHAPTER XVI

INTO THE FIRE

When Kennedy awoke he could see shafts of sunlight coming into the cellar. He could not see his watch because his hands were still tied behind his back, and the ropes were cutting painfully into his bare arms and knees. He rolled over and looked upwards. He was lying at the bottom of a ramp used for rolling beer barrels. At the top was a pair of wooden trapdoors, hinged to open upwards at delivery times. The doors were firmly bolted from below, but between them was a gap of around half an inch, which allowed a shaft of light to penetrate the gloom. There was a strong smell of beer mingled with petrol fumes from a metal barrel that stood by a small pile of motor cycle tyres. At the far end of the cellar, by the steps leading to the ground floor of the public house, were dozens of wooden crates marked 'Best Scotch Whisky'. Kennedy could see that the supply of whisky, stacked almost up to the ceiling, was far in excess of anything that the Saracen's Head might require to supply its own clientele. The crates were marked 'Bonded for Export'. Of course! He recalled the conversation he had overheard from behind the

'HE WAS LYING AT THE BOTTOM OF A RAMP.'

balustrade. The whisky had without a doubt been pilfered from the docks and would be sold on illegally at a cost of many thousands of pounds in lost excise duty to the Treasury.

Kennedy began to reflect on his situation. Fat Sam and his accomplices must be aware that he had overheard their plans; and the fact that they had imprisoned him within sight of the stolen whisky meant only one thing. They were determined that he would not survive to testify against them. He was in the kind of predicament often suffered by the plucky boy heroes of scouting novels. Lying trussed like a chicken on the oily floor of the cellar, he tried hard to be plucky but felt only cold and scared. His arms were aching, his new scout uniform was torn and filthy and he realised with a pang of shame that he desperately wanted a cigarette. He shifted position again and felt an excruciating pain in his bare knee. Looking down, he saw he had rolled onto a broken whisky bottle. At that moment, he heard the door at the top of the steps open. Quickly he closed his eyes.

'Sleeping like a baby,' said a rough voice. ' Shall I bring him up?'

'No, we'll take him to the canal when it's dark,' came the reply.

The door closed and Kennedy suddenly had an idea. If he could only jam the broken bottle between his feet, he might be able to bend double and use it to cut through the thick cord binding his wrists. How many hours of daylight did he have left? He wriggled backwards until the bottle was wedged between his rubber-soled shoes. He twisted his body forwards, stretched his wrists towards the bottle and began to rub the cord along the jagged edge. After a few seconds he was in agony and was forced to pause for breath. When he looked up, the sunlight coming through the trapdoor was growing dimmer. Then he bent forward, gritted his teeth and tried again.

The platoons of boys in khaki marched down the High Street, their boots crashing on the cobblestones. It was a Sunday evening, and all the businesses were closed, with the exception of Berlusconi's café, where the proprietor stood in the doorway sheltering from the wind. The king of the jam puffs waved his arms and shouted his support, but the boys looked straight ahead and ignored him. 'You come-a back for hot chocolate whenever you like,' he shouted. 'Is-a no problem.'

They sang another chorus of 'Tipperary' and followed it with 'Soldiers of the King'.

War clouds gather over ev'ry land
Our treaties threatened east and west,
Nations we've shaken by the hand
Our honor'd pledges try to test.
They may have thought us sleeping
Thought us unprepar'd
Because we have our party wars,
But Britons all unite
When they're call'd to fight
The battle for Old England's common cause,
The battle for Old England's common cause.

But there was no applause on the streets. The inhabitants of Coalhaven looked curiously at the noisy marching boys and went about their business, some returning from evensong and some heading for their local snug.

When they arrived at the mission, the ammunition and

other supplies were unloaded from the carts and the boys were told to rest.

'Can we fix our bayonets just in case they attack us?' asked one young lance-corporal. 'And what about some ammunition? We'll be sitting ducks without ammo.' Boys sat around on the floor, fiddling with their boots and puttees. Ashdown took Hoon for a discreet reconnaissance around the back of the Saracen's Head and pointed out the lie of the land. They agreed that it would be foolhardy to try to rescue Kennedy by storming the building during the evening, and it would be better to wait until the enemy might be asleep.

By the time Blair arrived at the mission, the boys' mood had changed. They were impatient to get into action and could not understand why they were being made to wait. To make things worse, they had missed dinner. Some boys were openly asking how long the night operation would last, and what was the point of it, if there was not to be a good scrap. Veterans of the half-term camp at Fairhaven told stories about the roasted sheep and the splendid thrashing they had given to Hattersley the gamekeeper. But the storytelling could not disguise the fact that stomachs were beginning to rumble. Soames offered to share his two kippers, but with more than a hundred mouths to feed, his generous gesture appeared futile.

Blair went from group to group, chatting and shaking hands with his usual bonhomie. He promised friends of Kennedy that their chum would be rescued safe and sound. The St. Stephen's Rifle Corps was, he assured them, the best in the country and Hoon was the best regimental sergeant-major. They would most assuredly prevail. Hoon invited Blair to climb the stairs to the roof of the mission to get a better view.

Beneath them they could see the front door of the Saracen's Head, which was positioned on a corner site where two streets met. On one side of the public house was the gated yard and the music hall, on the other a four-storey brick tenement. Of Fat Sam himself there was no sign and there was no indication of anything untoward. But appearances were deceptive; Blair knew that somewhere in that building Kennedy was being held captive and the missing rifles were concealed. After his encounter with Fat Sam's motorcycling son, Blair was more certain than ever that Percy was the poisoner who had fed arsenic to the luckless Horatio. Who would be the gang's next victim?

'We can't keep the lads hanging around here all night,' said Hoon. 'Presumably you and the Doctor have worked out a plan?'

'A plan? You're the one who's supposed to be responsible for the plan,' Blair countered.

At this point in the conversation an upstairs window in the Saracen's Head was opened. Hoon and Blair strained forward to see if Fat Sam might stick his head out, but in the murk they could distinguish nothing at all. Then the wind blew aside the clouds for a moment and in the moonlight they glimpsed a hand with a gun. There was the sharp crack of a revolver and a bullet whistled over their heads.

'Get down,' cried Hoon, pushing Blair on his face behind the low parapet. Hoon extracted his own revolver from its leather holster, but realised he had no ammunition for it. Another bullet whistled past. It took them what seemed like an eternity to wriggle along the roof to the staircase and descend to safety.

In Hoon's absence the sergeants and corporals had ordered all lights to be put out. Candles, electric torches and the oil lamp in the scullery were all extinguished. In the dark a cry went up: 'Ammo time!' and the boys scurried round the ammunition boxes, dragging them to the four corners of the room and opening them. It was too dark to distinguish between blank and live rounds and there were no clear orders. So most of the boys filled the magazines of their Lee Enfields with live bullets and stuffed the pockets of their tunics with spare ammunition.

In the cellar of the Saracen's Head, Kennedy heard the two shots and redoubled his efforts to cut through the rope binding his wrists. With a final stretch, he severed the last strands and rubbed his hands to get the circulation back. Within a minute he had untied his ankles in the dark. He climbed up to the trapdoor and pulled back the bolts, but the doors would not move. He was still trapped! If only he had read the advice in *Scouting for Boys* on how to mimic the cries of wild animals! Sooner or later, Fat Sam's gang would be back for him, but he would never be able to fight them off single-handed. His only hope was to wait until he was out of the cellar, then make a dash for it. They were stronger than he was, but he knew that in a short sprint along the cobbled streets he would outpace his captors. Deliberately, he picked up the rope and wound it loosely around his ankles again, hoping the men would not notice. Then he replaced the rope around his wrists and lay down where they had left him.

He did not have long to wait. The door opened and his two captors hurried towards him. 'The old man seems in a right lather,' one of them said. 'I don't like this one little bit,' the other interjected. 'Trust Percy to start playing around with his revolver.' The men put Kennedy into a sack and carried him up the stairs. Though he could see nothing, he could feel the fresh breeze on his face and realised he was in the yard. They dumped him roughly on a handcart and covered him with a tarpaulin. Beneath it, Kennedy carefully loosened the ropes and drew his scout knife from his belt. He heard the gate being unlocked and the handcart began to move across the cobblestones towards the canal.

Luckily for him, he was not entirely alone. Ashdown and the remainder of the Beaver patrol, displaced from the mission by the arrival of the corps, were keeping vigil in the shadows. When they saw the handcart covered in a tarpaulin rolling out of the gate, they slipped silently into Indian file and followed it at a distance.

The boys of the Rifle Corps, their weapons loaded and their hearts pounding with anticipation, crept out of the mission as silently as their hobnailed boots permitted. Some mounted the stairs to the roof and crouched behind the parapet, keeping their weapons out of sight. Some slid out of the back door and round to the front of the mission, where they knelt behind the remains of the brick wall which the rioters had demolished. The boys without rifles picked up half-bricks as weapons. All this came not from military training, but from the native cunning of British public school boys, honed in years of night-time ragging between houses and dormitories. The spirit and teamwork they had learned on the St. Stephen's rugger field came into play. As the survivors were later to tell the police, nobody ever gave the order to open fire. But after a certain point in the proceedings, there could be no question of retreat. How could these descendants of Francis Drake and Robert the Bruce look each other in the face, if they returned the ammunition to its boxes and marched meekly back up the hill to school without firing a shot? It would be an exceptionally brave commander who would risk giving such an order. The boys' blood was up and they were determined to do their duty, not for St. Stephen's or for Blair or for the Union Jack, but for each other. They hummed a tune under their breath.

> *But Britons all unite*
> *When they're call'd to fight*
> *The battle for Old England's common cause,*
> *The battle for Old England's common cause.*

Within five minutes, the Saracen's Head was surrounded on three sides. On the fourth side, the tenement formed a solid barrier. It was at that moment that the front door of the public house opened and three figures came running out. There was a volley of shots, and the three fell motionless on the pavement. 'They're firing at us!' shouted the boys at the back gate, who could see nothing of what was happening at the front of the building. They fired their bullets over the gate into the first floor, from where they imagined the shots were coming. There was a tinkling of glass and the windows gaped open. A woman began to scream and a white net curtain flapped in the wind. Behind it stood the yellow glow of an oil lamp, but then a gust caught the curtain and the lamp disappeared from sight. By now the boys at the back of the house had emptied their magazines, and paused to reload. By the time they took aim again, the rear of the building was billowing smoke. The wind brought a crackling sound and flames began licking towards the roof. The boys ran forward, pushed open the gate and found themselves facing an inferno of flames.

Hoon and Blair were back on the roof of the mission. 'They're firing back. They must be using our missing Lee

'THERE WAS A VOLLEY OF SHOTS.'

Enfields,' Blair surmised. He sneaked a look over the parapet and swallowed hard. The rear of the building was ablaze. There was shooting from the front and shooting from the rear and small explosions from the side. Two boys ran forward across the street, heading for the front door. But as they approached, a giant ball of fire spiralled upwards from a wooden trapdoor set in the pavement and they were lost from sight. The smell of burning petrol engulfed the street and every boy within a hundred yards covered his face in his sleeve to keep away the heat.

It was at this moment that the handcart carrying Kennedy's prostrate form reached the canal, some two hundred yards away. Under the tarpaulin, he had wriggled out of the sack, knife in hand, and was ready to confront his captors. 'Be prepared,' he muttered to himself. 'Say your prayers, you young scallywag,' said a voice. The tarpaulin was pulled away and he saw a hand clutching a piece of heavy iron rail. Quick as a flash, Kennedy rolled off the cart, lunging with the knife. He was halfway down the street before his two captors realised what had happened, and began to give chase. They found their way barred by Ashdown and the rest of the Beaver patrol, standing four square across the road, bearing their staves. The men turned tail and fled with the scouts in hot pursuit.

'Go back to the mission and tell them you're safe!' shouted Ashdown.

Kennedy sprinted away from the rest of the patrol, towards the orange glow of the Saracen's Head. As he rounded the corner, he felt a hot blast strike his face. The fire was sucking in air from all sides and getting fiercer and fiercer. There was a smell of burning alcohol and Kennedy realised that the flames had now reached the stolen whisky bottles, which were exploding in quick succession. He felt a terrible ache in his chest and began to cough.

He sat down on the pavement, his legs giving way beneath him. He was a peaceful boy, who had joined the scout troop to indulge his love of country walks and botany, not to get mixed up in a violent confrontation like this. He blamed Baden-Powell for writing *Scouting for Boys*, he blamed his parents for purchasing it, he blamed the inhabitants of Mesopotamia for living in such a mean slum and he blamed himself for being one of life's volunteers. If this was Scouting, he had had enough of it. He got up and resumed his route towards the mission, when he heard a roaring sound above him and slates falling on the cobbles. The fire which had gutted the Saracen's Head was spreading to the tenement next door. He could see the desperate figures of women and children at the upper windows, shouting vainly for help. The front wall began to bulge alarmingly towards the street. Kennedy began to sprint for safety towards the mission, which he could see dimly through the flames and smoke.

Among the boys who had their weapons still trained on the Saracen's Head from the mission roof was one who shall remain nameless, at least in this narrative. The boy was an enthusiastic marksman who had shown exceptional promise competing for the school at Bisley. Instead of firing his weapon aimlessly like the others, he was waiting for a target to show itself, scanning the scene with his field glasses. In nearly half an hour of mayhem and destruction, he had kept his powder dry while others had blazed away with impunity. Then he heard a shout: 'There goes another anarchist! Let him have it!' He took aim at the shadowy figure running through the smoke and squeezed the trigger.

The bullet hit Kennedy in the right temple. He fell dead like a stone, though the smoke closed over him and nobody saw him fall. 'I think I got him,' said the sharpshooter on the roof. Then he looked again. The burning tenement had collapsed into the street, lighting up the scene. The sharpshooter raised his field glasses to his eyes, saw the lifeless form in scout's uniform on the cobblestones, and let out a terrible cry.

By now the heat was so great that the mission building had to be evacuated. 'Take the ammunition!' someone shouted. Hoon looked across the road and put his head in his hands. 'Oh my giddy aunt!' he muttered. 'I suppose I shall get blamed for all this. I shall be lucky to make Sandhurst now.'

Blair clapped him on the shoulder. 'Cheer up, old man. You can trust old Sooty. I take full responsibility for everything,' he said. 'The main thing is that we won't have to worry about Fat Sam any more. Coalhaven is going to be a better place.'

CHAPTER XVII

THE STORMY PETREL

When Hoon looked up a few seconds later, Blair had vanished. He rose to his feet and surveyed the scene. The walls of the Saracen's Head were still standing, though the roof had caved in and the building was gutted. The heat from the burning whisky and petrol was still so fierce that from the broken front window of the mission he could only look out for a few seconds. 'Cease firing,' said Hoon. The order was superfluous, because after the shooting of Kennedy, the boys had put down their rifles. Some were retching. There could be no question of recovering the burning bodies from the street while the wind continued to fan the blaze. 'Get the ammunition!' screamed a corporal, struggling to make himself heard. The boys dropped their rifles and began loading the handcarts at the back of the mission in preparation for a withdrawal back to the High Street. The mood was sombre and there was no more talk of 'a jolly good scrap.' With the passage of time, however, many of the boys were secretly glad they had volunteered. They found the sight of death bound them together like an invisible cord. As one of them subsequently told the

Rocket, 'I wouldn't have missed it for anything.' When Prescott wrote a poem for the newspaper about how the heat of the flames had forged boys into men, his verses seemed to sum up the feelings of many.

The boys withdrew to the sound of wailing from the neighbouring streets, whose inhabitants appeared strangely ungrateful for the way in which the St. Stephen's College Rifle Corps had risked their lives to bring them a better future. As dawn approached, the grey light revealed a smoking heap of rubble some ten feet high, which was all that remained of the destroyed tenement. Crowds of people were passing buckets of water from the canal in a human chain. Others milled around, yelling for vengeance. As the Rifle Corps left the mission and marched away in orderly fashion, a mob of angry Mesopotamians barred their path. The boys scattered in confusion, using the butts of their Lee Enfields to clear a passage. They fled in the direction of the High Street, desperate to regain the safety of the lighted thoroughfare. Two boys without rifles who were pushing a handcart found themselves cut off, and were beaten and thrown into the canal. Their bodies were recovered later by the fire brigade, whose horse-drawn engines arrived on the scene too late to save any lives. The Coalhaven police, depleted by their duties elsewhere, were even slower to appear. By noon, however, the combined efforts of local residents and the forces of law and order had succeeded in recovering a total of nineteen bodies. Five were from the school, four were found in the shell of the Saracen's Head, and the remaining ten were buried in the smouldering rubble of the tenement. Five of the dead were infants and five were women.

The tragedy filled the front page of the *Coalhaven Gazette,* whose dramatic photographs of the devastation also appeared in the metropolitan press. Regular readers of the *Police Illustrated News* will no doubt remember the photograph of two smoke-shrouded policemen bearing a child's body on a stretcher under the headline 'Great Loss of Life in Coalhaven: Anarchists' Lair Besieged'. Kennedy and the other St. Stephen's boys who perished in the tragedy were pictured on an inside page, under the headline 'They gave their lives for Mesopotamia'. A subscription fund was announced by the Marquess of Coalhaven to assist the destitute victims of the conflagration. The victims' funeral attracted a crowd of several thousand mourners. St. Stephen's College sent a wreath, but it was thrown in the canal. The school mission to Mesopotamia was boarded up.

We are, however, getting ahead of our narrative. What of our hero, Anthony Blair? After leaving the mission, he doubled back by a roundabout route which took him along the river bank, past Ma Mowlam's yard. He buried his face in his scarf, but when he looked round in the darkness, he realised he was being followed. Twenty yards away, he saw a shadow flitting between the bushes. He thought he recognised the boy with the fishing rod who had scrutinised him and Mandelson so strangely after their meeting with the Fenians. When he stopped the boy stopped. When he walked on the boy followed. To shake off his pursuer he began to sprint along the towpath until he reached the bridge leading to the High Street. There was gas lighting here and he slowed down to a walk. Blair halted outside Berlusconi's café and rang the bell. After a minute or so a familiar figure wearing a silk dressing gown and a hairnet greeted him. 'Somebody been havin' a nice bonfire,' Berlusconi joked. 'You come-a upstairs and have a nice hot chocolate. It's on-a the house.'

Blair sank onto the couch. He had not slept for two nights and his mind was in turmoil. On the wall of the parlour hung a crucifix, an engraving of the Pope and a coloured print of a Venetian gondola. On the mantelpiece stood a silver cup. He closed his eyes and dozed for a minute, dreaming that he was not in Coalhaven but in Venice, a simple gondolier drinking ginger beer from a silver cup. Berlusconi woke him with a mug of cocoa, and he began to reflect on the night's dramatic events. Looking at the red glow over the rooftops a mile away, he wondered whether God was looking down on Coalhaven and what He might be thinking of the whole business. At the moment when Hoon had asked him what the plan was, Blair's usual presence of mind had deserted him. But now he realised the obvious answer: the plan was in God's hands and he was only the humble instrument of the Lord of Hosts. *Deus vult!* He felt somehow purified. Babylon had been thoroughly disquieted, in no small part as a result of his own firm leadership. He had conducted himself well under fire, dodging the volley of shots fired by the anarchists from their Lee Enfields. *Fortiter in re, suaviter in modo.* He had been resolute in action, gentle in manner. Now the Saracen's Head and Fat Sam had been properly dealt with, the inhabitants of Mesopotamia would show due respect for honest citizens. When he returned to school he would make sure that due credit for the success of the operation was shared among all those involved. Should the grateful residents of Coalhaven propose a medal or an award in his honour, he would politely decline. When Dr. Bush congratulated him, he would briefly acknowledge his own modest part in the operation, for this was not a time to boast. He would tell the *Rocket* and the *Coalhaven Gazette* he regretted the fate of Kennedy and the other boys caught in the crossfire. If there had been mistakes during the course of the operation, they could not be laid at his door.

His thoughts were interrupted by the sound of knocking from downstairs. Peering around the curtain, he saw in the half-light of dawn the familiar figures of Brown, 'Flogger' Williams and the mysterious boy who had been following him. Blair leaned over the banisters to listen as Berlusconi, still wearing his hairnet, descended the stairs.

'Is-a no rest for the wicked?' he said as he opened the door. Blair could not hear all that was being said, but the word 'Blair' was clear enough. Then he heard Brown's voice: 'Well done, Charlie. You can go home now.' So the boy was called Charlie. And Brown had betrayed him once again.

Berlusconi's reply was audible. 'No, no, I have not seen him. Why should he come here?' At least Berlusconi was a man of integrity, who would not sell him to his enemies for thirty pieces of silver! Brown, on the other hand, had revealed himself in his true colours as a slave to personal ambition who would do anything to usurp his place as captain of school.

He heard the voice of the padre, calling up the stairs. 'Blair, put down any weapons you have and come downstairs with your hands above your head. I will do my level best to see that you get a fair trial.' For a moment, he was tempted to escape. But to run away would be tantamount to a confession of guilt. This was a test of his character and he was determined not to fail.

There was a pause. 'He may have gone back to school by another route,' he heard the padre say. The door closed and all was quiet again. Blair stretched out again on the couch under the crucifix and the picture of the Pope and slept the sleep of the just.

By the time he awoke, the shadows were lengthening. Berlusconi brought him a cup of tea and a jug of hot water to wash his blackened face. This time, Sooty really did need a wash, he reflected ruefully. Blair immediately started to feel better and began to turn over in his mind the interview he would give to the *Rocket* describing the night's events. Then he thanked his host with his usual politeness, slipped on his overcoat and began walking back towards the school.

He headed straight for Dr. Bush's study and knocked on the door. 'Come in,' said the familiar voice. The headmaster's welcome could not have been more sincere, and he ushered Blair to a chair, taking his overcoat and hanging it on a peg. 'You are safe and well, dear boy, I trust?'

Blair gave his account of the assault on the Saracen's Head, making sure he gave praise where praise was due. Hoon had been particularly cool-headed and courageous and the sergeants and corporals had proved their mettle. As he had predicted, the Rifle Corps had come through with flying colours.

'And the missing rifles?'

'I have no doubt, sir, that a forensic examination of the scene by detectives will confirm their presence. After all, we were fired on during the siege. The important thing is, Fat Sam and his son will no longer be able to give shelter to anarchists and hardened criminals.'

Dr. Bush nodded and picked up his Bible. 'You remember the siege of Jericho? *And they utterly destroyed all that was in the city, both man and woman, young and old, and ox, and sheep, and ass, with the edge of the sword. And they burnt the city with fire, and all that was therein.*'

Blair nodded. 'I do feel it's a shame about young Kennedy,' he said. 'He was very plucky.'

'You must not reproach yourself. The police have been here. They want you to give a statement. Apparently they have found the bodies of four other boys as well.'

'Perhaps I should address the school and explain that their sacrifice was not in vain?'

'I think that would be an excellent idea, Blair.'

When he returned to his study, he found two notes pushed under the door. The first was from Mandelson, who as usual seemed to have access to private information. 'Brown's going round saying he's found the paperwork that proves the missing rifles weren't missing at all. There's a chit from the War Office confirming they got them back. He wants to know if you're going to resign as captain of school. Of course, he says he'll stand by you through thick and thin, whatever happens.'

The second note was from the padre.

> *Dear Blair*
>
> *It gives me no pleasure to tell you that my misgivings about your character and judgment have been fully vindicated by your ill-judged expedition last night. Nineteen people have lost their lives without cause, and you must take the main share of the blame. I would like your assurance that you will cooperate fully with the police investigation and do your best to make amends.*
>
> *Yours in sorrow*
> *Canon Williams*

Blair scratched his head in puzzlement. How could old Flogger be so short-sighted? Of course, the casualties were to be regretted, but there was a wider picture to be considered. Certainly, he took full responsibility for the operation, although, with the benefit of hindsight, it was possible that Hoon's planning and tactics had been less than optimal. But he did not feel that blame was an appropriate word. He did not like the implication that he should be made a scapegoat for something which all the school, including Salisbury's house, had enthusiastically supported. Blair threw the note into the waste paper basket.

At dinner that evening, Blair was his normal cheerful self, determined to lift the morose spirits around the table. But even the other prefects showed a certain reserve when he spoke to them and, when he approached the table where most of the Gladstone's boys were sitting, there was a low murmuring. As he turned his back he heard an unmistakable hissing sound. Then a boiled potato hit him on the arm.

The next day when the boys assembled in Big School Blair stood and went to the lectern. He was confident that his powers of persuasion would be more than adequate to dispel any lingering misunderstanding or mistrust.

'I think it's fair to say that you all know me well enough by now,' he began. 'You men have had to put up with me since last September and we've had our ups and downs. But I've listened and I've learned. You know I've always been sincere and straight with you and you've been loyal to me as well. The longer I spend at St. Stephen's, the more convinced I am that it's the best school in all the world. Does anyone disagree?'

Blair paused to look at his audience. They were silent, watching him with a mixture of curiosity and scepticism, waiting to hear what he had to say. There was still everything to play for. He raised his hand and pointed in the general direction of Coalhaven.

'You men are truly fortunate. You are not only British subjects, but lucky enough to be taught by some of the best teachers in the land. You will go on to Oxford, or Cambridge, perhaps to the Army or the Indian Civil Service. You will always be able to hold your heads up in pride as St. Stephen's men. Proud to be honest. Proud to be fair in your dealings with rich and poor alike. Proud to be chivalrous, like knights in shining armour. Proud to be wise. Proud to be generous. Proud to be humble.'

Blair caught an approving glance from Dr. Bush, seated to his right. He was hoping that Brown, seated behind him to his left, would start to lead the applause, but his hands remained firmly folded and his face was inscrutable. The third formers were beginning to warm to his words and were flattered to be addressed as 'men'. But the blank gaze of the older boys told him that his oratory was falling on deaf ears.

'What about Kennedy? Are you proud of what happened to him?' came a voice from the back. The cry triggered a wave of movement in the hall, as the boys looked round and began whispering to each other. Blair held up his hand and the noise faded.

'Yes, Kennedy. It's about his sacrifice and that of the other boys that I want to speak to you today. He knew that not everyone in Coalhaven was lucky enough to have three square meals a day and sound boots on their feet. He wanted to help the less fortunate. And he died a hero's death facing the enemy. Did he complain? No! Did he falter? No! Did he ask that the cup pass from his lips? No! And the best way we can honour his memory...'

At this point there was another shout from the back of the hall, somewhere on the crowded green benches. It sounded to Blair like the familiar Scottish voice of Cook, who had already resigned his prefect's cap and had nothing to lose by further treachery. 'What about the missing rifles? You haven't found them, have you?'

Blair cut in immediately. 'I know for a fact that the missing rifles were in the Saracen's Head. I saw them myself. In fact, they were being fired at me! And I have to tell you, even if we never find them now, that doesn't mean they weren't there in the first place. It just shows what a cunning devil Fat Sam was.'

He lowered his voice and adopted a conspiratorial tone.

'Do you know something? Even if there hadn't been any missing rifles, we would still have been right to do what we did. Fat Sam was a criminal and we were upholding the law of England by going in to sort him out. Is there anybody here who doesn't believe it's the duty of every man to uphold the law?'

This bold invitation to the audience was something of a gamble. Blair paused for a second, intending to resume, but he found himself unable to do so. All round Big School, boys were on their feet, shouting and waving pieces of paper. 'Charlatan! Liar! Murderer!' they cried. Dr. Bush looked alarmed and rose from his chair. 'Assembly is over. You will now return to your classes,' he shouted, trying to make himself heard. The headmaster headed for the door, inviting Blair to follow him.

At the foot of the stone staircase the jeers and shouts were still ringing in their ears when their path was blocked by a man in a brown bowler hat. 'Inspector Annan, sir. I have a warrant for the arrest of Anthony Charles Lynton Blair.'

Behind the inspector stood two motor vehicles and five uniformed policemen. Blair smiled gravely and stepped forward. 'Of course, inspector. I shall be delighted to assist you with your enquiries.'

At the Coalhaven police station, Blair found himself in the cell recently vacated by the anarchist Mandelbaum. The bed was hard and the food was lukewarm, but no worse than at St. Stephen's. Unlike Mandelbaum, he was neither hooded nor threatened with a red-hot poker and nobody poured cold water over his bed. He was taken to the magistrate's court, where the Marquess of Coalhaven presided. Blair smiled in the direction of the bench and gave the Marquess a friendly wave of recognition, which was not reciprocated. The inspector referred to the serious nature of the offences under investigation, and bail was summarily refused. Blair found himself at a loss to understand the logic of the proceedings and began to regret that he had never opened his father's copy of the *Introduction to the Law of England*. A solicitor came to visit him and counselled that his best chance of avoiding a lengthy term of penal servitude was to plead guilty.

After several days his normal bubbly optimism was beginning to go flat, like a stale bottle of aerated water. Was this how British justice treated a man who knew he was innocent? What had happened to the Magna Carta and the mysterious *habeas corpus* thing his father's lawyer friends talked about? Then his gaoler, the kindly Constable Hutton, brought in a parcel. 'Here you are, young gentleman, someone's been sending you extra food.'

When Blair examined the package, it contained a note from Murdoch, telling him not to despair. 'Here's some tucker mate, for old times' sake. Don't drop your bundle just yet.' Wrapped in brown paper was one of Thatcher's renowned veal and ham pies.

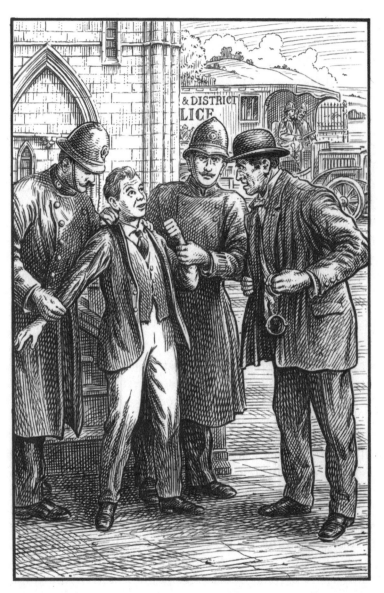

' "I HAVE A WARRANT FOR THE ARREST OF ANTHONY CHARLES LYNTON BLAIR." '

Later that night, when his cell door had been locked for the last time, Blair picked up the pie and took a large bite. But his teeth felt something hard and metallic. A closer inspection revealed a three-inch section of file secreted inside the pastry.

Blair looked up at the window of his cell. There were three wrought iron bars on the outside of the glass. Standing on tiptoe, he could just open the glass and reach high enough to touch them. After listening carefully for Constable Hutton's patrolling footsteps, Blair got to work. After some hours of painstaking effort he managed to file through the bars and ease them out of position. He rolled up his overcoat into a ball and pushed it through the window, then scrambled up and pulled himself through the narrow opening. There was a drop of around six feet to the ground and he landed on all fours in a deserted alley parallel to the High Street. Without looking behind him, he began to run.

It was roughly a mile to the Coalhaven docks. The streets were no longer in darkness and Blair knew he could cover the distance in a few minutes. At the halfway point he paused for breath and looked around. But there was no sign of any hot pursuit. Was he being too hasty? Should he perhaps have remained to face down his betrayers? After all, he had nothing to feel guilty about. He could see himself standing in the dock at the county assizes, defending himself with passionate sincerity against the trumped-up charges and telling the jury that his conscience was clear. Then he thought of the distress a court case would inflict on his parents and Lizzie. It would be far better for him to disappear and make his fortune somewhere under an assumed name. Perhaps he might join the Foreign Legion? He spoke passable French, but the description of the Legion he had read in the *Boy's Own Paper* made it sound too much like the Rifle Corps for comfort. Where was it that Ernie had been sent to make his way in the world? Yes, Canada might be the answer. But Australia, the home of his loyal friend Murdoch, was perhaps a better possibility. He would volunteer to work on a sheep farm as a smackeroo, or whatever the Australian term was. And one day he would return to Coalhaven and to St. Stephen's in triumph to clear his name. He would loop the loop over the clock tower in his aeroplane, land on the cricket ground and rip off his flying helmet and goggles to reveal his true identity. Hundreds of curious boys would pour down the stairs to see him. The grizzled padre would clap a hand on his shoulder and admit he had been wrong to doubt him. He would address the school on Founder's Day as guest of honour. In Coalhaven a thankful population would deck the streets with banners and hold a subscription banquet for him, with toasts to 'Good Old Blair'; and rival parties would compete for the honour of inviting him to stand for parliament. Yes, it was better to make a clean break with the past and move on.

So as not to attract attention to himself in the grey light, Blair slowed to a walk. The road to the docks ran parallel to the railway track and Blair joined a straggling procession of stevedores. His overcoat, once so smart, was pockmarked with the stains of burning debris. He stuck his hands in his pockets and fell into step with the rough-featured men in cloth caps, doing his best to imitate their hunched shoulders and shuffling gait. One or two glanced in his direction and Blair smiled politely back.

At the end of the road was a pair of iron gates where the men queued up to show their work documents. Several policemen were on duty. Beyond the gates, Blair could see a line of ships tied up at the quayside. There was a vessel with a load of Baltic timber and a couple of much smaller coastal freighters loading up with coal. Behind him he heard the hissing rumble of a small shunting engine hauling a long line of coal trucks. The train was travelling at hardly more than a walking pace, and Blair ran alongside it, looking for something to grip on to. One of the coal trucks had an iron ladder and he used it to climb upwards, swinging his legs over the side. As he lay flat on the coal, he felt the same exhilaration as on the night he escaped from Matron Boothroyd's sanatorium to take part so triumphantly in the Christmas concert. How far away it all seemed now! What would happen at St. Stephen's when they discovered that the captain of school was missing? How would Dr. Bush steer the old College without his wise counsel? He frowned as he imagined Brown taking over the school captain's study and rifling through all his possessions. But there was no point in pursuing such thoughts. His mind was made up. It was always better to look forward than back. As he knew from the Bible, the righteous who followed the laws of God often faced persecution for their beliefs. He was happy to be a voice crying in the wilderness.

The train clanked to a halt, and he peered over the side of the wagon, making sure he was not seen. Coalhaven was an old-fashioned port where the coal wagons were tilted on their sides to spill their contents on the quayside. Then a crane with a shovel and bucket picked up the coal and transferred it to the hold of the ship. There were four or five men standing on the forward deck of the first freighter, shovelling stray lumps of coal into the hold and preparing to close the hatches. Black smoke was rising from the funnel, a sign that the *Stormy Petrel* was preparing to sail. Near the stern of the rusty ship, a steep gangway linked it to the wharf. Blair climbed down and crouched beneath the wagon to see if the coast was clear. He wondered what to do after he sneaked aboard. Should he offer his services as a cabin boy? After all, his hero Nelson had begun as a midshipman. But he was unsure if small freighters employed cabin boys. On reflection, it might be better to march boldly up the gangway and then stow away. If he was challenged, he could always make up some yarn or other about his friend the Marquess of Coalhaven, who owned both the docks and the coal.

Blair strode forward to the foot of the gangway. The men shovelling coal ignored him. He walked confidently upwards and on to the deck. He turned a corner and there, leaning on a ventilation pipe, was a Lascar in a grubby white steward's jacket, smoking a cigarette. 'A fine morning,' Blair remarked with a smile. 'Yes indeed, sir,' the Lascar replied, with a bow of the head. Then he tossed the stub of his cigarette into the oily water and was gone. Blair moved swiftly to inspect the single lifeboat. From a seafaring story he had read in *Chums*, he knew that lifeboats always had some iron rations and drinking water aboard. To cover his tracks, he climbed around the far side of the boat, overhanging the rail, and prised open the ropes holding the tarpaulin. He wriggled under the canvas, then pulled it back over his head as best he could. So far, so good. He wrapped himself in his coat, rested his head on a coil of rope and began to think about the future. Where would it take him? What oceans would he cross? The vessel vibrated as the screw began to turn and there was a loud blast from the funnel. Blair knew that from now on he would be charting his own course through the stormy seas of life, with only God to watch over him. Within a minute or so he was fast asleep, hearing neither the noise of the engine nor the spray of water along the hull, as the *Stormy Petrel* passed the lighthouse and left behind the unhappy town of Coalhaven for the open sea.

EPILOGUE

Five years have passed since the events described in the last chapter. They are still painfully remembered in Coalhaven, but the headlines they generated in the London press have been forgotten. When the morning newspapers tell us daily of the gallant sacrifice of thousands, who remembers an incident in which a mere nineteen perished?

At St. Stephen's College the clock tower still looks proudly above the clifftop, but many things have changed. The rugby pitches have been ploughed up for vegetables and on the spot where Blair scored his famous try against Salisbury's, a line of boys, pale-faced from their wartime diet, is busy weeding carrots. The name of Blair is missing from the honours board listing the captains of school. For the year in question the space where his name should appear in gold letters has been left unaccountably blank. All the boys involved in the Mesopotamia events have now left the school, leaving only tribal tradition, the voice of the bard at the camp fire, to tell the awful story to newcomers.

Dr. Bush is no longer headmaster. Shortly after the dramatic events we have described, he was found one night in his pyjamas reciting the Book of Revelations from the rooftops. He has now been transferred to an asylum in Switzerland run by a noted professor, whose progressive views on treatment of the insane have attracted worldwide attention. The professor often accompanies Dr. Bush as he strides along the mountain paths, declaiming long passages from the Old Testament to an audience of ruminating alpine cows.

At St. Stephen's he has been succeeded by 'Flogger' Williams, whose grey beard has turned white with the burdens of his post. In the evenings the old padre mostly sits alone in his lodgings. Unlike his predecessor, he is neither theologian nor scholar, and finds little comfort in books. Recently he has been seen going through old volumes of the St. Stephen's College Record, marking names in pencil. Of the generation of boys with whom we have become acquainted in the telling of this story, a quarter has now been reported dead or missing. The sixth formers gather each morning around the noticeboard marked 'Pro Patria' to read the names of the Old Boys killed in France or Flanders. 'Wasn't he captain of squash?' 'I used to fag for him. Decent sort of cove, always let me take away the leftover cake when he'd finished tea.' Some of the boys reading the noticeboards are wearing black armbands, indicating that their fathers or brothers have made the ultimate sacrifice. When the chapel bell tolls, the boys file in to hear the headmaster intone the names of the fallen. The kneeling boys look up at the stained glass windows and secretly pray for different things. Some ask God for the chance to leave behind the make-believe battlefield of school and 'do their bit' in France and Flanders. Some pray for the opposite – for the chance to let the cup pass from their lips.

In the staff room, many familiar faces are missing. The younger men have mostly joined up to 'do their bit', including the maths master who drove Kelly to his fatal station on the cross-country race. 'See you all again by Christmas!' he pronounced jauntily as he drove away for the last time from St. Stephen's. He was the first to go missing in action, but others have followed. One or two lucky ones have returned as amputees to resume teaching. The gaps in the curriculum have mostly been filled by masters plucked from retirement, though the school has been driven to the temporary expedient of engaging a woman university graduate to instruct the lower forms in Latin. It is Cherie, the stepdaughter of the Famulus. She has also taken responsibility for the vegetable crops on the playing fields.

On the Fairhaven estate, the news is also bad. The Marquess's coalmines and his other business ventures are doing well, though the new licensing laws have reduced the profits of the Black Pig Brewery. But it is now two years since the Marquess's only son Ernie, a Royal Flying Corps pilot, was reported missing behind enemy lines somewhere in France. Hetty and Clemmie are both nursing somewhere near the front. The big house is half-shuttered, the gardens are neglected and in the stables Pumpkin has long ago been taken to the knacker's yard. Ecclestone the chauffeur, too old to join up, still meets the Marquess at Coalhaven station in the Rolls-Royce when the London train arrives on Friday afternoons. Neither man speaks.

In Mesopotamia there is a large empty site where the Saracen's Head and the adjoining buildings once stood. The St. Stephen's mission, however, has been repaired and is now a soup kitchen run by Methodists. Plans for a discreet memorial plaque to the dead were dropped after a long argument about the words to be used. But Fat Sam and his son Percy are buried in the nearest cemetery, and those who have seen their monument say it is a fine example of the stonemason's art.

I am told there are also changes in Coalhaven High Street. A 'To Let' sign hangs over the door of what was once Berlusconi's café, vacated without warning by the owner one summer night. The establishment's long queue of creditors found its only real assets were some tubs of perishable Italian ice-cream. In the upstairs bedroom they found a selection of wigs, hairnets and theatrical greasepaint, leading to suspicions that the café proprietor might have fled the country in disguise.

Thatcher's grocery store survives, however, and flies the Union Jack proudly in every corner of its window. The famous veal and ham pies are made only infrequently, as good quality meat is in short supply, and the grocer and his daughter are not ones to lower their standards. Anyone who complains about shortages is asked to leave the shop immediately and is accused of helping the Kaiser.

Enough! Enough! The patience displayed by faithful readers of this small volume has its limits. What kind of epilogue is this, they wonder, with no mention of the fate of the central character? When is virtue going to be rewarded and vice punished?

To which your humble narrator can only offer his usual excuse: we are treating here of real life, and real life does not follow the neat rules of boys' fiction, however admirable they may be. It has taken some considerable time to piece together the story of Anthony Blair after he fled Coalhaven as a stowaway, with the police in hot pursuit and an international warrant out for his arrest. Many details of those five years will forever remain shrouded in mystery, but a plausible account has been obtained of his fate.

–o000o–

They were a mile away from the coral island, and it looked just as perfect as the hundreds of other islands, some large, some small, in this far corner of the South Seas. From a distance of two miles, they all looked the same – just a greenish smudge on the horizon. At one mile, there were coconut trees as far as the eye could see, a yellow strip of sand and a few dark dots which were undoubtedly canoes, proving that this particular small island was inhabited.

A quarter of a mile from shore, just outside the reef, the small barque dropped anchor just long enough to lower a rowing boat. Two men in linen suits clambered down into the boat, clutching light bags made of sailcloth with a change of clothes and other essentials. They reached upwards to grasp two heavy wooden boxes, which they placed in the centre of the boat, then removed their jackets and ties and with a practised air began rowing in the direction of the shore.

'I'll be back for ye twa Sassenachs on Saturday,' shouted the skipper. 'Mind yerselves wi' ma wee boat on that reef, now!'

'Don't worry. You can trust me,' shouted one of the oarsmen, a slim man in his early twenties with an engaging smile.

'God bless!' shouted the first mate, a Liverpool man who made no secret of the fact that he was an atheist. 'Missionaries!' he muttered to the skipper as the rowing boat moved away. 'How many souls do you think they'll save by Saturday?'

The skipper grunted and waved to the man on the winch to pull in the anchor. The barque had a full load of sail to catch the morning breeze, but it was now so still that without the engine they would hardly have moved at all. The skipper watched the rowing boat to make sure it cleared the reef safely, then yawned. 'Ye know where to find me if I'm needed.' Then he vanished below deck and nobody gave the island or the rowing boat another glance.

After several days as passengers on the barque, the two oarsmen were enjoying their little outing. It was like being on the Serpentine. Once they were through the gap in the surf that marked the reef, the water around them was calm. Instead of deep blue, it was now pale and clear in the lagoon and they could see tiny tropical fishes swimming all around them.

'Hang on a moment, Archer,' said the man with the smile. 'Stop pulling for a second. I need to see where we're going.'

'Puffed out again, Sooty?' enquired the other. 'If you had ever done serious training for the Arbuthnot-Jones you wouldn't be complaining now.'

The chaffing between the two old friends followed a familiar routine. Whenever one was tempted to be irritated with the other, the warm shared memories of schooldays came flooding back.

'Don't start criticising your skipper, or you'll be made to walk the plank,' Blair retorted. 'When we get there I shall show how fit I am by carrying both boxes of Bibles. You can carry the parasol.'

'Now you've got your breath back, perhaps we can start rowing again,' said Archer. They were following a route parallel to the shoreline, aiming for the beached outrigger canoes.

'Funny that nobody seems to be about,' said Blair as he lifted his oar. 'Perhaps they've all gone off to Berlusconi's for an ice-cream.'

The two pals had been together in the South Seas for some months, travelling on small trading vessels which traded cooking pots and cheap trinkets for copra. Missionaries, like farmers in the Canadian prairies, are always looking for virgin soil to plough. There was no use trying to distribute Bibles on the larger islands, where others had preceded them. More than once they had walked ashore on seemingly remote beaches, only to find that the inhabitants were already devout Protestants. Sometimes the islanders turned out to be Catholics and chanted 'Hail Mary' to them as they disembarked. Archer and Blair knew that within a week they could turn the islanders into Anglicans, but the Bible Society back in London strictly forbade such practices. So each month they scoured the chart for ever smaller and more remote islands.

This particular dot was too small to appear on any map, but it was in a part of the South Seas over which the British Empire held sway, at least in theory. In practice, there was no way of telling what seafaring visitors had preceded them, or what kind of welcome they might expect. The natives were almost always friendly and responded to a few well-chosen words in pidgin English. Blair sang hymns in a tuneful tenor voice, while Archer was a dab hand at storytelling. On most islands they found that a week was quite long enough to teach the inhabitants the fundamentals of revealed religion, without going so far as to claim fully-fledged converts. At the end of each voyage Blair and Archer scrupulously sent their reports to the Society with an exact tally of Bibles distributed and islands visited, baptising each one with a name drawn from the past register of St. Stephen's College. There was a Soames Island, a Mandelson Island and even a Prescott Island. The Bibles themselves were printed in large editions in Bombay on paper suitable for the tropics, with numerous colour illustrations.

By now they were approaching the shore, resting on the oars as the boat coasted gently through the shallows past the occasional floating coconut. 'Very strange,' said Archer, shaking his head. 'You'd think they'd be down on the beach by now to welcome us.' They scanned the line of coconut trees above the beach, but there was no sign of life. Yet the giant outrigger canoes showed every sign of being in good repair.

They pulled the boat on to the sand, unloaded their modest belongings and lay down in the narrow strip of shade given by one of the canoes. It was nearly noon, and if the islanders were too nervous to meet them, it would be foolhardy to plunge into the interior. Far better to wait on the beach and allow time to give them confidence to approach. Then with the exchange of a few trinkets, the missionary work could start.

'F-a-a-g!' shouted Archer without warning. This was an old joke between them. But on this occasion Archer kept his voice low, so as not to alarm any natives within earshot.

'Yes, sir?' replied Blair, entering into the spirit of the game.

'Fetch me two of Berlusconi's capital jam puffs and a couple of coconuts. And make sure you look sharpish.'

'Rightee-ho!'

Blair drew a small panga from his bag, strolled up the beach, picked up two coconuts and neatly chopped away the end of each one, leaving a hole small enough to drink through. 'There's a terrible jam puff crisis at the moment. They're blaming it on the Kaiser. But here's your coconut, sir,' he said.

'Thank you, young Sooty. By the way, there's no need to call me sir.'

After they had finished the coconuts and a few biscuits, they dozed for a while. When they awoke, there was still no sign of human life. The sun was falling from the sky and they moved to the other side of the outrigger to remain in the shade.

'Why did you leave the old Coll. when you did?' Blair felt he should use this rare moment of intimacy to ask a question which he had never quite dared pose before. Archer, like himself, was a difficult man to embarrass, but Blair knew the subject he was raising was a sensitive one.

'It wasn't beastliness or anything like that, if that's what you're thinking,' Archer replied. 'It was some nonsense over a missing postal order. To be honest, I don't remember all the details. But they asked me not to come back for the final two terms. Actually, that suited me fine, though I would have enjoyed a final crack at the school mile record.'

'So you made your way in the world?'

'That's right.' Archer paused. 'I had my own motor within a year.'

'Did they really send you down at the Old Bailey? What happened, exactly?'

Archer paused again. He drew a circle in the sand and continued.

'Some business about share certificates, and loans, and promissory notes. I won't bore you with the details. Take my advice, never trust a lawyer and especially not a judge. I now know the prisons are full of innocent men who have been tripped up by the law.'

'How awful,' said Blair, shaking his head. 'And the real criminals go scot-free.'

'When they let me out, I travelled here and decided to stay. And how about you? I heard about the Mesopotamia business.'

'I was innocent too,' said Blair. 'But I managed to stay one step ahead of the lawyers. The way I see it, you have to follow God and your conscience. *Veritas prevalebit*. What counts is knowing, deep down inside, that you're doing the right thing.'

'Good for you, old chap,' said Archer. 'I tried to do that. Of course, I wasn't religious like you. But at least I never got anyone killed.'

Blair was unsure what Archer meant by this, but decided to change the subject. 'Did you ever get that novel published?' he asked.

'Not yet. Publishers are such duffers. But I'm going to persevere.'

'I might try writing a novel some day. The dear old mater always said I was good at making things up.'

There was another long pause as the sun continued to sink, and the water in the lagoon began to turn a golden colour. A slight evening breeze began to blow, moving the coconut trees and making a handful of nuts drop on the sand.

'My turn to fag, I think,' said Archer, scrambling to his feet. He walked up the beach to the line of trees and bent down for the coconuts.

There was a single piercing cry, and a hail of arrows flew out of the dark green shade. Blair saw his chum stumble and fall forward. Before he could draw breath about thirty natives armed with bows and arrows, sticks and spears had surrounded Archer's crumpled figure and were pounding it to a pulp. The men wore no trace of clothing, just leaves and bones tied together with rough

'THE SAVAGE WITH THE CUTLASS LET OUT A FULL-THROATED ROAR.'

ropes of coconut fibre. Their leader carried what appeared to be a rusty naval cutlass. Blair understood in an instant that this was an island on which no white man had ever set his foot and survived to tell the tale.

As the savages ran towards him across the sand, he clasped his panga and took to his heels, but realised there was nowhere he could escape. He ran into the water, hoping to slow their advance somehow. Did it all really have to end like this? Wasn't Captain Cook killed by natives on the beach of a Pacific island? Then at least he and Archer would be in good company. But he would never return in triumph to St. Stephen's to rout his enemies, he would never acknowledge the cheers of the adoring populace from a Rolls-Royce, he would never play Henry V at the Theatre Royal Haymarket, and he would never become prime minister, a job for which he considered himself well suited. Perhaps if he offered to put down his weapon and smoke the pipe of peace, they might spare him? He was tiring now and the war-whoops of his pursuers were getting closer. He turned, dropped his panga in the water and held up his empty hands.

Above the tops of the coconut trees rose the smoke of a cooking fire. Blair grinned his most persuasive grin. In response the savage with the cutlass let out the full-throated roar of a man within sight of his dinner, who knew, deep down inside, that he was doing the right thing. Blair turned again and tried to run into deeper water, but he felt a stinging pain between his shoulderblades and a blow which knocked him forward. He was gulping seawater and sand, and trying to get back on his feet, when another blow on the side of the head left him groggy. He turned on his back, opened his eyes skywards and tried to think of something beautiful before he lost consciousness completely. Cherie! He wanted so much to see the girl in the blue dress, whose photograph he had kept in his desk wrapped in tissue paper. Cherie! Cherie! But try as he might, he could not conjure up her features. Instead, a nightmarish image swam before his eyes as he slipped below the water. He saw a carving knife cutting into a joint of meat and behind it, a pair of staring eyes. It was the face of the grocer's daughter.

THE END